ISBN: 9781651492635

ENFORCING BOUNDARIES

Eva Harper

Book 1 of the Boundaries Series

*Dedicated to my loving and supportive family.
I owe everything I am to you.*

PART 1

WHEN I WAS 4

"Margo."

My eyes snapped open in the dim room, and my mother came into view. She looked worried, but a small smile graced her pink lips as she spoke to me. In my sleepy haze, I didn't realize what she was whispering as she grabbed my hand and pulled me out of my bedroom. My father was waiting in the hallway, dressed in his black coat and work boots. His skin nearly blended with the coat, something I used to tease him about, but he would remind me that my own skin nearly blended with my tan coat, and I would giggle at the thought.

His face was stern as he bent down in front of me and grabbed onto my shoulders.

"Margo, I need you to be a big girl, honey," he whispered, stroking the side of my face. "Listen to me and Momma and be very quiet."

"Daddy," I whimpered, looking between him and my mother.

"Shh," my mother hushed, pulled my arms into my coat, and handed my father my old black shoes. He lifted me into them and buckled the latch around my foot. They each took one of my hands in theirs and pulled me down the hallway of our tiny apartment building. As we exited the building, they looked out at the guards that stood watch over our small human compound.

There were only a few of us left in the building after that winter. My mother told me the other family had moved to a different pack, and the older lady that lived next to us had gone to visit her son. Now there were only twelve of us, including our small family.

The werewolves lived around us in big homes. Some of them lived in the packhouse on the edge of the territory; they were important, and I was told never to speak to them.

"Which way?" my mother whispered to my father.

"East," my father told her, pulling us along the perimeter of the building. I stumbled between them, but they held me up by my arms and pulled me along. They exchanged a few whispers, but I continued to stare at their feet, wondering why we were leaving our home in the middle of the night.

We made it halfway across the territory before one of the guards saw us between the trees. He called out for us to stop and began running towards us. My mother picked me up in her arms and started running, my father right next to us. My head faced over her shoulder, and I watched as the wolves slowly closed in on us. My father had placed his hand on my mother's shoulder and told her to run as fast as she could before he stopped and faced the wolves.

My mother faltered and turned around to look at my father as the guards tackled him to the ground and forced his arms behind his back. She whimpered and placed a hand on my head, running faster.

The shifters caught us seconds later.

I was ripped from my mother's arms as they pulled her hands behind her and tied her wrists with rope. One of the guards held his hand out for me, and I naively took it and began walking beside him, behind the guards who were guiding my parents. They walked us back to the packhouse, where the Alpha had been alerted of our escape and was waiting with his guards.

He glared down at us as the guards forced my mother and father to their knees and placed me beside them. The Alpha declared that we would be punished in the early morning when more of the pack could see us. They carted my mother and father off to the cells in the basement of the packhouse. We were rarely allowed inside the packhouse, and as we walked, I looked around in wonder. It was a grand place, filled with beautiful things, none of which I could touch.

The guard who held my hand pulled me a little quicker and allowed me to share a cell with my mother. I fell asleep in her lap, playing with her long blonde hair, tired from the running, and being woken up; I don't think she ever slept.

In the morning, one of the guards came and removed us from the cells. The same guard who held my hand came back and walked me behind my parents, again, to the front of the packhouse. There, a large pole was placed in the front yard with a rope sectioning off the area. Most of the pack stood around it, watching us arrive from the basement. I had never seen so much of the pack before. Each time they gathered, we were not permitted to attend.

The Luna, an older lady who always had a scowl on her face, motioned to the guard to bring me to her. He walked me over and waited for me to let go of his hand. I didn't want to, and the Luna peeled my fingers from him and placed her clawed hand on my shoulder to keep me in place.

They dragged my father to the pole and tied his hands

around it. The Alpha walked up beside him on the small, makeshift stage and began speaking loudly. I wasn't paying attention to him; I was looking at my father, who had tears streaming down his face. He never cried before. My mother was on the other side of the rope, calling out his name, "Levi! Levi!" but her voice was drowned out by the Alpha's loud tone.

My father called her name and mine, trying to find out where we were. "Viviana! Margo!" he cried, turning his head to either side, searching for us in the crowd.

The Alpha picked up a long, brown object, and the crowd around us cheered. I looked around in confusion until the Luna turned my head forward. The Alpha raised the object and struck it hard against my father's back. My father cried out as his shirt split open, and blood started running down his back. I whimpered, afraid to cry out.

The Alpha continued whipping my father for several more minutes, growing excited as the crowd around us cheered. My mother fought against the guards with tears streaming down her face, crying out my father's name as he sunk further and further down the pole.

Eventually, the Alpha stopped and set down the whip. My father was no longer moving when the Alpha stepped off the stage and allowed the guards holding my mother to bring her up to the pole. They tied her around the same pole as my father and called out for the other guards to join them. My mother sobbed loudly as she stood over my father, his bloodied and battered body in shreds on the floor.

Eight or nine guards surrounded my mother and began tearing her clothes off. She screamed, but no one came to help her as they took turns raping her and beating her. The Luna behind me grabbed my chin and forced me to watch as they tore my mother apart. Tears silently dripped down my cheeks, but my mouth remained locked shut.

I don't know how long it was before one of the guards

hit her in the back, and her spine snapped in two. She was instantly quiet as her body fell to the ground on top of my father's body. They left her there as the guards climbed down from the stage and retreated to the packhouse.

The Luna let go of my shoulder and stepped away from me, walking towards her mate, the Alpha. They were in charge of all the werewolves, and incidentally, the humans in the pack. They began speaking, pointing, and staring at me, trying to decide what to do with a newly orphaned four-year-old.

I continued to stare at my parent's bodies until a boy with honey-colored hair stepped in front of me. He smiled, revealing his missing front teeth and waved his hand slightly. I lifted mine and waved sadly before I tucked my chin into my chest. He grabbed my hand, and I looked up at the boy who was still smiling, blissfully unaware of what had just happened. In a way, I was too.

"My name is Caddy," he grinned.

"I'm Margo," I whispered, wiping the tears from my ruddy cheeks with my palms.

"Do you want to be my friend?" he asked, tilting his head to the side. I nodded my head and allowed him to pull me behind him. We walked past the Alpha and Luna, who seemed fine with our arrangement.

"I don't have a lot of friends," Caddy babbled, leading me into a room with toys and play structures. "Mommy says it's because I'm gonna be Alpha one day. Maybe you can be Luna!"

I shook my head, and he frowned.

"Why not?"

"I'm human," I said softly, staring at the ground.

The boy walked towards me and placed his hands on either side of my head, rougher than he intended, and smiled at me.

"Well, then, I'll protect you. We can be best friends."

THE ENFORCER

"Margo!" Caddy's voice called for me from the other room. I sat up from my position on the floor, where I was watching the wings of the fan on the ceiling spin around in boredom. "Come here. I need your help!" he called again.

I walked to the adjoining room to find him with his paintbrushes in his hand. "What are you painting?" I wondered; the canvas was blank.

He shrugged his shoulders and turned around towards me. "I don't know yet. My uncle asked me to paint something as a gift to the new Enforcer when he visits in two days, but I don't have a clue what to paint." His uncle, whom the rest of us now called Alpha, was a strict man but was nowhere as intimidating as the new Enforcer.

The canvas was large, about seven feet wide by five feet tall; he would never be able to finish the work in two days. I told Caddy this, and he glowered at me.

"If I start right now, I can finish it," he groaned. "But I

have no idea what to paint. It has to be good; this is a peace offering. We all know very well that Dorian isn't always the best with other leaders."

"What do you need help with? You know I can't even draw a flower, I'm not sure what you want me to do," I said carefully, not wanting to anger him in his anxious state.

"I know you aren't a painter, but you are the more creative one out of the two of us. Tell me what to paint. I can do the painting, but my mind is going in ten different directions," he pleaded. His hazel eyes looked sad and scared instead of his usual cheeky manner.

"I can try," I sighed. His smile grew tenfold. "You'll have to give me a few minutes to think of something. I need to plan."

He nodded and left me alone.

I sank to the ground, resuming the same position I had before, and closed my eyes. "Pick up the brush," I ordered. I could hear his hands grasp the tool. "So, from the left corner, start with a deep purple."

His fingers began to paint, not fully understanding where I was guiding him, but trusting me enough not to question it. I didn't look at the canvas, just stayed on the ground with my eyes closed for the next several hours. We took a small break to get food from the kitchen on the first level of the packhouse. He accompanied me so the others wouldn't cause me trouble as they sometimes did.

It was difficult being the only human in a pack full of werewolf shifters, but Caddy did his best to make things seem normal for me. After my parents were killed, I was kept to be Caddy's companion since he had few friends. His parents did not want him playing with a lot of other children in fear it would corrupt him when he was older and it was time for him to take the Alpha position. His parents didn't think a small, human girl would have much influence over him, and allowed me to stay.

Caddy's father was killed a few years after my parent's murder in a rogue attack. His brother, Dorian, was handed the Alpha title when Caddy was fourteen and I was twelve, although Caddy would take over for him one day.

Although I was raised alongside Caddy, I held onto my human qualities as best I could. I taught Caddy art and literature from the books in my parent's apartment, and in return, he kept me safe from the other wolves who wanted nothing more than to rip me apart. He had a steady hand, which made painting easy for him. I was not blessed with an artistic hand, so I usually posed for him, set up his scenes, or described things for him to paint.

The canvas took us seventeen hours to complete, and another six hours for it to dry. Caddy's uncle seemed pleased with our work and sent it to be framed for his guest, who would arrive in less than ten hours. Caddy thanked me, hugged me closely, and then sent me to my room to rest before the festivities.

My room was plain, like many others in the packhouse. It had slate stone walls, a medium-sized window on the far wall, a small bed covered in afghans I found in a storage room, and a desk-which I had built from a slab of wood and metal poles. It wasn't much as my comfort was never a priority for the pack, but I was thankful they even allowed me to stay.

Caddy shook me from my sleep in the morning, looking excited. I grumbled at him.

"Get up; you have to get yourself ready. Mom says we all need to be dressed nicely for the Enforcer when he gets here in an hour, so get yourself up and tame your mane," he chuckled, ruffling my curly hair.

I sat up, stretched, and wandered over to my desk,

where I had a small mirror and some hand-me-down makeup Caddy's mother gave me. My hair was kinky, curly, and thick. Caddy called me a lion when we were little because the volume of my hair used to dwarf my tiny body. I had managed to tame it as I got older and parted it to the right of my head, which framed my face nicely. I didn't wear much makeup on my face usually, simply did my lashes and put on a bit of blush, but this was a pack event, which meant I needed to do a bit more. I finished quickly, despite the effort, and went to my small cedar chest to pull out a dress.

Caddy's mother had given me most of her old things from before she birthed Caddy, which was nice of her. Aside from her son, she was one of the only people that looked after me.

I dressed in a lilac-colored frock with thick straps and a classic neckline. It flowed to my knees, and I slipped on a pair of white sandals as Caddy returned to my room. We walked down the three flights of stairs and joined the rest of the pack in front of the house. There was a large crowd, the entire pack was required to attend the gathering, and many of them were excited to see the newest Enforcer.

Caddy grabbed my hand as we pushed our way through the crowd. He was obligated to stand next to his family, several feet in front of the pack, to greet the guests. I stood close to the front, tucked in between a few of the taller wolves.

A series of cars approached, large SUV's that came in a stream of black. The atmosphere shifted, and everyone became quiet. The vehicles stopped short of fifteen feet away, and there was a moment before the doors opened simultaneously.

Each man was dressed similarly in a black suit, white shirt, and black tie. They were muscular, tall, and showed no emotion on their faces. Finally, they gathered around one car in the middle, and opened the door.

A man stepped out, buttoned his suit, and scanned the scene. He was dressed in a navy suit with a white shirt and walnut colored shoes. He stood taller than the rest of the men; his presence seemed to fill the entire area. I kept my head down after looking at the men. It was disrespectful for a human to make eye contact with wolves of power.

"Dorian," the Enforcer loudly greeted as he walked closer to clasp arms with the Alpha. It was a common greeting, and as the sound of arms meeting rang through the air, the pack relaxed visibly.

"Theo, I see you're settling in the role well," Dorian commended.

"Yes, well, someone has to keep order," he responded vaguely and halfway grinned.

"Caddy," Dorian called. "Fetch the offering."

Caddy stepped back, glanced at me, and gathered the painting from another member of the pack who stood behind him.

"My nephew has a gift for art," Dorian boasted. "We hope that you will accept our offering. We wish you the best in your future." Caddy stood behind his work, looking wearily at the Enforcer, who showed little emotion on his face.

"You certainly do have a talent for this." The Enforcer nodded. "I thank you, truly."

Caddy smiled and turned his head to look at me once again.

"Why do you keep turning your head to look back?" the Enforcer asked. A cold chill settled over my spine despite the mild air outside. My hands shook; I prayed he wouldn't notice me. I knew he was aware there was a human; wolves could sense those things immediately.

Caddy cleared his throat and lowered his head. "I meant

nothing by it," he offered. The Enforcer wasn't satisfied with his answer and scanned the crowd accusingly.

"Theo," Dorian tried to reign in his guest, wanting to be in control of the situation like most Alpha's do.

"Quiet," the Enforcer commanded. We were all shocked that he spoke that way to someone with Dorian's status, but the Enforcer position was high above any Alpha, and he had the right to speak as he wished.

I wrung my hands together, using my hair to shield my face from his view.

"Who are you looking at, boy?" the Enforcer turned back to Caddy.

"Sir," Caddy said softly. He didn't like the tone in his voice, I could tell by the way his neck strained despite his softer tone.

"Who?" the Enforcer growled.

"No one," Caddy denied, shaking his head adamantly. The Enforcer growled again and stepped closer to Caddy.

"Margo," Dorian shot out. I stopped breathing.

No, you could have said any other wolf's name.

"Margo?" the Enforcer looked between Dorian and Caddy, whose face was red and angry. Dorian gave one nod of his head, and I closed my eyes and squeezed hard. "Margo, join us, won't you," the Enforcer called loudly. I looked up slowly and glanced at the two wolves standing next to me, who gave me the same stern look they always did.

"Margo!" he said again, looking around. "I don't like waiting."

HUMAN CONDITION

I sucked in my breath and took one step forward, breaking past the few wolves in front of me, but stopped once I saw his face. He stared at me, threatening me not to come forward as if it would give him a reason to snap my neck.

His entourage came towards me and grabbed me by my arms to drag my body forward. I stumbled to stand and walk with their large hands pulling me but failed, and they threw me at the feet of the Enforcer. I got onto my hands and knees and looked up to see his face in front of me. He squatted down and grabbed my chin in his hands.

My lip wobbled; I could feel it although I tried to look strong like the wolves I grew up with.

"A human girl," the Enforcer mused. His light cerulean eyes bore into mine. I didn't dare glance anywhere else. "I've never met one before."

I stayed quiet. He grabbed me high on my right arm and forced me to stand along with him. He pushed me back towards Caddy, and I rushed to his side. Caddy looked livid, wanting nothing more than to smash the painting over the Enforcer's head.

"What is she to you?" he asked Caddy.

"She's an orphan, we allowed her to be a companion for young Cadence," Dorian explained. The Enforcer turned his head slightly.

"I asked your nephew, Dorian," he stated. He turned back to Caddy and took a step closer, the painting now out of the way. "What is she to you?"

Caddy lowered his eyes to look at me again.

"Is she your mate? I've never heard of a human mating with a strong wolf like yourself," the Enforcer questioned further.

"No," Caddy murmured.

"A servant, perhaps?"

"No."

"Does she provide a service here for you?"

"She does her share like we all do," Caddy said stronger, fighting for me.

"But she provides no purpose, being human. Why have you not turned her?" he asked, although he already knew the answer.

"Sir, only a mate could do that," Caddy said, confused.

"So, she is of no further use to this pack," the Enforcer said, staring at me, although my gaze remained at my feet. He was going to kill me; there was no other way out of it. I knew humans were nothing to wolves if they had no mate. "Girl," he addressed me. I stiffened at his voice, which urged him to step closer to me, only a foot away now. "Do you not speak?"

I opened my mouth, but I didn't know the words to say.

"Tell me why you should stay here."

"I've lived here since I was four," I whispered, not able to make my voice louder.

"And because you've lived here, that means you should continue to live here?"

I looked up at Caddy, wanting him to help me, but knowing he couldn't. The punishment for disrespecting a wolf like him was death, no matter your ranking in your own pack.

"Don't look at him, little girl, look at me and tell me why I should allow you to keep living here." His voice was rough, sending shivers down my spine. I looked back at him, noticing for the first time how young he was for someone so entitled.

"I don't know," I answered honestly. My mind was stricken with fear; there was nothing else to save me but honesty.

"You don't know?" he scrutinized, eyebrows coming together, leaning down to study my face closer. I tried to remain as calm as I could.

"No, sir."

He straightened himself and turned around.

"I really must be on my way," he informed Dorian.

"You won't stay for our festivities?" Dorian offered, hoping to make a bond with the Enforcer.

"I'm afraid I have a lot to do, the old Enforcer left me with my work cut out. You were my last pack in the area to visit." The Enforcer turned to the men who traveled with him and gave them a curt nod, which propelled them to start the cars again.

"Well, you are certainly welcome in our territory, Theo. I hope to see you again soon." Dorian stuck his arm out, and Theo grasped it strongly.

"Thank you, Dorian."

The Enforcer turned slightly, nodding at the painting. His men came and gathered it, and loaded it into the back of a vehicle.

"Oh," the Enforcer turned, looking smug. It was the first time his face changed from his stone exterior. "The human girl comes with me, as well."

My hearing drowned out, one ear at a time. It sounded like ringing, like a loud siren going off right next to me, and my vision went out of focus. I looked to Caddy, shaking my head slightly, grabbing onto his forearm.

"Theo," Dorian reasoned. "You would have no use for a human girl. Allow her to stay in our territory. We will care for her." Caddy put his hand over mine, warming it slightly. He was always warm.

The Enforcer grinned. "No use for her," he chuckled and wandered over towards me. He sauntered around my body and Caddy's since I was latched to him. "I've never met a human girl before. She intrigues me." He continued circling and stopped behind me, lifting, and sniffing my hair.

I ground my teeth together, cringing as his fingers skimmed my neck.

"I wonder how long it would take to make her scream." His lips grazed the curve of my ear. I whipped my body around, wanting his hands off me and glared at him.

"Oh," he purred. "She has a backbone after all."

"I'm not going with you," I ground out. I knew the consequences for what I was saying, but I would've rather died than allow him to take me back with him. I would surely be torn apart like my mother. I was too young then to do anything, but I was older now, and I wasn't going to stand silent.

"You are." He smiled back at me calmly.

"I'd rather die than go with you."

Caddy cursed my name behind Theo. He was shaking.

"That's enough, little one," the Enforcer scolded and grabbed my arm again in his strong grip. He began walking us towards his cars. I jerked and fought against his grip; unlike Caddy, who was afraid to bruise me, this man wasn't.

"Caddy!" I screamed, turning around to look at him. Caddy was shaking, his arms being held behind his back by Dorian and another guard as he screamed my name. Tears streamed down my cheeks, and my hair flew around violently.

The Enforcer grabbed my other arm and pushed me to the car door. I refused to go in willingly and threw my legs on either side of the door, pushing off the frame with my feet. Another man inside the car grabbed my ankles and pulled me in as the Enforcer shoved my body in the rest of the way.

He climbed in after me, and a moment later, the car jolted to life, and we rolled away from my home. I struggled out of the hold of the other wolf and climbed over the Enforcer to place my fists on the dark window and beat on it. The wolves looked shocked, not upset, apart from Caddy, who was mid-shift as we pulled out of the driveway.

The Enforcer's hands came around my waist in front of him and pulled me back to sit in his lap. I wiggled and threw my body around aggressively, slamming the back of my head into his nose roughly.

"Little one," he growled in my ear, grunting as he wiped the blood away from his nose. I froze, squeezing my eyes shut and allowing the tears to fall down my freckled cheeks. "You will be much happier here if you don't fight me."

I slumped my body over, trying to get off his lap. He allowed me to move freely in the spacious back. I curled myself in a corner, away from the Enforcer and the other wolf, and hid my face in my hands.

He stared at me for most of the ride. I think he expected me to lash out again, but I kept silent, wary of him and the other shifter. Once my crying stopped, I leaned my head against the seat and stared blankly at my shoes.

The once white sandals Caddy's mother had given me were caked in dirt and grass and mud. I counted the blades of grass. One. Two. Three. Four. Five. Six. Seven. That didn't distract me long enough. The ride was long, hours long, and eventually, we stopped and allowed the other wolf shifter to change cars, leaving the Enforcer and me alone in the separated cavern.

"Are you tired?" the Enforcer asked after some time. I glanced up at him confused, after all that time, that was the question he had wanted to ask? I shook my head and continued to play with the hem of my dress. "Hungry?" Again, I shook my head. I lost my appetite the moment I looked into his eyes.

Finally, we stopped, sometime in the morning near a large house in the forest. I didn't move when the doors opened.

"Margo," the Enforcer called out, his legs outside the car, but his head was looking back at me. "Come along." I remained frozen. "I will drag you out of here if I have to. Just come inside, and I will explain everything to you," he threatened. It didn't faze me; if I was going to die, why did it matter where it happened?

His hand came around my ankle, and rapidly I was thrown on top of his lap once again. He sat me up the best he could and grabbed my jaw. "Don't make me repeat myself," he warned, and then pushed me out of the car towards the only house within view.

THINLY VEILED

I tumbled into the body of another wolf much larger than me; he stiffened but didn't move. I scampered away from him, turning to look at the large building in front of me.

It was exquisite, much more lavish than the packhouse back home, although not as large. It was dark, fitting into the forest behind it, covered in polished wood, stacking stones, and windows that sprawled out across entire rooms. A frigid wind blew, sending a shiver up my arms. It was much colder here than back home.

The Enforcer stood beside me, allowing me to take notice of his mansion. I looked up at him, and he smirked back down at me. Even though I wasn't short, he made me feel small. I was lanky, taller than some other human girls, but wolves tended to be larger than most humans.

He walked forward towards the front doors. I stayed back a moment until he turned and opened his eyes a little wider, beckoning me to come forward. A man opened the door for us, and we walked in slowly. He took a scan of his home, making eye contact with the other men inside, and then relaxed visibly.

He shrugged out of his suit jacket and placed it on a nearby gray couch. He walked forward again, grabbing arms with the two men who sat at a glass table along a light-colored wooden backdrop. I stayed back by the foyer, breathing nervously, not knowing what to do in the unfamiliar environment. He spoke for a few moments with the men, smiling and laughing, looking happy and relaxed. I glanced around nervously, looking at the muscular men who stood next to me, staring down at me blankly.

"Margo," the Enforcer called for me, extending his arm to welcome me. I stumbled forward slowly, flattening my dress, and took my place a foot away from him. He smiled at me and reached a hand up to run it affectionately over my hair; I flinched.

"This is the human girl, Margo, from Dorian's pack," he introduced me. The men at the table looked me up and down, smiling at the Enforcer again. I shook under their gazes, desperately looking around the room for a door to escape through.

"She won't last a day with you," the fair, blond one smirked, laughing loudly. His counterpart smacked his arm and rolled his eyes.

"I'm sure you two will have a lot of fun together," the dark-skinned one chuckled, trying to be less crass than his friend. It did little to comfort me, and tears formed in the corners of my eyes though I willed them not to drop.

The blond took notice of my tearful state and looked down sorrowfully. The Enforcer grabbed my arm again, wanting me to turn towards him, but I struggled to stay stationary.

"Hey," he said softer, trying to gain my attention. My lip wavered once more. He sighed, put his arm around my back again, and began to lead me to a set of floating, wooden steps. I looked back as I took the first step, begging someone to save me. They all looked down as a whimper escaped my throat, and Theo pressed on my back more firmly.

When we reached the top of the steps, we went down a long hallway and turned right. There was a room at the end of the hall, glass covered with privacy shaded frost. He opened the door gently and held it until I walked in. The room was dark apart from the far wall, which was all glass and allowed light to enter the room. The walls kept with the smooth wood from the first level; a bed sat in front of us, large, white, and covered with gray and white pillows. On the opposite wall from the bed was a television on a large, slate gray, metal dresser. There were doors opening to a closet and a bathroom on either side of the television.

The Enforcer stood behind me, near the door, observing me as I looked around the room. I noticed him staring and turned back to him, bowing my head to show my submission.

"Margo," he said lightly, stepping forward. I took a step back, and he stopped momentarily before stalking ahead. "You're afraid of me," he noted.

I glared accusingly but said nothing.

"Why?"

"You tore me away from my family," I spat, the nervous fluctuation in my voice making my words appear less intimidating than I meant them to be.

"Those people were not your family," he said back. "You're an orphan, correct?"

"They were the closest thing I had. They cared for me."

"I will care for you from now on, little one," he said softer now, placing a hand on my shoulder, stroking the exposed skin with his thumb. I pulled my shoulder back, but he didn't let go.

"I don't want you to care for me in *that* way," I growled.

"In what way?" he asked sincerely, dropping his hand.

"I know how you wolves are. You bring me up to your bedroom within five minutes of us being here," I gestured around me.

"I wanted to give us some privacy, you seemed rather intimidated by my friends, and we need to have an important conversation," he explained.

"They said I wouldn't last a day with you," I wailed, the emotional toll beginning to take over. "You said you wondered how long it would take to make me scream!"

He shook his head in regret, untucking his shirt from his slacks. "Margo," he whispered.

"Don't you dare say my name," I told him, wrapping my arms around my stomach.

"I realize my words may have seemed a bit harsh, and I apologize for that, but I had a reason. I needed your Alpha to think I was going to kill you," he said, sitting on the edge of the bed to undo the buttons around his wrists.

"You aren't going to kill me?"

"No, Margo."

"Then why say those things?" I asked, shaking my head in confusion, curls falling in my eyes at the movement.

"Because if the world around us knew I found my mate, they would use you against me," he said, standing up and folding his shirt sleeves up to his elbows. I stepped back, trying to make sense of his words.

"What?" I breathed out.

"I knew you were my mate the first moment I stepped out of that car. If they saw me be gentle towards you, they would use you against me, hurt you, take you, and I couldn't allow that to happen. Not until I have security measures in place, not until I know I can keep you safe."

"I can't be your mate," I said accusingly. "You're lying. You said you never heard of a human being mate to a powerful wolf like this." I glanced around me, stumbling back towards the door.

"Margo, I know this must be confusing. I will explain everything to you, come sit on the bed. I'll find something for you to wear other than that dress, it's filthy." He stood up and went over the closet, rifling through some clothes. I turned quickly and threw the door open again, running down the hallway, trying to find my way back to the stairs.

I heard him curse loudly, and his thunderous footsteps followed mine twice as fast. I saw the staircase and rushed down it, missing a step towards the bottom, which only propelled me faster. I didn't care what the wolves on the main floor thought about me. This wasn't about my reputation; this was about my life.

"Margo," the Enforcer called, standing at the bottom of the stairs.

I raced to the front door and pulled it open. The same man who opened the door for us now stood outside, guarding it against intruders, or possibly escapees. He looked surprised when he saw me, and I took that moment to jump down the three steps and towards the open woods around us.

Someone grabbed my arm, another guard, who pulled me to a stop and held me until the Enforcer approached us. I begged the man to let me go, but he held me firmly, bruising my freckled arm.

The Enforcer nodded to the guard and took me from his grasp. I fell to the ground as they transferred me. I crumbled down, burying my head in my arms.

"Margo," he whispered as he knelt next to me, his hands

stroking my hair soothingly. I didn't make any attempt to move, and he said my name more assertively.

"Enforcer, please," I whimpered, the sound muffled by my arms.

"Theo," he said softly, sounding pained. "My name is Theo."

When I didn't respond again, he gathered me in his arms and brought me back inside the house. My curly hair shielded me from the other wolves downstairs as the Enforcer brought me back upstairs and set me on the side of the bed. I pushed his arms away, and he set them right back on mine, forcing me to sit still.

He knelt in front of me, taking the dirty sandals off my feet, setting them next to the nightstand on the side of the bed. His hand lingered on my skin, taking notice of a bruise his hand created in the car. He gathered the clothes he pulled out from the closet and set them on the bed beside me. His hands parted my hair, pushing it back so he could see my red, tear-stained face.

"Would you like to have a bath? It might calm you down," he offered. I looked up at him through my tears. I shook under his steady, sad gaze. "Come on." He helped me stand and led me to the bathroom where there was a large, curved, soaking bathtub in the right corner. He drew the water, pouring some soap in it as it filled, so bubbles covered the surface of the water.

"Do you need help?" he asked, noticing I was still visibly shaking. I shook my head quickly, no. He nodded. "I'll be back in a moment then." He left the bathroom, shutting the door most of the way behind him. I pulled the string that held the back of the dress together and slid it down my body. I took my bra and underwear off and placed them under the dress, out of his view. The water was warm as I slid into it, sinking far enough down, so the bubbles covered everything up to my shoulders.

The Enforcer knocked on the door once and then entered, walking over to sit beside the tub on a small stool. I kept my gaze on the bubbled water until I felt his hands touch my hair. I lurched forward, leaning over so that I was hunched over my knees.

"Margo, please, I'm not going to hurt to you," he said gently, resting his hands on the edge of the tub. "Let me take care of you, that's all I want." I didn't dare move.

He grabbed a soft sponge and dipped in the water and began to run it down my spine, brushing my hair aside to reach my shoulder. He continued to do this until he was satisfied and then moved his stool, so he could wash my hands and arms. He continued to wash my fingers, gently scrubbing the dirt from beneath my fingernails, and then moved to the end of the bathtub to do the same to my feet. My leg emerged from the water, only up to the knee. He cleaned my toes from the dirt and a few cuts I got from running outside.

With his hands on me, it was hard to focus on anything other than the claws that lurked on the other side of his skin.

Once my body was clean, he came behind me once more and washed my hair. I closed my eyes and tried to relax, but it was difficult. Under his touch, I would surely perish, why should I allow him to bring me comfort before? I was completely clean, my skin soft and warm from the bath. He left the room for a moment, so I could change into the clothes he brought me: a pair of gray sweatpants and a black shirt. The clothes were large on my frame, but they were warm and modest.

I stepped out from the bathroom, finding Theo sitting on the edge of the bed waiting for me. He stood up quickly, coming to meet me as I stumbled in his clothes like a fawn. He bent down and started folding the sweatpants up, so my feet were exposed. When he was finished, he stood up again and looked over me.

"Would you like to sleep? You didn't at all on the drive. You must be exhausted."

I shook my head no, not wanting to have my guard down around him.

"No one will hurt you, I'll make sure of it," he promised adamantly.

"It's not everyone else I'm worried about," I said quietly but with strength against him. He looked sad again and began shaking his head.

"Margo, I won't ever hurt you."

I held my wrist up, showing him the bruise he left on me earlier. The one on my upper arm hurt as well as the one on my ankle.

"Little one," he all but whimpered.

"Don't call me that," I said softly.

"Margo," he tried again. "I'm sorry. I didn't know how fragile you were before. I didn't mean to hurt you, I promise. I will do better."

"I'm not fragile," I hissed. He went and sat against the bed again.

"You are, Margo," he insisted. "Come sleep. I won't touch you."

I waited a few moments, allowing my tired muscles and eyes to persuade me into sleep. I went and stood on the other side of the bed. Theo reached over and pulled the cover back, revealing soft, silky sheets. I climbed in slowly and laid on my side, away from him. He pulled the covers farther over me and pushed my hair back before leaving the room. Though the sun streamed through the room, I fell fast asleep, allowing it to heal my body and mind.

CONFINEMENT

When I woke up, it was darker outside, maybe late afternoon. I stretched, rolling my aching shoulders, and threw my legs off the bed. I stood up and looked around, wandering around the room to see if the Enforcer was lurking somewhere. He wasn't. I went to the bathroom and looked in the drawers, to the closet to look behind his clothes, in his nightstand, trying to find any secret of his.

I found nothing, despite my intrigue, and sat on the edge of the bed. Minutes passed, maybe twenty of them before I decided to leave the room. The cold wood touched my feet, and I wished Theo had left me socks as well. I followed the same path to the stairs and descended slowly.

There were fewer people downstairs; now, I only noticed Theo sitting at the glass table with his two male friends. Theo noticed me first, his eyes lit up, and he stood up as I finished the last four steps. The other men turned to face me, watching as their friend met me at the bottom.

"Did you sleep well?" Theo asked. I nodded and looked

at my hands, stationary at my stomach. He placed a hand on my back and walked me over to the table, pulled out a chair, and waited until I sat down in the seat next to his. I sat cautiously, looking at the other men who were confused as well. "I'm going to go get you something to eat; I'll be right back." And he disappeared out of the room.

I turned and faced the two men, both around the Enforcer's age, who wore deep smirks seeded in confusion.

"So," the blond one spoke. "You're human."

"Yes," I said blankly, sliding down into the chair.

"Are you really Theo's mate?" he asked, his nose scrunching up in disbelief.

"I guess," I said stiffly, looking over my shoulder, wondering where Theo had gone. "Who are you?"

"His friends," the other one said.

"His best friends," the blond one spoke again, a little boastful.

"Do either of you have a phone?" I asked softly. They cocked their heads back, and the one on the right pulled out a phone from his pocket. He slid it over to me across the table, and I reached for it greedily, wanting to call Caddy.

As I picked up the small device, Theo's hand reached over my head and plucked it from my fingers. He threw it back at his friend and set a plate of pasta in front of me. He shook his head and slumped into the chair next to me, scolding his friend. "Not until we have a talk," he told me, staring at me until I picked up the fork and took a bite.

"Why?" I asked, chewing a piece of tomato. "I should call Caddy."

"Your friend?" I nodded. "You can call him after we talk. There are certain things you need to know. Security matters. You can't go around telling everyone that you're my mate until I make arrangements."

"You told them," I pointed out, sticking my fork in their direction.

"They're my friends," he answered. "They won't do anything that compromises either of our safety."

"Caddy wouldn't say anything."

"You can talk to him later," he promised, a tone of finality settling over us. I finished eating quickly and slid the plate a few inches in front of me. The two men left, leaving me alone with Theo and whatever guards were stationed outside of the house. I stayed sitting until the Enforcer came back into the room.

"How about we talk, Margo," he offered. I nodded softly. He sat down on the gray couch where his suit coat once laid, and I followed him. I sat gingerly on the edge of a soft chair, uncomfortably full and curious. "You have questions," he stated, leaving the conversation up to me.

"How?" I whispered.

"How what?"

"How is this even possible? If it is even possible. Is there some kind of mistake?"

Theo stayed quiet for a few moments, processing my question. "This isn't a mistake, Margo. A wolf only gets one mate; there are no substitutes or mistakes that occur in that process."

"But why me?" I asked, pulling at the hem of the shirt I was wearing.

"Every mated pair is chosen carefully." He reached his hand out to touch mine, but I pulled it away nervously.

"By the 'moon goddess?'" I fought not to roll my eyes.

"Something like that," he clenched his jaw. "We were

36

meant to be together. We fit for some reason. We make each other better, stronger. That's what mates do. They challenge you, protect you, love you, strengthen you. Margo, I promise you, this is going to be the best thing that will ever happen to us. You just have to give it some time; you have to adjust."

"You don't know that," I whimpered. "You took me away from Caddy, he's my family, he's the only person I have, and you took me from him."

He slid off the couch onto his knees in front of me, placing his hands on the armrests of the chair. I sat back further in my chair to put distance between us.

"I'm sorry that the way we met was so...rough. But I don't regret meeting you. Many shifters don't meet their mates, and I've been blessed with you. I understand your frustration, your anger, your skepticism, but you will make friends here. I will care for you. I will love you. I will take care of you. You are my world now, Margo. You will never be safer than you are with me; you will be treated like a queen."

I shook from the proximity, nodding my head to appease him.

"Margo, I don't want you to be afraid of me. I might be stern around others, but it's only to keep you safe. I don't want anything to happen to you."

"So that's what you were doing yesterday when you yelled at me and bruised me in front of the whole pack, you were keeping me safe?" My voice was thick with emotion, the back of my throat beginning to burn with the raw, rough scream that was building under the surface.

"Yes," he pressed on. "If I could go back and do it differently, maybe I would, but it's the only way I saw us getting out of there without anyone knowing you're my mate."

"What is so bad about that?" Tears began collecting in my eyes. "You said I was a gift, that I'm your world. Why does it matter if other people know?"

"I'm an Enforcer, Margo," he slumped tiredly on his knees. "The only one on this entire continent and I worked really hard to get this position, but that doesn't mean it comes without threats. There are a lot of people that want this job; it comes with a lot of power. That's why I have those guards standing outside. That's why no one can know about you until I make sure you are absolutely safe. I wouldn't know what to do with myself if you got hurt because someone was trying to hurt me."

His words sunk into my skin like a lullaby, and I nodded understandingly. He was only trying to make sure I was safe, and there was nothing to fault him for. I studied his face as he knelt before me, his thick, dark hair, the tan skin that sat with two wrinkles between his gunmetal, blue eyes as he stared at me anxiously. Soft pink lips tilted in a frown, two freckles that sat on his right cheekbone, all of which melted into the humble man who sat on the ground in front of me.

When I stayed quiet, he left for a while, going upstairs and closing a door. I wandered around the first floor, finding a stainless-steel kitchen, a small den that looked like the Enforcer's office, a few large bedrooms, another office, a few storage rooms, and then I found myself back in the large open space near the front door. His house was open, and the floor plan didn't allow many places to hide, which I suppose was the point of it.

I found a space near the wall of windows and curled up in the closest chair, watching the world around me. The men near the door never moved, constantly watching for signs of an intruder. There was a small space of grass around the house, and then the tree line started about one hundred feet away.

In the distance, a squirrel ran up a tree. I never thought I would be jealous of a squirrel, sitting on the other side of the glass like a caged animal. I sighed and turned my attention back to the interior of the house. It was beautiful, designed with quality and masculine, refined taste, but it was a cage around me.

"Margo," the Enforcer greeted as he came downstairs again. I looked over apprehensively. "Would you come upstairs with me? I want to show you something." I untangled my legs from the seat and trailed after him. A few doors before his bedroom, he opened a door.

There was nothing inside.

"You wanted to show me an empty room?" I wondered, stepping inside a little.

"I cleared it out. It used to be a guest room. I thought you might like it, and you can turn it into whatever you'd like. I'll help you."

"So, this could be my bedroom," I thought softly.

"We will be sharing the bedroom. I can't have you sleeping in another room, but you can turn this into a library, a craft room, an art studio, wardrobe, a place where you hang your hate mail towards me," he chuckled.

"I don't have anything," I realized, the weight of that sentiment pushing down on my shoulders. "I have nothing with me."

"I will get you whatever you want, anything, everything," he promised, tucking his thumbs into the pockets of his pants. "This job does have some perks, we, uh, have plenty of resources."

I looked around the room. It had one wall of stone, and the rest were a smooth, chestnut color wood. The far wall, just like the bedroom, was made of windows, and thick grey curtains draped the sides.

"I want this to be your home too," he said softly, shrugging his shoulders, hands still tucked in his pockets, eyes following me as I trailed along the spacious room.

"Okay," I agreed half-heartedly.

His smile grew, and he nodded his head, trying to contain his excitement. He slowly walked out of the room, muttering a soft, "yes," under his breath as he walked down the echoing hallway.

LINEAGE

In the evening, Theo put an old movie on the television and sat on his couch, eating a hearty meal of braised beef and sliced potatoes. He ate his quickly; his plate was empty within minutes. I was used to eating lighter foods, fruits, and vegetables since the meat and large things were reserved for the wolves. The food Theo gave me was filling, and I struggled to finish even half.

"Do you not like it?" he asked when he noticed I hadn't eaten much.

"It's not that, it's good, I'm just not used to eating so much meat," I tried to keep my voice soft. I realized when people raised their voices, Theo raised his, and I didn't want to anger him.

He got up from his seat and went to the kitchen, banging around in his fridge and cupboards until I called out, "This is fine! I'm sorry."

"How do I not have any fruits or vegetables in this house," he said dumbfounded. "I'm sorry, Margo, we can go into town tomorrow, and we can get things you like as well."

"We can go into town?" I asked, hopefully.

"Of course." His eyebrows tugged together. "You aren't a prisoner here. I hope you know that." I looked down, shamefully, and he sighed loudly. "Margo, I'm not going to lock you inside all day. We can go out; I don't want you to think of this as your cage or your cell."

I continued eating, watching the black and white film on his television. Outside, it grew dark, and the trees began to look like people. I had never liked the dark; something about it made me weary. Wolves could see in the dark, unlike me, and it scared me that I had even more of a disadvantage.

I looked over at Theo, who was staring outside as well, looking farther in the distance. He stiffened, sat up straighter, and then relaxed in his seat again. I looked at him in confusion.

"Deer," he stated, picking up the remote to turn the volume up. We sat there for most of the night, not saying anything to each other, and somewhere around eleven o'clock, I found myself dozing off on the plush couch.

I was almost asleep when Theo shifted his weight on the couch, and I jolted awake. He apologetically grinned as I sat up and stretched.

"Do you want to go to bed?" he asked. I nodded, standing, and following him upstairs. He gave me another change of clothes to sleep in and waited for me to change in the bathroom. The covers were pulled back when I came back, and he was taking a pillow from his side of the bed and throwing it on the ground next to the bed.

I crawled into my side of the bed, and he pulled the covers up around my chin, tucked me in, adjusted my pillows, and then sat on the edge of the bed. He brushed my hair back, like he always seemed to, and touched my forehead with his thumb. He looked like he wanted to say something but didn't.

Instead, he took a blanket from the edge of the bed and slid down to the floor, curling under the blanket and resting his head on the pillow.

I perked my head up and looked around, peeking over the side of the bed, still hidden by the covers. Theo laid on the ground, looking positively uncomfortable as he closed his eyes and tried to sleep.

"I can feel you looking at me, little one," he said smiling, eyes still shut. I shot back to my position and closed my eyes.

* * *

In the morning, I woke before Theo and crept quietly to the bathroom, where I washed my face and used the toilet. When I flushed, I heard Theo groan outside.

He sat up on his elbows when I opened the bathroom door, stretching and groaning loudly before he stood up and trudged over to the closet. As he walked, he looked at me, sizing me up. I waited in the doorway to the closet as he rifled through some pants, finding a pair of athletic, black sweatpants, and a worn, blue, crewneck sweatshirt with a town name on it.

"These are the smallest things I've got," he said regretfully, holding them out for me. I nodded and took them, changed in the bathroom, and came out to the side of the bed to roll the pants and arms of the clothes up so they didn't trip me. "I thought we could go into town for some breakfast, and then we could go shopping," he offered. I nodded, okay, and he smiled, grabbing a pair of socks and slippers. "We can buy you more things while we're out. I'm sure you don't want to wear my clothes forever."

I nodded again, sliding the slippers on my feet; they

slipped off my heels as I walked, and I almost tripped over my foot. Theo put a steadying hand on my shoulders, leading me downstairs, where he grabbed two coats, a scarf, and a pair of gloves.

"It's a lot colder here," he said, wrapping the scarf around my neck several times despite my grimace. "I don't want you to get cold."

We walked outside, nodded to the guards, and climbed in the back of a large SUV. We traveled for about fifteen minutes before we reached the small town. It was quaint, small shops with a few people walking down the street. They stopped and stared as the stream of black cars passed them.

Three guards followed us as we exited the car and walked into a bakery, where I was immediately greeted by the smell of fresh bread.

"Theo!" A woman called affectionately over the counter. Theo smiled back and brought us to the counter while the guards took a seat in one of the corners near the entrance. "Where have you been, boy? I know you're busy, but I haven't seen you in weeks! Was it something I fed you?"

"Emily," he chuckled. "You know everything that comes out of your oven is heavenly. I've been traveling, but I'm back now. I promise I'll come in more."

The woman smiled; the lines around her full cheeks showed prominently. She was older, maybe in her fifties, her brown hair tied back with a ribbon.

"Margo, this is Emily. Emily, this is my mate, Margo." Emily smiled at me warmly.

"Oh my gosh, you must be so happy," she gushed, leaning her elbows on the counter. "I have to call your mother; she must be over the moon."

"Could you wait to call her?" Theo's eyes narrowed as Emily placed her hand on her hip.

"You haven't told your mother, boy?"

"This is only her second day here, Emily. I wanted her to get settled in before I throw her to the shark."

"Well, okay," Emily conceded. "But if you haven't told her by the end of the week, I'm going to have to hit your behind with this rolling pin."

"Emily, I am a grown man." His bottom lip pushed out.

"And you're still afraid of your mother," she reminded him, setting the rolling pin down.

Theo smiled softly, and we took a plate of raspberry scones and pistachio shortbread to a pastel-colored table. The guards looked at us longingly, but Theo assured me they would get a lunch break after our excursion.

"Theo," I whispered suddenly, glancing around us. He looked at me in concern. "Whose territory are we on right now? I thought you needed permission to bring a human into a pack's territory?"

Theo chuckled, leaning back in his seat lazily, and continued consuming his meal. "Little one, this is my brother's territory. Even so, I can go where I please; I am the Enforcer."

"Just like that?"

"Just like that," he smirked, wiping a stray crumb from his lip. "I would never do anything to put you in danger." My head ducked, and I felt a warm blush crawl onto my cheeks from my neck. "How much do you know about Enforcer's?"

"Not a lot," I pursed my lips, embarrassed that I didn't know more. He didn't seem bothered by my lack of knowledge and proceeded to tell me the inner workings of his job and how his position came to be.

"So all the other Alpha's voted for you, and now you get to do whatever you want?"

Theo chuckled in amusement. "No, sweetheart. I don't

get to do whatever I want. There are five other Enforcers, one on each continent except for Antarctica. We keep each other in check. There is no one person above everyone else."

"Well then, what happens if you go rogue and start killing everyone?" I threw the question out, my mind buzzing with hypotheticals.

"Well, the other five would probably come and hold a trial. They would decide what would happen to me."

"But what if all six of you went crazy at the same time?"

"Is this really what's going on in your mind all the time?"

"Kind of," I mumbled, looking away.

"No wonder why you're so quiet," he teased.

"That's mean," I said softly, not knowing how he would react. He smiled largely and set his food down.

"I'm sorry," he mumbled, looking over his shoulder at the guards.

"So, just one brother?"

"Three actually, all younger than me," he said a little pridefully.

"What are they like?" I rested my cheek against my hand.

"Curious little thing, aren't you?" He smiled, sliding the plate away from him towards the middle of the table.

"I'm an only child," I offered, biting my lip. "I never had any brothers or sisters."

"Well," Theo began. "Gabriel is twenty-eight, he's the Alpha of this pack now. I handed the title to him a few months ago when I got this position. He's a lot like me, we have the same views, but he's a bit stricter than I was. He takes his job very seriously. And there's Reese, he's twenty-five, and the

Beta of the pack-although sometimes I don't know why," he chuckled.

"Why?"

"Reese sometimes isn't as serious as we'd like him to be. He'd rather make jokes than do his job most days, but when Gabriel needs him to be, he's a good Beta. And then there's Eli; he's the youngest, he just turned twenty-three. He doesn't really know what he wants to do yet. He's not as rugged or competitive as the rest of us. But he's only twenty-three, he's got time."

"If Gabriel is twenty-eight, how old does that make you?" I said hesitantly.

"Old?" Theo scoffed. "I'm only twenty-nine, I'm not 'old.'"

"You're older than me," I nodded.

"And how old is that?"

"Twenty-two," I said firmly.

"You and Eli will be best friends," he chuckled.

"And your other brothers?"

"They'll love you, too," he assured me seriously. "Just don't take anything Reese says seriously. And I promise you, Gabriel isn't nearly as scary as he tries to seem."

I nodded, thinking his parents must have been patient to raise a house of boys. Theo stood up from his seat and held his hand out for me to grab. I did, hesitantly, and we said good-bye to Emily before leaving the bakery. The guards followed us out quietly and remained a few feet back as we strolled down the street.

"What would you like to do first?" Theo asked, tugging me closer. "We need to get you clothes, food that you like. I'm sure my mother will want to take you shopping for makeup and dresses and things, but we'll make a good dent for now."

"Um," I stuttered, looking around to the various shops.

"How about we go get you some clothes? You're falling out of mine."

"I don't have any money," I whispered sideways towards him, hoping the guards wouldn't hear. Theo's smile grew, and he squeezed my hand.

"Well, I guess it's a good thing your mate is a very important official with money to spare," he smirked. "Whatever you want is yours, Margo, just say the word."

We stopped into a few shops, and Theo began grabbing everything from thick leggings and snow boots to socks and pajamas. I stayed at the sides of the shops near the guards, watching him and the ladies who worked in the stops pick items out.

"Margo," Theo smiled apprehensively. "Will you please come help me pick out things you want? I've got some of the basics, but I don't know what you like to wear, and I'm pretty sure you don't want me picking out your undergarments."

I cautiously walked over to him, trailing my fingers over the racks of clothing. I had never picked out my own clothing. Sure, Caddy had bought me a few things for my birthday or a special occasion, but most of my clothes were hand-me-downs, what little clothing I did have.

Theo held up a crème sweater in one hand and a silk top in the other, looking at them like he wasn't sure what they were for. I glanced at them and back to the rack in front of us. I ran my hands over a denim shirt, a plain gray sweater, a distressed pair of stone-washed jeans. Theo set what was in his hands down and picked up anything that my hands touched. Nothing I ever owned was sparkly, flashy, or audacious, and I greatly preferred things that were subtle and comfortable.

I didn't notice Theo's arms were full until I had maneuvered around the entire shop. I stared at his arms, piled up to his shoulders with clothing, and to the guard behind him that had become Theo's lacky when his arms grew too full.

"Theo," I hesitated.

"Margo, whatever you want is yours."

"It's just so many things."

"Yes, and we have three more shops to go to today, and if you don't have this much clothing after each, I'm going to take you back out tomorrow. So, you might as well fill up now."

I nodded, scared that I was asking too much of him. Somewhere in my head, a thought reminded me he took me; he was the one forcing me to stay here. In a new haste, I grabbed another pair of shoes, four pairs of socks, a headband, a soft cotton jacket, and a stack of plain, gold bracelets near the cashier.

Theo smiled encouragingly, not realizing I was punishing his wallet for his actions. He paid for everything, and true to his word, we did the same in the next three shops. He stayed close to me, deliberately watching me to learn what kinds of things I liked or disliked. I had to sneak away to look at undergarments, though when he found me again, he blushed, and called a store worker over to help me.

I decided to make my room in a quiet sanctuary, filled with books, art, and embroidery tools. Theo gathered as much as he could, promising that when we got home, I could pick furniture out online to be delivered.

By the time we got home, we had eaten dinner and filled up the entire car with my new belongings. Theo and the other guards carried everything inside and set the bags in my new room.

Theo had paperwork to finish, so he left me upstairs to sort through my new things. There was a box of hangers to hang my clothing in Theo's closet, where he had cleared out half of the rectangular room for me. I stacked the books and paintings against the stone wall and began sliding my clothes on hangers when I noticed a faction of men walking quickly through the woods towards the house.

BLOOD TIES

They looked up and saw me in the window, and their smiles grew. They quickened their pace as I raced to the stairs and called Theo's name loudly.

He rushed to the stairs, climbing them in three motions, and grabbed my shoulders to check if I was injured. I stepped out of his reach and pushed his hands off me.

"Theo," I panted. "Men were coming toward the house."

He turned his head quickly, listening to the sounds outside, and then went down the stairs in the same motion as before. The door flew open, and three men, along with a nervous guard, came in. Theo growled loudly, but the three men only laughed.

"Why are you in my home?" he fumed.

"Emily told Mom you had a human girl with you today, buying her all sorts of things," one said humorously.

"Got yourself a little human plaything, have you?"

"She's none of your concern," Theo shot back.

"Theo, we just wanted to make sure you aren't torturing the girl," the smallest one said, peeking his head around the tallest. "We saw her in the window. She's really pretty."

I took two steps down, peeking over the banister to look at the men. They were tall with the same dark brown hair as Theo; I assumed they were his brothers from the way they spoke.

"She is nothing to worry about for now," Theo said calmly, straightening his back.

"Come on, we've never met a human girl before," the middle one said. "What's she like?"

"She is a human, that's all you need to know for now."

"She is not just a human," the middle one rolled his eyes. "You've never had an interest in them before, so why is she here? Come on, tell us."

"Maybe she'll tell us," the smallest one pointed towards me, spying from the stairs.

"Human girl," the biggest one called. "Come down here; we won't hurt you."

They chuckled while I shivered and looked to Theo, who only nodded his head sadly. I slowly descended, and my eyes never left their faces.

"My, our big brother has such a sweet pet," they joked. Theo growled, turning to find me standing close to his back.

"Reese," Theo warned.

"Oh, we're just messing around," he laughed, reaching a hand out. "What's your name?"

I gulped and whispered back, "Margo."

"Margo," he grasped my arm roughly. "I'm Reese, Theo's favorite brother. Has he been treating you kindly?"

I nodded, grabbing the back of Theo's shirt hem. He noticed my distress and quickly wrapped his hand around mine, giving it a light squeeze.

"Well, she certainly seems like more than just a girl," the smallest one noted.

"Don't worry about her," Theo scolded, moving to sit me in a plush chair out of view. The men followed, throwing themselves on the couches comfortably.

"I mean, Margo is very pretty. If he doesn't want her, I'm sure she wouldn't mind spending the night with me, hey Eli?" Reese joked, kitting the smaller one on the leg.

Theo growled again and moved closer to Reese. He grabbed the boy's arm and hauled him up to his feet.

"You. Will. Not. Touch. Her," he heaved out, body shaking, veins expanding.

"Theo," the biggest one called calmly.

"No one touches her, Gabriel!" Theo screamed as his brother struggled to escape his grasp. Theo began shaking, and I knew from experience this happened when they were fighting the urge to shift.

"Okay, Theo. But you need to calm down," Gabriel warned.

Theo's head snapped over. His usually blue eyes were a dark onyx. I shrunk back in my seat as far as I could, blocking my face as I pulled my knees up to my chest.

"Theo, you're scaring her," Eli said softly. That was enough to stop him. He released his brother in a clumsy drop and relaxed his shoulders. He started moving towards me slowly, keeping his hands in front of his innocently.

"Hey," he whispered as his eyes returned to their normal hue. "I'm sorry. I wasn't thinking, Margo. I'm not going to hurt anyone. I'll never hurt you." Slowly, he made his way to my side, moving cautiously.

"Brother," Gabriel beckoned. Theo turned his head but didn't move from his place in front of me. "Is she?"

Theo nodded his head before turning and kneeling by me. His eyes begged for my forgiveness, but I was still shaken from seeing him in his raw stare.

"Is she what?" Reese whispered to Gabriel.

"His mate," was all he said.

The room fell silent until I unraveled myself from my contorted position, allowing Theo to sit on the edge of the large chair with me.

"No one can know," Theo said.

"The pack should know," Gabriel insisted, leaning forward over his knees and interlaced his fingers.

"They can't, not yet."

"How are they supposed to protect her if they don't know about her?" That made Theo think.

"I don't want anything to happen to her before I can put security measures in place. I need to hire and screen more guards, I need to go over safety procedures with her, I need to-" Theo rattled off, only to be interrupted by Gabriel.

"Theo, I can't think of a better security measure than introducing her to the pack. Fifty thousand wolves will be protecting her; there would be no safer place for her."

Theo closed his eyes, weighing his options. He never once asked me for my preference and made the decision to introduce me at the end of the week. His brothers nodded in agreement, perking up at the talk of a pack meeting. No one noticed my discomfort.

"I don't want to meet any more wolves," I murmured, blocking my face with my hair. Theo set a hand on my back, gently brushing the long curls that rested against my spine.

"Did we really make that bad of an impression?" Eli joked softly.

"No," I said quickly, afraid to offend them.

"Then what is it?" Theo asked.

I fidgeted with my fingers while they stared at me. "It's just all a bit much. I know shifters like to do things fast, and I get why you want to introduce me, but could we please wait a few more weeks?"

Theo's eyes softened, and he instantly nodded his head. "Of course, we can. I'm sorry, Margo, I wasn't even thinking about how stressful this has all been on you. We can take all the time you need." My frantic heart stopped beating quite as fast, and I settled back into the chair.

"Mom's going to kill you," Reese spoke, breaking the silence. "You didn't introduce her to your own mate. Emily was the first one to meet her and see you after you've been gone for weeks."

"Mom can wait. No one was supposed to meet her yet. You bunch just came barging through my door."

"Rightfully so," Reese joked. "You were hiding something from us. Isn't that punishable, Gabe? Hiding a human from the Alpha?"

"You know very well Theo can do as he pleases," Gabriel scolded his younger brother.

"Big, bad, Enforcer man," Reese grumbled. "Thinks he's all that."

"I can still take you down with one arm, kid," Theo snorted, watching Reese's face turn to a scowl.

"So, what are you going to do with her?" Eli asked suddenly.

"What do you mean?" Theo asked.

"I mean, are you going to turn her?"

Theo narrowed his eyes at the question. "No," I answered for him. My eyes got wider as Theo looked at me in confusion. "No, you aren't turning me."

"Margo," Theo whispered.

"You aren't turning me." I shook my head. "I don't want to be a shifter."

"Margo, it's not a bad thing," Gabriel assured me.

I continued shaking my head as my heartbeat sped up again. My hands shook as I tried to brush the hair from my clammy forehead. Theo reached his hand down to steady me, but I shot out of the chair and turned around to face him.

"No," I panted. "No, I won't do it."

"Margo, calm down," Theo said softly, eyeing me nervously.

"I can't 'calm down,' Theo. Please don't make me do that. Please."

"We aren't bad people," Reese said with a slight smile on his face.

"Why don't you want to be a shifter?" Theo questioned. I didn't reply. "Tell me," He prodded more when I remained quiet. He stood and moved closer to me, grabbing my chin between his thumb and finger, forcing me to look at him.

"I watched my parents die," I whimpered. His grip on my chin loosened, but he kept his fingers against my cheek. "The old Alpha and Luna of my pack murdered my parents in front of the entire pack when I was four. They whipped my father until he bled out, and then they raped my mother over his body until her spine snapped. That's why I don't want to become a shifter," I spat.

"Sweetheart," Theo sighed, letting his hand drop.

"Our pack doesn't harm humans," Gabriel said sorrowfully.

"No one will ever hurt you here, Margo," Reese bit his lip.

"We'll leave you two," Gabriel murmured, grabbing his older brother's shoulder sympathetically. Theo's brothers left, and we remained a foot apart in the living room, staring each other down.

"I'm sorry," Theo eventually said. "I'm sorry they did that to your parents. You should have never had to see that, but that doesn't mean all shifters are like that."

"I know that," I told him. "I know there are good shifters, and there are bad shifters, just like there are good humans and bad humans. Caddy is my best friend, trust me, I know what most shifters are like, but I can't do that to them. I can't willingly let myself become what killed them."

Theo nodded tiredly. "Okay," he relented. "Can we go up to bed?"

I followed him as he went to the bedroom and laid on top of the covers. I crawled in next to him, laying at the far edge of the bed. His hands found their way behind his head as he stared at the ceiling.

"A lot of Alpha's used to do horrible things because they were arrogant," he said unexpectedly. "They thought they were the most powerful people on the planet. That's why my position was created. If there had been an Enforcer when you were little, your parents would have never been killed. Or there would have at least been consequences."

"I can't let them down again," I said back, keeping my back turned so he couldn't see my tears. "I was too young before, but I can't do that to them."

"Margo," he sighed, tugging on my arm until I rolled flat on my back. His face fell when he saw my red eyes, and he lifted one hand to stroke my forehead lightly. "I won't do anything you don't want me to do, but if it comes to a choice between turning you or letting you die...I'm going to do everything I can to protect you."

"You should let me go, Theo," I said softly with conviction, looking up at him with immense guilt. "It won't be worth it."

"I can't wait to show you how wrong you are," Theo smiled crookedly. He leaned down and placed a kiss on my hairline, closing his eyes as he did so. "Go to sleep, Margo. We can argue to your heart's content tomorrow."

INTOXICATION

The next weeks were quiet, with no intrusions, no stress. Theo worked on paperwork and made phone calls while I decorated my room, hung my clothes, and read in front of the fireplace. I was trying to find where I fit into this new life, but it was more difficult than simply changing packs. I was somebody's somebody now, and with that came new rules, new routines, and new feelings.

When Theo wasn't on a business call, I stole the phone and called Caddy, who was always excited to hear my voice. He wept when I first talked to him because he believed I would end up dead in Theo's control; they all had believed that. As angry as Caddy was at Theo, he also understood his actions.

After a while, Theo found it bothersome to only have one phone in the house and bought me my very own. The shifters could communicate through mind-link if they were acquainted, and they only made phone calls in business settings. Caddy, Theo, and Theo's brothers were the only numbers programmed into it, which was more than I needed since

I only called Caddy. Theo was always with me.

Although I tried to keep my distance for my own selfish, unavoidable reasons, Theo was starting to grow on me. He didn't speak to me like I expected an Enforcer to, he was patient and respectful, and as much as it pained me to admit, I found myself opening up to him. He was easy to talk to, and I didn't have anyone else to talk to besides Caddy, who was busy with his Alpha training. Even when he asked to mark me, he was considerate of my hesitations and explained everything to me multiple times.

"Marking is sort of like me asking you to be my girlfriend," he had chuckled as I sat on the edge of his desk. "It's not as serious as mating, by any means, but it's a step in the right direction."

"Well, what does it do?" I bit my lip, immediately releasing it when Theo's eyes darkened.

"In very blatant terms, it puts some of my DNA in your body, and you will put some of your DNA in mine. It binds us so that we can feel each other's emotions and pain. If you were ever in trouble, it would help me find you faster. It's also very sacred to shifters because it shows that you are spoken for; any shifter will be able to smell my scent on you and know that your mate is a high-ranking wolf with Alpha blood."

"So, you want to mark me as your territory? Your property?"

Theo paused, noticing the spiteful tone in my voice, and moved his office chair closer to me. He placed his hands on my knees and cleared his throat. "I guess I didn't say that as well as I hoped. It's not me marking my territory; it's me claiming you as mine. It means that I want you all to myself, and I don't want anyone else's hands on you. It means I'm taking on the responsibility of a mate, and that you are as well."

His thumb moved circularly on my thigh as I peered at

him suspiciously.

"Will it hurt?"

His face scrunched up in guilt, and he ultimately sighed, dragging his hands off my legs. "Honestly? I don't know."

"What do you mean?"

"I mean, I've never marked anyone, Margo," he said chuckling, shrugging his shoulders. "From what I was told, it's very pleasurable for wolves. After the initial break into the skin, the marking bite releases all kinds of endorphins and chemicals in your brain. I've just never heard what it's like from a human standpoint. There hasn't been much research done on human mates because it happens so infrequently, and it's not like there's a blog about it."

"Well, what if it feels like you're stabbing me in the neck fifty times?" Theo laughed at my example. He reached for my hands, bending his head down to kiss my knuckles before looking up at me through his dark eyelashes.

"Margo, I would never do something that causes you pain like that. The worst it would ever feel like is an actual bite, but it would be over in thirty seconds, and I could give you some of my blood to heal you if you needed."

"Why do you want to feed me your blood?" I asked horrified. I knew I was only focusing on the negative parts of his explanation, but I couldn't help it. Watching Theo get flustered and try to reel back his statements was too fun. Most of the time, I was the one fumbling over my words, and I wasn't going to let this opportunity pass without evening the playing field.

"Did you learn anything from your pack?" he asked in exasperation, looking at me with wide eyes. I fought back a chuckle and kept my scared look. "Margo, it's not like drinking someone's blood for sport. One of the amazing things about finding your mate is their blood can heal wounds. I don't think it would work on me because you're human, so it's a good thing I never get hurt." He smirked. "But, a small amount of my blood will stop the pain from the marking bite, though I don't think you'll actually need it."

"So, you bite me, then I bite you, and then we're marked?"

"Essentially, yes." He pursed his lips, waiting for my next remark.

"And how do I know that you won't give me the shifter's bite instead?" I raised one eyebrow and crossed my arms over my chest.

"Do you really think I would do that to you?"

"No," I admitted. "But I'd like to know the semantics of that as well."

Theo chuckled, squeezing the bridge of his nose as he settled into his seat. "This is going to be a long night, isn't it?"

"No. I just want to know what I'm getting myself into. If you were a human and your big, scary mate asked to bite you on your neck, you'd feel the same way."

"Well, if my big, scary mate was half as cute as you, I'd let them," he teased, loving the dark red blush that crept onto my face. "And then my big, scary mate would reassure me that the marking bite and the shifter's bite are completely different. In order for a shifter to turn their human mate, the shifter has to be...shifted for lack of a better word. I'd have to be in my wolf form to turn you. I think that would give you a little heads up, so if I suddenly shift in front of you and go for your neck, you'd have plenty of time to find a lamp or something to bash over my head."

"That's comforting," I noted sarcastically.

"The hardest thing is going to be you trying to bite through my skin with these little baby incisors," he said, reaching to move my upper lip, and run his thumb over my tooth. I shoved his hand away as he laughed. "Can you even bite through an apple with those little guys?"

"Of course I can," I gritted, clenching my jaw tightly. "Sorry, I don't have dog teeth like you."

"Wolf teeth, sweetheart. Not dog." I rolled my eyes. "I guess you'll just have to bite really hard, find some pent-up aggression and let it out."

"Because I have no aggression towards you at all," I smirked. "And it can't be that hard."

"Shifter's skin is a bit tougher than human skin. It'd be pretty hard to be fierce predators if we got paper cuts and slivers," he chuckled.

"Well, fine," I declared, sliding off the desk. "I can do it."

"Not here, Margo," Theo shook his head. I grabbed his hand and tugged until he stood up from his chair and followed me to our bedroom. I dropped his hand and stood with my hands on my hips as he sunk into the bed. "Don't you think it's a bit strange that we're about to mark each other and you still haven't kissed me yet?"

"I know where you're going with this, and you can have your kiss after we do this," I said determinedly.

"Why not now?"

"Because if we wait too long, I'll chicken out, and also because you said I couldn't do the bite."

"So, that means we have to do it right now?" Theo concluded. I nodded. "Of course."

"Why?" I asked, stepping back. "Do you not want to?"

Theo grabbed my hips and pulled me onto him, my legs between his and my hands resting on his shoulders. "Of course, I want to. I'd love nothing more than to bear your mark. I just want to be sure you're okay with this."

"As long as it's not the shifter bite, I'm fine with it."

"Well, okay." He nodded, digging his fingers into the soft skin of my hips where my shirt rose up. "Do you want to go first, or do you want me to? Traditionally the male goes first, but I don't mind either way."

"That's okay with me," I whispered. A bout of nervousness hit my stomach as we finalized everything. Theo saw it and kissed my cheek softly before lifting me up and gently tossing me on the bed beside him. I let out a squeak and the sudden movement, but before I could comprehend, he was above me.

"If you want me to stop, now would be the time to tell me," he warned, leaning over me.

"I don't," I said quickly, smiling for a second before it disappeared. Theo grinned calmly, leaning down the place a kiss on my collarbone. He moved the black sweater I was wearing down my shoulder along with the strap of my bra, which at any other moment would send him into a lustful fit. Now he was calm, sensuous, loving, unperturbed by the strap of my brassiere.

He trailed two kisses up the left side of my neck, gently trailing his tongue along the line of my veins. It was important that his bite did not nick an artery or vein, because no amount of his blood would be able to stop the pain of me bleeding out on his bed. He paid careful consideration to that and found his opportune place in the crook of my neck, two inches below my ear.

He kissed the area firmly. I felt his shifter's incisors grow as he placed his mouth over the area. He took a deep breath and lifted his left hand to hold my cheek in place as his teeth dove into the soft skin of my neck.

I let out a small noise of discomfort as the pain of his bite seared into my skin. Once he stopped moving and allowed the bite to take action, a rush of happiness flooded into my brain. I nearly felt drunk as his teeth slowly receded, and he licked the area clean of my blood. I closed my eyes as he gently set my head back on the bed and sat up straighter.

"Margo?" he whispered. I moaned lazily but didn't open my eyes. "Margo," he chuckled, shaking my shoulder softly.

"What?" I breathed.

"Are you okay? Did it hurt?"

"It felt," I slurred. "Delightful." Theo laughed loudly, his booming voice startling me, and I jumped slightly.

"I'm glad it felt good. It's your turn now," he told me.

I groaned and reached up for his help. He grabbed my hand and pulled me into a sitting position. When he noticed me slumping backward, he lifted me up and placed me on his lap with my legs and arms around him. His hand came around the back of my head, and he positioned my mouth over the point on his neck that I was supposed to bite.

"Okay, whenever you're ready," he prompted, stroking to back of my head. The gentle motion lulled me, and I fought to keep my eyes open. "Margo, you're almost done, and then you can take a nap, but right now, I need you to open that cute little mouth of yours and bite me."

I opened my mouth and sat up in his lap, grabbing onto his shoulders to steady me as I placed my teeth in the correct position. The first time I tried to mark him, he laughed at my attempt and told me, "You're going to have to bite a little harder than that."

I gritted my teeth and bit down harder, getting frustrated that my incisors weren't sinking in as easily. "It's okay, Margo," he soothed, gently rubbing my back. "Just bite a little harder, you won't hurt me, I swear. Just a bit more, there you go," he cooed as my teeth finally broke the surface.

A rush of his blood came into my mouth, and I choked back the urge to gag, knowing it would only be a few more seconds. His blood tasted like metal, but when a small bit of it glided down my throat, I felt my own mark tingle as it healed.

"I think you're fine now," he whispered. I slid my teeth out of his neck and wiped my chin of the line of blood that cascaded down it. He smiled brilliantly and tilted my chin up towards his mouth. His lips gently pressed against mine, and he added just a touch of pressure. It wasn't a long kiss, and it wasn't deep and seductive, but I felt a small sizzle in the pit of my stomach.

He pulled away after a few seconds. I kept my eyes closed, and my lips slightly pouted as he leaned me back against the bed.

"That was my first kiss, you know," I said breathlessly as he lifted a blanket over me.

"It was not," he denied, looking down at me in shock.

"Yeah, no one in my old pack wanted to kiss the poor, weird, little human girl. I was sort of the black sheep. Although Caddy kissed me once when I was seven, I don't think that counts, do you?"

"No," he laughed. "I don't think that counts."

"So, yeah." I nodded, never opening my eyes. "That was the first one. Do you feel special now?"

"Of course, I do," he said sincerely, kissing my forehead as he stood up. "Get some sleep, sweet girl. I'll give you your second and third and fourth kisses when you wake up."

THE VALKYRIES

With my eyes still closed, I felt Theo's warm breath on my face. I groaned, scrunching my face up, and then opened my eyes to see Theo staring at me.

"Come on, sleepyhead. We've got a big day ahead of us," he encouraged, getting out of bed much too cheerfully.

"Go back to sleep," I whined, covering my head with the comforter. He yanked the covers off me, pulling them down by my feet. I instantly pulled my legs up to my chest as the cool air hit me.

"We can't, Margo. You've got to get ready. Gabriel is gathering the wolves, and they'll be ready for us in about an hour."

I shot up, nearly bashing heads with Theo. "He's gathering them now?" I wailed. Theo nodded, walking into his closet. "Why didn't you tell me about this sooner?"

"I reminded you last night before I went to bed, but you were still kind of bite-drunk, so it doesn't surprise me you don't remember."

"Ugh," I growled, fighting my way past him to my side of the closet, fishing through all my shirts and pants and dresses to find something suitable.

"Margo, are you okay?"

"No!" I shouted with my head in a pile of clothes. Theo chuckled and walked over to me, removing a shift from my head and fixing my hair. "What do you wear when you're going to be on display in front of thousands of wolf shifters?"

Theo crouched down and smiled at my disheveled appearance. "I don't know what to tell you, little one. Dress warm; we're going to be outside of the packhouse, there's a sort of stage and podium area where Gabriel talks, but it's in the open, and it's windy today."

I nodded and started sorting things into piles of warm and cold clothes. Eventually, I found a calf-length olive dress with bell sleeves. It was very chic, something Caddy's mom would be proud of me choosing, and it was longer than most of my other dresses. I fixed my hair in the bathroom mirror, cursing that I didn't know how to put on sophisticated makeup, and settled for mascara and lipstick, the only staples I was ever taught how to use.

As I pulled a pair of tan, ankle boots on my feet, Theo wandered out from the closet in his usual black slacks, and his white shirt rolled up to his elbows.

"Margo, your legs are going to be cold," he scolded.

"The few inches that are bare," I giggled. "I wanted to look nice, Theo." He nodded, grabbing my hand to lead me downstairs, where we put our coats on.

The drive was shorter than the trip to town. Theo held my hand in his lap, stroking it gently as I watched the trees pass by us. Once we got close enough, I could see the packhouse was larger, by far than any structure I had seen.

It was like a castle in its grandeur, standing several stories high with different wings and adjoining buildings that could house my entire old pack. We arrived in the back, where Gabriel stood on a podium, not speaking yet, and his pack surrounded the area.

I wiped my forehead nervously. Theo noticed and moved to put his warm hand on my shaking knee.

"It's going to be fine, Margo. They'll love you."

"But what if they don't?" I asked frightfully. He smiled a little and kissed the side of my head as the driver parked alongside the building. We walked towards the side of the stage area with Theo mainly dragging me behind him.

"Thank you for being here today," Gabriel spoke through the microphone as we approached. "I called you all here for an important purpose. As you all know, we rarely call everyone together except in wartime, but this is not wartime, this is a grand occasion." Gabriel smiled, glancing over towards Theo and me. Theo stood behind me, his hands on my shoulders to prevent me from running off.

"As you are all aware, my brother Theodore has taken over the position of Enforcer. It is with great pleasure that I invite him up here to speak and introduce you to his lovely mate."

A roar of whispers and intrigue surfaced as Theo climbed the few steps, dragging me by my hand behind him until we reached the center of the podium.

"Quiet," he spoke sternly. The crowd hushed, staring at me. I stood next to Theo, completely exposed as he kept his hand firmly around my wrist. "Gabriel has called you all here today so that I would be able to introduce my wonderful mate to you all." Theo smiled down affectionately at me. "Valkyrie Pack, please welcome, Margo. I trust you will all treat her with the same kindness and respect as you have always shown me and my family."

The crowd was silent for a few moments, taking in the news. I stilled while my heart continued its rapid beating in my chest cavity.

"She's human," someone said loudly, slightly off-put and confused.

"Correct," Theo noted flatly. "Any other observations?" If I wasn't so terrified, I probably would have laughed. I looked around the crowd some happy, some confused, others angry.

"Well, I think it's wonderful," a woman's voice shouted close to us, and the majority of the wolves gathered in an uproar of cheers, hoots, and clapping. I blushed and tried to hide my face in Theo's arm. He chuckled, stroking the back of my head softly. Gabriel resumed his position after patting Theo's back happily.

"The reason we have gathered here today is to celebrate our previous Alpha and newest Enforcer's happy news. We have also gathered to ask something." Again, the wolves stilled. Gabriel turned his head towards me and placed his hand protectively on my shoulder. "I have only known Margo for a few short weeks, and I know for most of you this is the first time even hearing of her, but she deserves the same protection, respect, and love we show all our Lunas. I know Margo will find her place here, in time. Valkyrie Pack, Margo is one of us now, and we protect our own."

With his words, the wolves began to howl loudly, shouting into the air. Gabriel and Theo stood at my sides, staring into the crowd of wolves victoriously and joined in the howl. The pack dispersed around the grounds, many staying to introduce themselves to me, although I hid behind Theo the best I could.

"So, Margo," a girl a few years older than me greeted, holding my forearm gently with hers. "Has Theo been treating you kindly? I know he has to be a softie underneath all this brutish, steely exterior," she said giggling, pushing Theo's arm comically.

"He's been very accommodating," I responded. She laughed, grabbing onto Theo's arm more to hold herself from laughter.

"Accommodating?" she howled. "I've known Theo since we were infants, and no one has ever described him as 'accommodating.'"

I glanced at Theo, who smiled down at the woman. "Margo, this is Albia James, Emily's daughter. Our mothers are best friends. She's practically my sister. Albia, this is my beautiful mate, Margo."

"It's nice to meet you," I smiled softly.

"It's great to meet you, as well," she gushed. "I'm sorry if I'm coming on a little much, but I had two too many cups of coffee this morning, and I'm a bit wired. I better go get a bagel or something to soak this all up. I'll see you both inside?"

Theo nodded and tucked me back under his arm. "What's inside?" I wondered.

"Your doom," Theo said dramatically, walking us towards the door.

"Is it your mother?" I guessed. He laughed loudly and opened the door for me.

"Guess you'll have to go in to find out." He smirked.

SCALDING

We wandered inside towards Theo's brothers, who were huddled around a document. Theo leaned over Eli's shoulders to examine it. His hand drifted out from my mine as I swiveled around and looked at the inside of the packhouse.

After a few minutes, I took a few steps towards another room where people seemed to be gathering. I looked back to Theo, who was still staring at the paper, talking heatedly with his brothers, and then I walked through the opening into the next room. In the middle was a makeshift arena, just a few lines set down in tape on the floor, and people formed around the perimeter. Two men were in the center, grasping each other's arms in the traditional greeting. A noise went off, and, in haste, the men began grunting, looking strained as they tried to force the other to the ground with the force of their grip.

Eventually, the man on the right won, forcing his opponent to the ground, and suddenly Theo's comment to Reese about forcing him to the ground with just one arm made sense. A woman and a man came into the square next; they were laughing and playful as they grasped arms. Again, the noise sounded, and they began sparing. The woman looked like she was exerting more of her energy, and the man laughed, humoring her. With one swift motion, the woman was on the ground with the man gently pinning her with his knee. He kissed her ear before standing and helping her up.

I heard my name being frantically called. The room quieted as Theo, Reese, and Eli stormed into the room. Theo rushed to me, grabbing my arms and glaring slightly.

"Where have you been?" Theo asked loudly. I opened my mouth like a fish repeatedly, not knowing what to say. "Margo?"

"I was just watching," I said. He sighed loudly, releasing one of my arms from his grip.

"You can't just run off like that," he breathed, looking relieved. "I turned around, and you were gone. I was terrified, Margo."

"I'm sorry. I was just watching them," I said dumbly.

"I know that," he sighed, strained like he wanted to stay calm, but his anger was bubbling just under the surface. "But you can't just wander off like that. You're human; you can't defend yourself. What if something were to happen to you, and I didn't know where you were?"

"I thought that was the point of the marking bite?" I pointed out. Immediately, I regretted my words as Theo's face relaxed into stone.

"That doesn't mean you can do whatever you want. I can't know if something has happened until it's already too late, and you're in pain, or you're scared enough that I can sense it. It's not a tracking device."

"Well, then what's the point?" I asked, honestly. Again, guilt settled in my stomach, and I wanted to start the conversation over. I wasn't trying to anger him or contradict what he was saying; I was just confused and anxious from the people around us staring.

"The point was that we claimed each other as mates, Margo," Theo hissed, dropping my other arm like scalding water. "Not for me to be your bodyguard whenever you're in trouble. I want to keep you safe, but because you're my mate and I care about you, not because it's my job. I already have a job. I don't need you to be one, too."

I bit my lip and stayed silent, trying to retreat from this battle I didn't realize I started.

"Theo!" a cheerful voice called from the opposite side of the room. He looked over with a hateful glare. "How about a spar from our former Alpha, for old times' sake?"

Theo groaned, rolling his shoulders back, before pressing me firmly into his brothers. Eli steadied me with a hand on my shoulder while Reese leaned his elbow on my head. I pushed Reese off, and he ruffled my hair before tucking his hands in his pockets.

We watched Theo play their game, sparing with a man who Eli whispered was the head of defense for the pack. Theo toyed with him, getting his frustration out before beating the man with one push. The crowd cheered while I looked around sadly, wanting to be anywhere else.

Gabriel entered the room, smirking as he looked at his brother. The wolves cheered as Gabriel stepped in the ring, smiling at his larger brother. Theo laughed loudly. The noise started, and they began pushing each other back and forth, bending each other as they gained the upper hand. Eventually, they let go of their arms, turning the battle into an old-fashioned wrestling match. After a few minutes, they conceded, lying next to each other on the floor, heaving in their tiredness.

Theo returned to my side with Gabriel trailing behind him. I kept my head down purposefully. Theo made a quick comment to Gabriel, and the boys started laughing.

"Oh, hey, I think Mom said she would be around here with Emily if you want to say hello," Eli suggested casually. I groaned internally.

"Yeah, thanks, we should see her before we leave," Theo said carelessly. The boys began moving, and with my body in the middle of them, I went along too. They stopped when they saw a brunette woman next to Emily, the woman from the bakery.

"Mom," Reese greeted kindly. The woman smiled, put a courteous hand on Emily's arm, and stepped forward to greet her sons.

"Hello, my boys," she said fondly. "And I hear we have a new little lady joining our family?" Eli pushed my back gently and forced me out in front of them. Theo's mother smiled, bringing me into a tight, warm embrace. I hugged her back, cautiously. "Margo, it is so nice to meet you finally," she spoke compassionately, taking my face in her warm hands to look at me. Her face turned into a perplexed scowl. "Dear, why are you crying?"

I quickly tried to wipe them away. I could hear Theo move behind me, placing his hands on my back.

"I'm fine," I tried to assure her, painting my face with a grin. She scowled at Theo and then the rest of her sons.

"What have you done to this poor girl?" she asked loudly.

"Theo may have been a *touch* more callous than he intended earlier," Reese said with a pained smile.

"Theodore," his mother scowled. "Have I not raised you better than making your mate cry?"

Theo looked down at me, and I didn't look up at him as he harshly said, "Mother."

"No, Theodore, listen to me. If I see that you cause this sweet girl any kind of pain, I promise you, no matter how high of a title you have, I will punish you more severely than anyone ever has. Is that clear?" She growled. I could instantly tell where Theo got his temper.

"Mom," Reese laughed uncomfortably.

"Reese, darling, be quiet. This is between Theo and his mate," she ordered.

Theo sighed and touched my arm affectionately. I pulled away but turned towards him. He looked down, and his eyes flashed with sadness as he placed his hands on my shoulders. "Margo," he pleaded. "I didn't mean to sound so angry with you earlier; I was just scared." I didn't say anything. "Little one, please, I'm sorry."

I knew it was a great deal for him to apologize to me, he didn't apologize to anyone else, and I also knew it was my fault for instigating the argument. "I know, Theo. I'm sorry, too," I murmured.

"We can talk more about this later," he promised, gently brushing his thumb over my cheek. "I promise I'm not angry. I know you're still confused, but I'll tell you everything you want to know."

His words were vague, not wanting to say too much in front of his family. I blushed a little at all the attention and the feeling of his thumb skimming the frame of my cheek. I nodded and stepped closer to him.

His mother giggled. "I never thought I would see the day my eldest son apologized for his behavior." Theo glared at her and began pulling me towards the door.

"It was lovely to meet you," she called, waving her delicate hand. "You can call me Sloane, or Mom, whatever you prefer! I'll see you soon, dear."

"You too!" I yelled, my voice fading away as Theo pulled us across the threshold of the building. "Your mother seems nice," I noted softly.

"She has the best intentions," he said pointedly, nearly laughing. "She's the best, and kind of the worst at the same time. She lives for humiliating us with love. It's like trying to hate a kitten who keeps biting your finger; it's annoying but difficult to be mad."

"And your dad?" I asked as the driver pulled the car around. Theo got a sad look in his eyes, and he smiled a strained smile.

"We'll talk about him another day."

A CHILLING EFFECT

We sat silent for the entirety of the ride; I was still a little hurt, and he was probably still angry. We arrived home mid-afternoon, and he immediately retreated to his office. I found my solace in my new room. I hadn't finished decorating yet, boxes of ordered belongings continued to arrive every other day. The boxes sat opened on the ground; my desk was in pieces.

I began putting it together, loudly clanking boards and dropping screws noisily on the wooden floor. I thought Theo would come upstairs to see what the noise was, but he never did. I figured out how to attach the sides, but when I stood it up, it was lopsided.

I groaned and began taking it apart, oblivious to Eli watching me from the doorway. He snorted, giving himself away, and I dropped one of the legs.

"Theo asked me to check on you. I had to drop some paperwork off from Gabriel," he explained. I smiled invitingly, and he walked in. "What are you doing? Or trying to do?"

"Attempting to put this desk together," I said apprehensively, holding up a metal leg. Eli chuckled and sat down on the ground next to me. He grabbed the directions and helped me attach the sides. We made small talk about my friends-or rather a friend-back home, his family, what the Valkyrie Pack was like.

"So, when you and your brothers were little, what did you do for fun?" I asked.

"Well, we all had to go through Alpha training when we were really young, I think when each of us was five, in case something happened to our parents and we needed to know how to act. I mean, we messed around and wrestled and played pranks on people. It was a lot of hard work being Alpha's kids. We had to go through more training when we were teenagers because Dad had to hand down his title one day."

"So, your dad handed his title to Theo, and then Theo to Gabriel," I pieced together, then paused. "What's your dad like?"

Eli's chin hit his chest, and he grinned somberly. "He's the best," he said, with some finality. We finished the desk quickly, and he stayed a while longer to help me build a small bookcase. As we stood it up, Theo slid the door open fully and stood in the frame with his arms crossed, watching us silently.

Eli situated the bookcase and wiped his hands on the back of his jeans. "Well, I should be on my way," he said kindly, grabbing my hand softly and giving it a squeeze before brushing past his brother.

I grabbed a few books and journals from a box and filled a shelf, trying my best to ignore Theo's staring.

"Margo," he beckoned after he got tired of waiting for me to acknowledge him. I turned to him and raised my eyebrows. "Talk to me. Are you still angry?"

"Angry that you yelled at me in front of the pack the first time I met them while I was just trying to understand more about shifters and our bond? No." I shook my head subtly, stacking more books.

"I didn't yell," he mumbled, looking at his shoes.

"Spoke very loudly," I amended. "I wasn't trying to say that I'm your job, Theo. I was just trying to understand more. I'm not a shifter; I never got to go to school like you all did. I don't know how the bond works or how mating works or the ins and outs of shifting. Caddy told me some stuff, but he's not so much an academic."

"I know," he nodded. "And I'm sorry. I didn't mean to make you more anxious than you already were. I know today was a big deal for you and for us."

"Well, you didn't need to get snippy," I murmured, biting my lower lip.

"And you didn't need to wander off," he shot back. "We're both at fault, can we just forget about it?"

"I didn't wander off. I was twenty feet away from you while you and your brothers ogled over some piece of paper."

Theo glared. "It wasn't some piece of paper, Margo. It was a very important letter that was directed at you if you must know. One of my guards probably leaked the information about me finding my mate, and the information got to some very bad people. Remember a few weeks ago when we first met, and I said I wanted security measures in place? It was for this very reason. That's why I got scared when I couldn't find you."

"What was the letter about?"

"It's nothing." He slumped against the wall. "Don't worry about it for now."

"Don't worry about it?" My voice scaled a few octaves.

"If it's a letter about me, I deserve to know what it said. Let me read it."

"You don't need to worry. I've got it covered for now."

I set the last book down and walked closer to him. His arms were tucked across his chest, and he regarded me with wary eyes.

"If there's a threat to me, I should know," I spoke slowly.

"Do you not trust me?"

"Well, I've known you for three and a half weeks now, so no, not really," I said between clenched teeth. "I trust that you care about me and that you probably won't kill me, but that's about as far as my trust goes."

"Good to know where we stand," Theo seethed as he walked out of the room.

"Can you blame me?" I shouted, walking out of the room after him. "I mean, can you honestly blame me?"

"Yes!" he screamed, stopping to spread his arms out by his sides. "I have done nothing but try to make you comfortable here, with me. Have I not bought everything you wanted? Done everything you wanted? I got you a phone to talk to Caddy, I gave you space, I answered your questions, and I waited to sleep in the bed next to you until you said it was okay! We marked each other, for the moon's sake, Margo. Does that not mean anything?"

"Yes, you've been very accommodating," I nodded. "But trust takes more than that. It takes time, Theo. I'm sorry I don't have the best track record with wolves, but I'm trying."

"Why would you let me mark you if you weren't sure?" Theo asked with glossy eyes.

"I was trying," I pressed. "I thought it was a step in the right direction. I wanted to give this a chance; I still do. But it's going to take more than some new clothes, and a few answered questions to make me trust you."

"What else can I do?" he asked tiredly.

"I don't know," I shook my head, fidgeting with my hands.

"Well, when you know," he started down the stairs. "Please, come tell me."

I stayed in my room until night. I knew Theo had gone to bed an hour before, and I weighed my options. In embarrassment, I settled for sleeping on the couch in the living room. I fell asleep despite the glare from the moon outside in the large window. I was woken in the morning by pounding on the front door. Theo stumbled down the steps, still shirtless and in sweatpants.

"Theodore!" Cam shouted cheerfully as Theo opened the door. Theo tried to shut it, but Cam and Beau forced themselves inside.

"Get out," Theo ordered sleepily.

"Now Theo, remember we made plans to go hunting today, you can't back out now," Cam winked. He strolled around the room, noticing me sitting up on the couch. He hitched an eyebrow at Theo.

"Leave her alone," Theo warned. Cam held his hands up innocently and backed away. "Just let me change."

Theo came down in a pair of athletic shorts and a black shirt. I knew when Cam said hunting they were not going to be in their human form, although if they shifted, a set of clothes would be handy. The men jogged out of the house without so much as a goodbye, as precedented by Theo, and left me alone in the large house.

I yawned, stretched, and wandered upstairs to ready myself for when Theo returned shortly. He didn't. I was alone until nighttime; I even opened the door to see what was happening, but the guards stared at me until I went back inside.

I knitted, cooked myself some squash and zucchini, and laid in front of the fire. Around six in the evening, the phone in Theo's office rang. I let it go to the machine. It rang again, and I went over to it, debating on whether I should answer. It rang a third time, and I picked it up.

"Hello? Theodore?" the voice said. It was a man's, most likely older than Theo.

"Theo's not here right now," I said back quietly. "Can I take a message?"

"Who is this?"

"Who is this?" I retorted.

"My name is Alpha Reed Porter, who are you?"

"Margo," I drawled.

"Ah." It sounded like he smiled. "I have not had the pleasure of meeting you yet. I'm calling about a document I sent your mate. I've not gotten a response; I just wanted to make sure it arrived."

I paused, wanting to put the phone down, but knowing it would be rude, and I would most likely have to meet the man one day.

"I don't see any documents on his desk. I can have him call you when he returns," I offered.

"I see he didn't tell you about my little note," Alpha Porter babbled.

"You're the one who sent the letter?"

"I am."

"What was it about?"

"You."

I rolled my eyes. "What about me?"

"That's something you'll have to ask your mate about. I wouldn't want to drive a wedge between the two of you. Now tell me, is it true you're human?"

"What does that have to do with anything?"

"I'll take that as a yes." Alpha Porter chuckled. "I'm sure we'll be meeting soon, Margo. Best to have your mate change you before we meet, dear. At least you'll have a fighting chance then."

BOLDER

The front door opened around nine in the evening and Cam, Beau, and Theo walked in noisily. Theo called out my name, to which I made some grunting noise in response. He came to the doorway of his office after saying goodbye to his friends.

"Why are you in here?" he asked, not upset, simply curious.

"Alpha Porter called," I said hesitantly. I didn't want to spark the fight again, but my curiosity and fear were getting the better of me. Alpha Porter's last comment was festering like an open wound I couldn't help but touch.

"Did you speak to him?" he asked, more concerned but trying not to look it.

"He called three times. I thought it would be rude not to pick up," I explained.

"I'm not mad you picked up, Margo. What did he say?"

"He asked about his letter," I ground out. "Wondered if

you got it." Theo nodded and let out a noise of approval. The festering wound split, and words poured out of me like puss. "And he also told me that I should have you change me so that I'd have a fighting chance when we meet."

Theo stilled and opened his mouth though no words came out.

"Are you still going to tell me not to worry?"

"Margo."

"Theo, this is about my safety. How am I supposed to stay safe if I don't know what's going on? How am I supposed to tell you when somethings wrong if I don't know what I should be looking for? How am I supposed to...to...to survive if I don't even know what I'm fighting against?"

"Okay," he soothed, taking my hands in his. "Okay, I get it. I'm sorry. Will you please sit down, and I'll tell you everything?"

"No," I said, yanking my hands out of his. "I've been sitting all damn day."

"Okay." He nodded quickly. He ran his hand over his face roughly twice before telling me everything he knew about Alpha Reed Porter. How the Alpha's had vetoed his run for Enforcer, how he was an outcast as a leader because of his aggression, and how he had a great hatred for humans because his mother had left his father for a human. Humans were weak to him, they were scum, and they had no place in the world of werewolves.

" So, that's why he hates me?"

"Pretty much," he said nodding.

"Wait, pretty much? Is there another thing?"

Theo bit his lip and tried to reach for me, but I sidestepped him and began walking out of the office. He called my name sullenly, and I stopped.

"I said I would tell you everything, and I will!" Theo said loudly. "Would you just let me get it out?" His shoulders took up most of the door frame, and the light behind him cast a shadow on the ground. He looked demonic, or angelic, something otherworldly. I didn't know if he was going to save me or damn me, but looking that good, I didn't really care.

"Reed Porter blames me for the downfall of his pack because I got the Enforcer position over him. If Reed were the Enforcer, he'd be able to give him pack more territory and power, which is exactly why the Alphas denied him the position. His pack lands were recently terrorized by forest fires that ruined forty percent of his land. Now, he either has to expand into someone else's territory or merge with someone else's pack. No one else wants to merge with him, and I've denied every request of his to take over another Alpha's pack lands."

"Why would you do that?" I hissed. "It sounds like he wants a fight, and he has a good reason. His pack lands are gone, that can't be good for their food production, and I'm sure some of his member's houses burned with the fire. Why wouldn't you allow him to expand?"

"And take land away from someone else who needs it? No matter whose pack I try to take the lands from, that pack will just ask for more territory. And if I start to give away free land, the other Alphas will have my head."

"Why? No one is using it?"

"No man's land is there for a reason. There is space between every pack to allow rogues and travelers to pass without crossing any boundaries. Wildlife also resides there. Without the free lands, animals would be herded into packs and either bred forcefully or killed off. There goes our main food supply."

"I had no idea it was so important." I let go of the harsh glare I had been donning.

"Everything is balanced." Theo held up his hands in a mock scale. "When one person oversteps, things shift, and their needs have to come from somewhere else. That's what my job is-to find the balance."

"So, Reed wants more, and you won't give it to him, he blames you and takes it out on me?"

"I think if there's one thing Reed hates more than me, its humans." He reached out and grabbed my shoulder, pulling me closer until our chests were flush. "I'm sorry, Margo." He breathed out, kissing the crown of my head. "I was trying to protect you."

"I understand," I said, though it was muffled by his broad chest.

"Did you have a good day?"

"It was...uneventful," I settled.

"I'm sorry." He moved away from me, and he took his warmth with him. The cool air of the house swept between us, and a shiver ran from the base of my spine up to my shoulders and down to my fingers. "I was just frustrated, and I wanted to give you some space."

"Space would have been fine. Ignoring me and then leaving all day?" I squinted. "Not as fine."

"Bad mate moment?" He cringed. His steely exterior melted away, and he looked like a scolded child.

"Bad mate moment." I smiled softly.

"Can I make up for it?"

"How?"

"Well." He brushed a piece of hair behind my ear. "I could wake up early and make your breakfast in bed, and I could show you more of the territory, we could spend the day together, and I don't know, whatever you'd want to do tomorrow."

I nodded, agreeing to his proposition, and headed to bed. In the morning, he woke me gently with a kiss on my cheek and softly said my name. I groaned and rolled over to go back to sleep.

"Margo, love," he said sweetly in the ear. "What do you want for breakfast?"

"Sleep, Theo, I want sleep for breakfast."

He laughed. "You can go back to sleep, love, but what do you want to eat when you wake up?"

"Eggs," I mumbled in my sleepy haze. "And bananas... and peaches...and toast."

"Okay," Theo whispered. He kissed my cheek again and tucked me back into the blankets. I slept for some time before I noticed that Theo was gone. I rolled over and looked around the room. I could hear his footsteps coming up the stairs, and I closed my eyes.

"Margo, I know you're awake." He laughed loudly when he walked into the room. I squinted up at him, unhappy that he called my bluff. "I brought breakfast."

I sat up and took the tray he handed me. On it were plates filled with fried eggs, sliced bananas and peaches, a piece of toast with jam, sliced potatoes, and a few strips of bacon. I looked at Theo, who sat down next to me with a similar looking tray.

"This is good," I complimented, smiling shyly.

"Yeah, except for the peaches," he said in disgust as he placed another peach slice on his tongue.

"Why do you keep eating them then?"

"Because this is what you're eating, and I told you we were going to do whatever you wanted."

We finished breakfast. Theo washed our dishes, and then we got dressed to go out on our walk. The air had gotten a few degrees warmer, which meant Theo stopped trying to put winter boots and gloves on me when we went outside. There was still a slight chill to the air, but it was refreshing.

The woods that surrounded the house were thick, pine, fir, and sequoia trees all blended together in a mix of shadows. Theo took my hand and led me down a dirt path that was cleared. We walked for ten minutes and then reached a small clearing where six large boulders were piled together. In three bounds, Theo had left my side and climbed up to the largest boulder and stood on the top childishly. He laughed boyishly and motioned for me to come up as well. I shook my head; my balance wasn't as good as his. I would certainly fall.

"What is all this?" I called to him.

"When we were little, my dad took us here, and there were only two, one for my mom and one for him. He said when we got older, we would have to prove our strength to the pack by getting a boulder from the cliff and carrying it here."

I stood in awe; the rocks were *huge*. I brushed my fingers over the smallest one, which was still three times the size of me.

"Which one is yours?" I said curiously. He smiled and pointed to the one he was standing on, the largest one. I raised my eyebrow. "Of course, you have the biggest one," I grumbled.

He laughed. "This one is my father's," he said, pointing to the second largest. "The only way I could take over my father's title was if I could carry a larger rock than his up here. That one is Gabe's, then Reese's, and Eli's, and the smallest one is my mother's."

"Will I get one?" I asked wistfully.

"You'll have to bring your own up here, sweetheart," he said happily.

"Theo, I'm never going to be able to carry one of these over a cliff and up here!" I shouted, laughing. He climbed down the rocks and stood next to me, looking at the rocks proudly.

"One day, you will be able to," he promised.

I sighed. "Okay, save a space for my pebble."

We continued our walk, stopping at the cliff, which was another ten-minute walk away. When we got hungry, we headed back towards the house. Theo made us sandwiches and sliced apples. We spent the afternoon lounging on the couch watching old movies.

I had my hands around Theo's, showing him how to knit, laughing as his eyebrows sunk together in frustration. A sharp knock on the door stopped us in the middle of a pearl.

A voice rushed out Theo's name as he opened the door. He stepped halfway out of the doorframe. I cocked my head back and watched him, the backside of him, tense. There were murmurs from both men, and then the door slammed shut.

Theo strode into the couch area quickly, stopped near the cabinets and television, and then began pacing back and forth.

"Theo?" I whispered. He didn't look up at me, just continued to pace. "Theo, what's wrong?"

"Nothing," he said quickly, not paying attention to the word.

"Something is wrong, tell me," I insisted, adding, "Please."

His breath hitched, and he closed his eyes, stilling himself. "Reed Porter," he breathed huskily. "He just invaded Duncan Trissur's territory with a group of a thousand warriors." The words were tense.

"What are you going to do?" I eventually asked.

"I have to go there," he said, almost surprised at his words.

I nodded. "When?"

"Tomorrow," he confirmed. "We'll leave first thing in the morning."

"We?" My face showed obvious concern.

"Yes, we, Margo. I can't leave you here. I want you with me," he smiled subtly.

"Okay," I smiled back.

We went upstairs and pack a few bags, clothes, tooth-brushes, and my knitting needles for the ride. We were rigid in bed, not wanting to break the small bubble of peace that was separating us from the rest of the world.

"I'm glad you're here," he broke the silence. I turned my head right to look at him.

"Me too," I said back, moving my body into his embrace before falling asleep.

PETRICHOR

We woke up the next morning before the sun had risen. I groaned and dragged my feet to the bathroom to get ready. Theo said we were going farther north, which meant it was only going to get colder and that we needed to look a certain way. He set out a dress he thought was appropriate-tan in the middle with black lining on the sides. I put thick black tights under it and tall, black, heeled boots that matched the dress.

Theo met me in the bedroom, wearing a dark gray suit, white shirt, and black tie. He took all but one of our bags downstairs, letting me carry my small bag of things for the car. Someone had fixed our breakfast already, which we took with us in the long line of black vehicles. It reminded me of the day Theo came to Alpha Dorian's pack. Now I would be arriving with the daunting stream of powerful wolves.

The drive took us somewhere between five and six hours. Halfway through, I fell asleep on Theo's lap. When I woke up, the cars were slowing down, and Theo's hand remained tense on my head. I sat up and looked at his worried face. He nodded to me, assuring me he was alright.

The car came to a complete stop, and Theo straightened up, fixing his tie around his neck. A few moments later, one of the guards opened the door, and Theo exited. I waited back until Theo's large hand appeared in the doorway, reaching for mine. I tried to maintain as much composure as I had as I stepped out of the car gracefully.

There was a large group of people at the front of the packhouse waiting for our arrival. They seemed to keep their gazes towards the ground except to steal glances of me as we walked past them. Theo walked strongly towards the front doors, where two guards flanked a man with graying hair.

"Enforcer Weston, I cannot tell you how pleased I am that you are here," the man said and bowed his head down to show his submission. Theo reached over and placed his hand warmly on the man's neck.

"Duncan, you're one of my father's greatest friends and a fellow Alpha, of course I came." He smiled graciously.

The man stood up and smiled back at Theo. He then ushered us inside his packhouse. The inside looked as rustic and warm as the exterior; exposed wood beams and metal fixtures covered their first floor. Alpha Trissur ushered us into a meeting room where a group of people sat.

Theo sat at the head of the table and motioned for me to sit next to him on the left. Alpha Trissur sat on his right and introduced us formally to everyone in the room. They each bowed their heads and then began informing Theo of the situation.

The meeting took a long time, most of it spent bickering about the ways they were going to reclaim their territory. Alpha Reed Porter set up camp on the south end of their territory and was threatening to attack if Alpha Trissur did not hand over his land.

Alpha Trissur sat back in his set, wiping his hand over his peppered beard. He looked tired, and I wondered why he hadn't handed over his position to his children yet.

"Alpha, we can't just walk right up to him and demand that he leaves. He'll attack on sight," a man at the end of the table growled.

"What do you suggest we do, let him stay there?" the woman next to him snorted.

"No, Willa," the man said condescendingly. "We need to think about the consequences before we decide our actions."

"I agree," Theo said lightly.

"So, what do we do?" All heads at the table looked to Theo. He looked down at his hands folded on the table.

"We contact Reed Porter first," he said, glancing at me out of the corner of his eye. "We ask him for a list of his demands, and then we make our next move after we know all the facts. We know he wants your land, but we need to know how much and when. Bring me up to speed when you know everything."

Alpha Trissur nodded in agreement and stood up, pushing his chair back. The rest of the table stood as well. Theo finally rose and looked at me until I did the same. He walked out of the room, and I followed after him.

A man escorted us to a room on the third floor and informed us a guard would be stationed at the end of the hallway for our protection and our privacy. Theo let out a big breath as he sat on the large, maroon bed. The room had the same rustic features as the rest of the house; exposed beams and candlelight fixtures warmed the room.

I slid off my shoes, feet aching from the tall heels, and limped over to Theo. He laughed as I dove into the bed face first, and he ran his hand lovingly over my leg.

"I'm sorry I haven't been as attentive today," he apologized.

"I understand, you've got a lot on your plate."

"I know, but that's no excuse," he stated firmly. I turned my head and rested it on my arms. He pushed my hair back from my forehead like he always did and set my feet in his lap. Slowly, he began rubbing my aching feet, and I groaned loudly in pleasure.

"This is a good apology," I practically moaned. He chuckled and continued soothing my feet. When he was done, he brought my foot up and kissed my ankle. I giggled and tried to sit up, but he released my foot and slumped back onto the bed next to me.

"Do you know what you smell like?" His warm words tickled my ear. I shook my head, no. "You smell like nutmeg and fresh rain."

I laughed. "I smell like nutmeg and rain?"

He nodded his nose into my cheek, inhaling my scent again. "Fresh rain, like the smell when you step outside right after the rain subsides. Like trees and flowers and everything covered in rain and dew. Everyone has a scent; humans just don't have the sensory receptors to smell it strongly enough."

His fingers gently ran across my exposed shoulder and drew lazy shapes on my skin. I closed my eyes and focused on the touch of his fingertips on me. I breathed happily, and as my breath washed across Theo's face, he leaned in. I felt the heat radiating from him as he gently parted his mouth.

I opened my eyes for just a moment before his lips pressed against mine gently. It didn't feel like the first time he kissed me. That kiss was loving and gentle, a few seconds of sweet reassurance. Theo growled playfully as my hands wove into the strands of his dark hair. His right hand gripped my waist tightly, my dress gathered in his hands.

His breathing quickened, and so did mine, but I didn't know my next move. All we had ever done was kiss, that was as far as it ever went, but Theo's strong hands seemed to be wanting more than just the touch of my lips. I pulled back as far as I could, unlocking my lips from his and took a deep breath. He kissed my cheek and then down to my neck.

"Theo," I burst. He skimmed his nose along my jawline and looked into my eyes. "I don't know what-"

"I know, love," he said in a soothing tone. "We don't have to do anything else."

"It's not that I don't want to," I rushed out.

"Little one," Theo smiled. "There is no hurry. We have the rest of our lives for everything else."

I nodded and rested my head back into his arm.

"Why don't I go run you a bath, and we can just relax for a while?" he suggested. I nodded. He left the bed, and I heard the knobs to a bath turn on. As I was waiting for Theo, someone knocked on the door.

"Come in," I called. The door slowly opened, but no one entered. I stood up off the bed and poked my head past a wall to look at the door from a safe distance.

"Excuse me, Miss. I'm looking for Enforcer Weston," a guard stated.

"Theo," I beckoned over my shoulder. He came wandering out from the bathroom, white shirt now rolled up around his elbows.

"Hello, can I help you?" Theo asked kindly as he wiped water droplets from his hands onto his pants.

"Enforcer Weston," the man greeted, bowing his head in respect. "I am to inform you Reed Porter has been contacted, and we have a list of his demands. Alpha Trissur would like you to meet him in his office."

Theo exhaled loudly and began unrolling his sleeves.

"We'll be right there, thank you."

The door closed, and Theo looked at me apologetically.

"I have to put the heels back on, don't I?" I guessed.

A FELLOW ALPHA

As I slid the tall boots back up my legs, Theo emptied the bathtub and slipped his suitcoat on.

"How do I look?" he said, standing before me, spinning slowly. I nodded, smiling a little, and he reached for my hand. We walked down to the office of Alpha Trissur, where two guards were stationed. They opened the door for us, and Theo pushed me in before himself. The office was smaller than the meeting room but still sizeable. Dark, mahogany wood coated the walls, desk, chairs, and the wall of books that fixated me.

"You're a reader?" Alpha Trissur spoke to me directly for the first time.

I tucked my head in embarrassment. "I love to read," I admitted.

Theo laughed and told him I had a whole room dedicated to books and art in his house. Alpha Trissur smiled and walked over to the wall, reaching for two books from a high shelf. They were weathered, and the spines were fragile.

"These are some of my favorite human books. They're from long before the exchange of power," he said as he held them affectionately. Most of the wolves I encountered referred to the time when wolves took over as "the exchange of power," so it didn't surprise me when he did the same. "I've read them so many times I could probably recite half of it back to you right now," he said chuckling. "Why don't you hold onto them for me?"

I looked in surprise but quickly averted my gaze in respect for him. Alpha Trissur and Theo both laughed boisterously.

"Margo, you don't have to lower your gaze." Theo touched my cheek as he spoke. "As my mate, you have as much authority as I do."

I continued to keep my head low as Alpha Trissur handed me the two books. I settled myself into a large, tub chair and gently caressed the frayed spines of the books. Theo and Alpha Trissur took seats close to me with a small table between them.

I was so intrigued by the books I didn't catch the first half of their conversation. I remembered things like, "Porter's demands," and "half the territory." It wasn't until Theo called my name that I honed in on their talking.

"Your previous Alpha, Dorian, he invaded a neighboring territory, correct?" Theo questioned.

"I believe so. I was only thirteen or fourteen when it happened, so I don't remember all the specifics."

"Do you remember if he was reprimanded?"

I shook my head, no. "I have no idea."

"I can't lose any more territory, Theo. I lost good ground to the north a few months back from a bad storm, and we have yet to rebuild. If I release this land to Reed Porter, it will force me to relocate my pack members, and I simply don't have the funds for that right now," Alpha Trissur admitted to Theo. The wrinkles in his forehead folded with concern.

"I know, Duncan. It's not right for him to demand this of you. His pack isn't growing enough to even consider an expansion of territory, let alone take yours from you."

"What will he do?" I whispered quietly to Theo, not wanting to upset Alpha Trissur further. Theo bent down to my ear.

"He's threatening to attack. Duncan has a large pack, but it is smaller than Reed Porter's, which would most likely result in the destruction of his pack altogether."

"I have an ally to the west that would fight alongside us. Francis Alban," Alpha Trissur said optimistically.

"That might work to our advantage," Theo nodded quickly. "We will meet with him in the morning. If he still does not concede, you may need to contact Francis."

Theo and I returned to our room, debating on drawing another bath, but I settled for a hot shower. I undressed in the bathroom and stuck my hand in to feel if the water was hot enough. Theo knocked on the door, and I quickly hopped in, letting out a squeal when the cold water hit my back.

"Do you want some help?" he called suggestively through the crack he had opened in the doorway.

"No," I said defensively. "I'm doing just fine without you."

"Water still cold?"

"How do you know that?" I peeked outside of the shower curtain.

"A guard just came by to tell me that the room hasn't been used recently and that we should let the shower run for a few minutes to allow it to warm up." I heard the teasing in his voice.

"That would have been nice to know beforehand," I grunted.

"Aw, do you want me to come warm you up?"

"No," I said, standing at the far end of the shower in attempts to hide from the cold.

"Are you sure?" His hand ruffled the outside of the shower curtain.

"Theo, get out of here." He chuckled. "I mean it."

"Okay, little wolf, put your claws away. I'm leaving."

"I'm not a wolf," I reminded him.

I swear I heard him mutter, "not yet."

I finished my shower and joined Theo in the massive bed. He was sitting up reading something on his phone. I slipped in next to him and began reading on the books Alpha Trissur had given me.

"Are they any good?" Theo murmured into my ear, startling me. I turned and found him reading over my shoulder.

"They're amazing."

"Really?" He smiled down at me. He didn't seem too surprised. "What are they even about?"

"Romance, society, ethics, mystery, all sorts of things," I rambled on. "This one is full of short stories about human days. It's amazing we got anything done with all the betrayals and love triangles."

"Things are simpler now." Theo pressed his lips against my head and turned over to go to sleep. I stayed up until I finished half the book and then curled myself opposite of Theo.

PREY

"Margo." My eyes flashed open, and I gulped in a huge breath. Theo was close to my face, out of bed, and standing next to me, fully dressed.

"Why do you never wake me when you first get up?" I grumbled unhappily. Theo laughed loudly and flipped the covers off me.

"Dress warmly. Try not to show a lot of skin. We're going to pay Reed Porter a visit this morning."

I got dressed in warm clothes and joined Theo at the small bistro table near the window where someone had delivered out breakfast.

"I want you to stay by my side today," he said with a bite of toast in his mouth. I nodded. "The only way I know you'll be safe is if I can have you right next to me. Not that I don't trust Duncan's pack, but if it came down to a choice of me or them protecting you, I'm always going to choose me."

"Okay," I assured him. He settled back in his chair until

I finished eating. We left the dishes on the table, much to my discomfort, and descended the stairs. Alpha Trissur and a group of muscular men and women were waiting for us.

"Enforcer, Luna Regina, whenever you're ready," Alpha Trissur greeted us. Theo jerked his head onward with a steely gaze, and we were escorted to a black vehicle.

"He does know my name, right?" I asked softly as I buckled my seatbelt.

"Of course, he knows your name," Theo smirked. "Luna Regina is the title given to an Enforcer's female mate. Everything is a hierarchy, remember? Because there are only six of us, we're often thought of like the Kings, which would make you my Queen. Luna Regina means Queen Luna. He means it out of respect. It would be Alpha Rex if the Enforcer's mate is male as in King Alpha."

I tucked my chin to my chest, not knowing how to respond. It was the first time someone had referred to me as a Luna Regina, and the title alone was enough to make my spine itch to sit up straighter and hold my head high.

"How is everyone else getting there?" I asked, noticing there was only one vehicle for the forty-some wolves.

"Margo, we're wolves. We're built to run." He winked. I scooted to the window and watched as the wolves began their transformation. It had always amazed me how shifters changed. First, they began shaking, almost like intense shivering that shook their entire bodies from their heads to their ankles. In one swift motion, the shifters would hunch over and begin to take their other form.

The normal wolves took slightly longer to shift into their wolves. Much like natural wolves, they came in a variety of colors and sizes, though most did not exceed five feet tall on all fours. It was easy to tell shifters apart from natural wolves since they were much larger and regal.

The Alpha wolves were much more exquisite, though. They seemed to shift effortlessly, painlessly into larger, more agile creatures. Alpha blood made their muscles bigger, their bones larger, and their stamina greater. Even in his older age, Alpha Trissur stood at six feet tall, with a tri-colored coat that blended into his territory. Human horror movies had gotten it wrong when they described werewolves as demon-like creatures who stood on their back legs, with fangs and blood dripping on their black pelts. Real werewolves were beautiful in the way most lethal things are.

The car started, and the wolves ran ahead of us. It was a short ride, only ten minutes before Reed Porter's group came into view. They had set up small shelters, fires, and stations for their food. There were a lot of wolves, Theo told me one thousand, but they weren't defensive upon our arrival.

The wolves from Alpha Trissur's pack shifted back to their human form apart from the two wolves. Theo exited the car and held his hand out for me. I was immediately pulled into his side as a reminder that I was to stay close to him at all times.

"So, you brought our wonderful new Enforcer with you," a man finally said. He was muscular, stocky, not as tall as Theo, but he had an aura of chaos that surrounded him.

"Reed," Alpha Trissur addressed him unkindly. "What do you want from us, honestly?"

"I've already told your guards what I want," Alpha Porter said calmly, stepping out from the group of wolves that circled around him. "Is that really so hard to understand? My pack is growing. Yours is shrinking- it simply makes sense. I don't understand why no one will even humor me and try to understand where I'm coming from."

"Reed, you know the territory lines were drawn many years ago. They can't be altered now," Theo said hesitantly.

"So, this is the little human I spoke to?" Reed wondered as he tried to peek around Theo's arm that was covering me protectively.

Theo didn't acknowledge his question. "You and your wolves need to leave Duncan's territory, Reed. There's no reason to keep them on edge like this."

"I don't mean to threaten Duncan's pack," Reed said, breathing deeply and loudly through his mouth. "I just want my pack needs to be met, and since you won't take me seriously, I had to go an alternative route. I know how close you and Duncan are, or was it your father?"

"My father has nothing to do with this," Theo growled.

"He does," Reed insisted. "He was the one that originally started housing humans, wasn't he? He should have done his job and gotten rid of them when he had the chance. Now, Duncan's pack is awarded extra land to house the humans in his pack while my pack suffers because we don't take care of the prey."

"You know that isn't the reason," Theo said placatingly.

"I understand the issue has more of personal touch now, Theo, but just remember your job is to do what's best for us. Not *them*."

Theo pushed me back softly behind the arms of two Warriors and stalked forward to Reed in the middle.

"You need to take your wolves and leave this territory," Theo demanded. "My choice has to do only with what is just for the people here. These are our laws, Porter. You and I both know you don't want to start a fight that goes against my position."

Reed receded two steps and chuckled, glancing at his feet. "You'd be surprised how many Alphas would disagree with you. I guess you're just a little too blind to see it."

"Too blind to see what?" Theo's body began quivering. I staggered in the hold of the wolves, but they held my arms firm, protectively.

"That little fawn is going to be the death of everything we stand for."

Theo immediately turned his back to Reed and walked towards me. His face was unreadable, a complete mask of stone and indifference. The warrior wolves released me into his hold, and he guided me quickly into the vehicle. The car pulled back as soon as the door was closed. The wolves from Alpha Trissur's pack shifted into their wolves, and we left the land as quickly as we'd come.

"Theo?" I asked gently. His body was still shaking, eyes clenched, the veins in his fists strained under his skin. "Theo?"

"I'm going to kill him," his low voice ground out. The sound came from his stomach, and I wondered how much control he had over himself.

"Is everything going to be okay?"

"No." His body relaxed in one motion, but his eyes stayed closed.

"What did he mean when he called me a fawn?" My voice was smaller than I wanted it to be.

"It's a dirty name for humans," he said sadly. His hand wandered until it found mine, and he held it tightly, almost too tightly.

"What does it mean?"

"Wolves like Reed Porter believe humans are only prey to werewolves. They serve no purpose to us other than the thrill of the hunt, much like deer."

His words sent goosebumps down my neck.

"Oh," was all that came from my mouth. Theo sighed and tugged my hand until I was close to him.

"I'm not going to let anything happen to you, okay? Ever. You know that, right?" he asked seriously. His eyes searched for something in mine.

"I know," I assured him, placing my hand on his cheek. His eyes fluttered shut, and he leaned into my touch.

"He's going to fight back," he told me.

"How do you know that?"

"Because I've known Reed for years, and there's nothing he hates more than being told no, even humans."

"He could surprise you," I tried to say cheerfully, but it came out strangled.

"Sure." He smiled placatingly. He didn't believe my words, but we both didn't want to argue.

"I trust you," I told him softly. He smiled at me, some light finally reaching his eyes.

"You don't know how much that means to me, little one." He grabbed the back of my head and brought my forehead to meet his lips. His hands wove into my curls and held me there, and for just a moment, it was like everything would actually be okay.

LET THE WINE FLOW

I started to notice the effects of the mate bond slowly, and then it was all at once that I realized how much had changed within me. Through the bond, we could feel each other's emotions, which was strange for the first few days. It felt like my own emotions, but I knew I wasn't frustrated or angry or excited. Seeing Theo and touching him immediately made the feelings dissipate.

Along with the emotions, I didn't fear Theo's touch anymore; in fact, I craved it, reveled in it. I pined for his fingertips on my skin, his breath on my neck, lips on mine. I always held myself back, though. I wasn't willing to let go of my human hesitations yet.

"Have any of your brothers met their mates? Or your friends?" I asked curiously. Theo was cooking us lunch, and I sat at the counter, watching his back muscles ripple under his clothing as he moved.

"None of my brothers, no," he confirmed, sneaking a look back at me. "Cam met his mate a few years back. They have a little girl." He smiled affectionately at her mention.

"Cam is the blond one, right?"

"Yes," Theo said, turning back around to his cooking. "His mate is Gemma, and their little girl is Tansy."

"Can I meet them?" My voice wavered. Theo turned the burner on the stove down and came to lean over the counter with me.

"Yeah, I'll tell Cam to bring them over for dinner," he said; his face looked confused. "Why the sudden interest in mates?"

"I just want to meet them," I said casually, playing with the tips of Theo's fingers. "I don't really know what it's like to be the mate to a wolf..."

"You like me," Theo teased, smirking. I frowned and pulled my hands away.

"It's not that, I just-"

"You like me, and you want to see another functioning mated couple so you can ease your stubborn mind into knowing we're going to be just fine," he practically sang to me as he turned around to stir his pot.

I spluttered out some unintelligible disagreements until Theo came to me and held me by my elbows that were covered across my chest.

"I like that you're trying to make this work." He smiled at me and the dimple in his right cheek appeared. "I think it's sweet."

I nodded and rolled my eyes, avoiding his gaze by looking at his hands on my skin. He gave my arms a squeeze and finished his cooking. I sat down at the counter again and watched him work.

"You're going to fall in love with me, Margo Anderson," he said playfully. "Just you wait!"

Theo invited Cam's family to dinner at the end of the week. All-day, I had been rushing around Theo's house tidying things, setting the dining table, and then resetting it when Theo made fun of the centerpiece I had chosen.

"I didn't mean anything by it," he told me, half-joking, half annoyed that I hadn't stopped moving since I had woken up.

I glared but continued to fix the knives and wine glasses.

"The table looks beautiful, Margo," Theo complimented loudly. I rolled my eyes at his flattery. "They'll be here any moment. Why don't you come and sit before you wear yourself out?"

"Theo," I exhaled, running my hand over my sticky forehead. "I just want everything to be perfect."

"Margo, everything is perfect. They're going to adore you, no matter what the table looks like."

"Why? Does the table not look good? I knew I should've stayed with the other setting," I rattled out frantically. Theo groaned and walked away from me, not knowing how to deal with my high anxiety.

The doorbell rang, and I froze. Theo walked back into the main room and looked at me, smiled reassuringly, and then went to answer the door.

"Theo!" Cam's boisterous voice filled the house. Theo chuckled and greeted him. I adjusted my top and joined Theo in the foyer.

"There she is," Cam smiled at me and pulled me into a bear hug I was not expecting, lifting my feet slightly off the ground. My face was in shock, and Theo laughed at me but made no move to save me.

"Nice to see you again, Cam," I greeted him softly. He chuckled and began to take his coat off. Theo was greeting a woman, Gemma, with a small brunette girl stuck to his leg.

"Gemma, this is my beautiful mate, Margo. Margo, this is Cam's mate, Gemma."

Gemma grinned cautiously, her full lips happy, but her eyes were weary.

"Hello, it's great to meet you," I told her, reaching out to grasp her forearm.

"Hell-lo," her voice stuttered. "Th-th-thank you for having us."

"It's our pleasure." I tried not to let my face show concern, but I glanced at Theo sadly.

"Once you get-t used t-to th-the st-t-tut-tt-ter, I'm actually quite funny. Funnier th-than th-th-at ass over th-there," she joked. I looked back at her in surprise and giggled politely.

"This is their daughter, Tansy," Theo told me, placing his hand on her small head while she stayed latched to his leg.

"Hi, Tansy."

"Hi," her twinkling voice called, muffled from Theo's pant leg. We began walking towards the table, Theo carrying Tansy in tow on his leg. Cam was already sitting down, pouring what looked to be his second glass of wine.

Gemma glared angrily at her mate.

"What?" he asked cheerfully. "It was just sitting there."

"Well-ll, you could-d've at-t l-least poured me a g-glass," she told him sassily. He chuckled at her, pouring her a glass of wine, and tugging on her hand to sit next to him.

Theo brought the food around, and we started eating, making small talk.

"So, when did you both meet?" I cleared my throat and set my fork down momentarily.

"We met seven years ago," Cam began telling me, before

stuffing his mouth full of steak. Gemma nudged him.

"He caught me tr-trying t-to cross the bound-dary line."

"Were you a spy or something?" My voice was full of surprise.

"No," Gemma giggled, looking down.

"Just a cute little rogue," Cam smiled happily, lifting his chin.

"Cute l-little rogue who you could-dn't catch," she said snidely.

"She's really fast," Cam grumbled, slightly annoyed. He reached over and took her fork from her hand and kept eating his meal. Gemma smacked his arm lightly and reached for her fork, which Cam held just out of reach.

I extended my arm, handing her the fork from Tansy's place. Gemma smiled victoriously at me and stuck her tongue out at Cam. Tansy refused to sit in her chair, even though her parents brought her a booster seat as well. She insisted on sitting in Theo's lap while he ate, climbing all over him and sneaking pieces of his food away.

"Can you hear me when I do this?" she called out right before sticking her fingers in Theo's ears.

"T-Tansy!" Gemma called in mortification. Tansy's small buns on either side of her head bobbled as Theo grabbed her around the waist and flipped her upside down.

"Yes, I can hear you, Tansy," Theo teased, tickling her stomach. He froze for a moment, staring at a spot on the wall while holding Tansy securely.

"Theo?" I called. He stared for a few more seconds, getting a mind link from someone in the pack. He snapped away and turned to look at me. I couldn't read his face, but he didn't look happy. He flipped Tansy upright and sat her on his lap, stroking her hair softly. "Is everything alright?" I said quietly, leaning over towards him. Cam and Gemma were looking down at their plates, busying themselves with eating.

Before he could answer me, the doorbell rang. I jumped in my seat, looking pointedly at Theo, who was fixated on Tansy's hands playing patty-cake.

"You should get that," he told me, not looking at me.

"What?" I asked, confused, and slightly irritated.

"Go," he said louder, more firmly. I pushed my seat back loudly; the loud scratch it created almost made me cringe. I shoved my seat back in, not as angrily as I wanted, and walked to the front door. I paused in front of it, not knowing why Theo was ordering me to open the door when he had never allowed me to before.

After a moment, a familiar feeling called to me from the other side of the door, and I threw it open quickly.

"Caddy?"

SUCCESSION

He looked up at me through his thick eyelashes. His face was red, blotchy, and tear-stained.

"What happened?" I asked frantically, pulling on his arms and shirt to bring him inside the door. He stumbled in and rested his back on the door as it closed.

"He's dead," his low voice whispered.

"Who?"

"My uncle, Dorian," he whimpered. I dove into his arms, hugging his midframe to me because that's all I could reach. "He's dead."

"I'm so sorry, Caddy," I soothed, an anxious wave tumbling down my body as I did so. "What happened?"

"We don't know for sure, but we know it was someone from another pack. We tracked the scent."

"Come in," I told him, grabbing his hand and leading him into the room where Theo and Cam sat, almost waiting.

Gemma had led Tansy away.

"Theo," I began to tell him.

"We heard," he told me sadly. I pushed Caddy's swaying body into the chair where I once sat.

"Are you okay?" I asked, running my hand down his back as he hunched over.

"I don't know." He shook his head and rolled his shoulders. His eyes looked far away. "They started talking about me and that I'm supposed to take over as Alpha now. I'm not ready for that, how could I be ready for that?" Caddy rambled, running his hands over his face three times.

"Everything's going to be okay." My words weren't convincing.

"No, it's not, Margo," Caddy wailed.

"We will find whoever did this," Theo promised.

"What does it even matter, you know how many enemies Dorian had," Caddy chuckled without humor. "Someone probably just got tired of dealing with his shit."

Theo looked at me sadly, pointedly, like he was waiting for me to realize something.

"Caddy, what pack did you say did this?"

"I didn't." He looked down at his shaking hands. "One of the trackers said it was someone from the Forte Pack."

"Theo," I said hesitantly, wavering. "That's Porter's pack, isn't it?" I took his silence as confirmation.

"Reed Porter?" Caddy perked up. I nodded. "I don't know that we've ever had contact with his pack. I mean, even Dorian knew that guy is batshit crazy. He wouldn't stick his nose in that."

"Theo, please tell me this isn't my fault," I whispered. Theo stood up and maneuvered around Caddy to hold me.

"Margo, how could this be your fault," Caddy said, grabbing my hand that was wound tightly around Theo's waist.

"Reed Porter has been creating trouble around here lately," Theo informed him. "He wanted me to approve his demand to take over a portion of Duncan Trissur's land. I told him no. He seemed to take a special interest in the fact that Margo is human."

"I mean, I know Porter hates humans, that common knowledge. What does that have to do with Dorian?"

"Your uncle took care of Margo, allowed her to stay in your pack. By killing Dorian, he not only sent every other Alpha a message that Alpha's who protect humans are at risk for attack, but he also made a threat to Margo directly," Theo said softly while pressing my head to his chest.

"Margo," Caddy said lowly.

"Caddy, I am so sorry." I fought my way out of Theo's arms and flung myself on Caddy.

"Margo, this is not your fault." Caddy ruffled my hair like he used to. "Reed Porter was looking for a target, it's not like you gave him the idea."

"But Dorian never would have been killed if it weren't for me."

Caddy snorted and sucked his lips into his mouth, shaking his head. "Sooner or later," he said spitefully. "He was cruel; he didn't care about anyone else and he never listened to anyone but himself. I don't even know why I'm so upset. He hated me. He only used me when he needed something."

"He was still your uncle."

"Yeah," he nodded, blowing air out of his mouth. I squeezed him tightly and released him.

"So, what do we do now?" I asked Theo. We sat down at the table, now joined by Gemma and a sleeping Tansy on her shoulder.

"Reed Porter just made a declaration of war," Cam stated. "Against Duncan, Caddy's pack, us."

"My pack," Caddy said strangely and shook his head. "I guess it is my pack now."

"Dorian trained you well." I touched his forearm. "You'll be a great Alpha."

"I'm only twenty-four."

"You're not the youngest ever," Theo said kindly, reminiscing. "You'll have the support. This is probably the best time to learn."

"Right in the middle of a war," he snorted.

"You're going t-to war?" Gemma asked Cam.

"Gem, there's no need to worry yet," Cam murmured, taking her hand in his.

"Yes, th-there is." Gemma's voice was loud, and it woke Tansy.

"Momma?" her tired voice asked.

"I'm right-t here, b-b-baby." Gemma kissed her head and rocked her softly against her body.

"We should reconvene tomorrow, get the council together," Theo suggested. Cam nodded in agreement and stood up. Gemma stood with him and passed Tansy to her father.

"Margo." Gemma came and took my hands in her cold ones. "It-t was wond-derful meet-ting you. I'm sure we will b-be seeing a lot-t of each oth-ther."

"Probably," I sighed, giving her a small smile. "It was nice meeting you as well. Your daughter is beautiful."

"Yeah, well, she t-takes aft-ter me." Gemma laughed at Cam's distraught face and kissed his cheek. They left quietly, sending their condolences to Caddy before exiting the house.

"Caddy's more than welcome to stay," Theo offered, tucking his hands in his front pockets.

"Thanks," Caddy noted.

"I'll make the guest room up for you," I promised, quickly running down the hallway to find extra sheets and blankets and pillows. I found some in a closet, carrying the large pile in my arms, unable to see around them. I heard Theo and Caddy talking as I set up the room down the hall.

"She's a really good friend," Caddy said affectionately. "She's always been there for me, especially when my dad died. You're treating her right?"

I almost laughed at the protective tone in Caddy's voice.

"She could ask me for my heart, and I'd carve it out of my own chest for her," Theo told him, chuckling slightly.

"Good," Caddy boasted. I blushed and tucked myself behind a corner, listening to the rest of their conversation. "You know she's been through a lot?"

"She doesn't talk about it," Theo sighed, grabbing two beers from the fridge.

"She won't," Caddy warned. "She lost her parents young. My grandpa was a cruel son-ova-bitch. Killed them right in front of her."

"How old was she?"

"Four."

Theo cursed under his breath.

"That's why she acts so," Caddy struggled for the word.

"Guarded?" Theo offered. Caddy nodded, taking a sip of his drink.

"It's not because she doesn't like you, I can tell she does. She normally doesn't touch anyone, let alone hug them, except for me. It's self-preservation. She's always had to look out for herself; she didn't have anyone other than me to protect her, and I couldn't always be there."

"And the human thing?" Theo grimaced.

"The human thing." Caddy nodded. "I think she knows not all wolves are bad. She has to; she's been my best friend for eighteen years now. She's never seen the good side of wolves, though. I'm the only exception for her. Her parents were murdered in front of her, and for twenty-two years of her life, she's been treated like absolute garbage. Would you want to become something that brought you so much pain?"

"I'm her mate, though," Theo insisted. "How are we ever going to have a life together if she could die from a cold next week? We won't ever have kids; we won't ever grow old together. Humans die at what, seventy? eighty if they're lucky?"

"Is another ten years and a couple of kids going to stop you from loving her?"

"No." Theo shook his head. "Her dying will stop me from loving her, and I won't let that happen."

I cleared my throat as I walked back into the room. "It's ready for you." I gestured to the hallway where the guest room was.

"Thanks, Mango," Caddy teased. I groaned.

"I thought we were done with that," I hissed at him, rolling my eyes. He shook his head and looked over at Theo.

"When she was little, she couldn't say her own name correctly, so I told her it was spelled the same as mango. So, until she was eight, she thought her name was actually spelled Mango."

"I hate you," I growled playfully. Theo laughed loudly as Caddy, and I playfully shoved each other back and forth.

"No, you don't," Caddy teased, raising his eyebrows provocatively. "You love us." He dragged out the word 'love,' nearly singing it.

Theo laughed and pulled on my arms until I fell into his lap, clumsily. I hid my face, half because I knew if they ever became friends, I would never have a peaceful moment again, and half because I didn't want to admit that Caddy's words might be true.

PLUMMETING HEART SYNDROME

The meeting reconvened in the morning, much like Theo suggested. The house was filled with people when I finally got up and made my way downstairs. I had the good sense to get dressed and fix my hair before I left the bedroom, unlike my usual messy hair and pajamas I lounged in.

I was surprised to see so many women in the living room waiting for Theo's council meeting. The world of shifters was often dominated by powerful men, but it gave me hope to see the council wasn't biased. Although an Enforcer ruled directly over the packs of their continent, they also had a council made of other dignitaries and retired Alphas meant to help with important decisions.

"Margo!" My name was shouted. Most eyes looked over at me slowly, trying to be coy, but many were shocked that I was still human. I excused myself around the groups of people and found Theo and Caddy waiting for me.

Theo greeted me by kissing my forehead. "Morning, little one. I fixed your breakfast." Reaching behind him, he grabbed a plate of food and handed it to me. I smiled my thanks to him and sat at the counter, eating quickly, and put my dish in the sink.

"What are we waiting for?" I wondered aloud.

"We're just waiting for Cam who was supposed to be here twenty minutes ago." Theo was peeved, scratching the back of his neck.

Cam came through the door a few minutes later with Tansy on his hip. "I'm so sorry I'm late, Gemma had speech therapy this morning, and our babysitter canceled on us last minute," he heaved out, tucking Tansy's hair behind her ears and adjusting her weight on his hip. "You're getting heavy," he told her quietly in her ear. Tansy's giggles filled the air, and she squealed, lighting the room's atmosphere.

"Okay, everyone, let's take this to the conference room," Theo announced, pulling me forward with him.

Everyone followed us back to the large room on the other side of the stairs. Theo sat at the head of the table, per usual, and I sat next to him on his left. Cam sat next to me on my left, Caddy next to him, and everyone filled into the empty seats and lined the walls.

Cam began to tell everyone the situation at hand, including every detail. The council started taking notes, profusely writing, whispering, and nodding along.

"When was the first threat sent, the document sent to Enforcer Weston?" a woman asked. She was middle-aged with faded red hair chopped short to her shoulders.

"The document arrived four weeks ago," Theo told her.

"You received a threat four weeks ago, and we're just hearing about this now?" Her voice was derogative to Theo; her eyebrows were raised.

"You didn't need to know four weeks ago, Keziah," Theo told her, trying to control his temper by tapping his pen on the table.

"An Alpha is making threats against humans, and you don't think we need to know?" she sneered.

"This had nothing to do with humans until two weeks ago," Cam stepped in. "When the threat to humans and other packs was made directly, the council was informed. Theo did nothing wrong."

"Well, that's very noble of you to step up for him, but now we have one dead Alpha, a pack on the verge of war, and a threat to humans. Reed Porter is not alone in his beliefs. This could separate packs everywhere," Keziah said, looking around at other council members who were nodding in support.

"There is nothing I can do to change the past," Theo admitted, dropping his pen and lowering his eyes. "If I would have known this is what would spawn from the document, I would have immediately brought the council together. I did what I thought was right. If you disagree with me, that's fine, but I'm the one who ultimately gets to decide. I called us here to create a plan of action to combat these injustices and protect the innocent."

Keziah settled in her chair, looking back to Theo, who had regained attention and dominance.

"I'm sure this issue is very close to your heart, Enforcer," another man said hesitantly from the corner of the room. He stepped away from the wall and bowed his head. Most eyes in the room shifted to me and my human-ness. "But most of us have grown fond of humans ourselves over the past years. They have been helpful and innovative in creating the kind of pack dynamic we had always hoped for."

"If Reed Porter wants to start a war against humans, he's

going to start a war against good wolves as well," the man next to him added, placing a hand on the other's shoulder.

"Well then, we're in agreement," Theo breathed out happily, placing his hand over mine on the table.

The next few hours were spent discussing strategy and plans. There were calls made to other Alphas near and far from us. The members of the council were not all from the Valkyrie Pack, only three out of the fifty were. The council made calls to their Alpha's asking support in their decisions.

Although most Alphas agreed with the council and Theo's decision, they were not ready to sacrifice their pack members to fight for it and remained neutral.

After some time, Tansy began squirming in her father's lap and begged him to take her to the bathroom. I told him I would take her and escorted her down the hall. I stayed on the other side of the door and helped her wash her hands when she was done.

"Where do you live?" she asked, tugging on my pant leg.

"I live here," I said softly.

"With Uncle Theo?" her voice cracked upwards.

"Yes." She looked down, confused, trying to make sense of it. "Your Uncle Theo and I are mates, just like your mommy and daddy."

"You're going to be my aunt?" she shouted happily. We were close to the conference room, and with their advanced hearing, the shifters inside looked out the window to us.

"Only if you want me to," I said, bending down on my knees. "Or you can call me Margo."

"Okay, Auntie Margo," she twiddled off cheerfully.

"Let's go back in and see your daddy," I suggested, taking her hand in mine, and walking towards the open door. Theo's body stopped me at the door.

"You're good with her," he complimented, casually slinging his hand in his pocket.

I glanced down at Tansy, smiling as I patted the top of her head. "Well, she's cute. It helps."

"Tans, your dad said you might be getting hungry, do you want a snack before we go back inside?"

"Yes, please," she said politely. He gestured, and we began walking down the hall to the kitchen. Tansy let go of my hand as it came into view and ran ahead.

"I can't wait to see how you'll be with ours," Theo imagined, sighing and rubbing his thumb over my arm. He looked over and saw the shimmer of fear in my eyes. "Not until you're ready, though," he added quickly.

I averted my gaze, blinking my eyes in an attempt to process his words.

"Are you okay?" he asked after a moment. I realized I had stopped walking.

"If you want us to have kids, that means you'll have to change me," I whispered. Anxiety crawled up my back and enveloped me in its gut-twisting stench.

"We don't have to do anything until you're ready," he told me soothingly.

"When I told you I didn't want to be turned, did you take that as, 'well maybe in five years she'll want to?'" My voice was dead and flat. I could feel sweat collecting on my neck. My mouth became too dry, and I bit my tongue to regain feeling.

"We don't have to talk about this right now," Theo soothed, touching the outer line of my arm as I stumbled back from him. "Margo."

"I'm sorry, I just," I panted. "I need a minute."

"Margo," he said pointedly. "Nothing is happening right

now."

"But it will." I shook my head as my vision became blurry. "Theo, I just need to know right now; are you planning on changing me?"

He chuckled, though it seemed more out of awkwardness than humor. "Do I really need to answer this right now? Let's go get Tansy something to eat. I'm sure she's opened every package of chocolate and candy in that kitchen."

"Yes, you really need to answer it."

He straightened and tugged on the collar of his button-up shirt. "Maybe, one day. But I want to wait until you're more accepting of it. I know it will take time-"

"It won't take time because there is nothing to consider."

"Can we-"

"No," I spoke quickly. "We cannot discuss this or think about it later. Just no."

"Do you think this is the best location and time to be having this conversation, with the council and our friends thirty feet away?"

"Honestly, I couldn't care less. I need you to know I won't ever be okay with being turned into a shifter. Ever."

"Okay," he breathed angrily. "You've made your point. Thank you. Can we continue with what we were doing now?"

"You should go back in there," I advised. "I'll find Tansy ad get her something to eat. I could use a glass of water anyways."

"Fine." He nodded.

I walked to the kitchen and looked around the nooks and crevices, trying to find Tansy. I called her name but heard no response. I left the kitchen and looked around the couches and chairs in the living room.

"Tansy?" I called louder. A gleam of sunlight hit me in the eye, and my head snapped up to find the front door swung open. No guard stood at the entrance, and I approached it warily. In the field in front of the house, Tansy was chasing a bunny that was hopping around the brush.

"Tansy!" I yelled. I could hear the wolves moving around in the conference room, and I was aware that Cam and Theo had probably come into the living room when I screamed, but it didn't stop me from running toward her. The guard was nowhere in sight.

Tansy was unaware of any threat and ran towards the tree line with glee.

"Tansy, stop!" I yelled, trying to catch up with the little girl whose legs seemed to be quicker than mine. She laughed and ran faster.

"Tansy!" I heard Cam yell behind me.

She paused, nearly tumbling to the ground as she came face to face with the amber eyes of a wolf that was not from our pack.

MOVING PARTS

"Tansy, don't move," I warned with tension in my voice. I reached my hand out towards her, still too far away, but needing to reach her. I took one step forward and the wolf whined. It was a warning sound, telling me not to move too fast.

Tansy whimpered and turned her head towards me. The wolf was ten feet in front of her, and I was ten feet behind. Cam and Theo approached the scene quickly, but when they were twenty feet from Tansy, the wolf growled and bared its teeth.

"Tansy, can you walk slowly back to Auntie Margo, please?" Cam called. His voice was calm and flat.

Tansy stumbled back on her heels, and she took a few steps before the wolf slinked forward, leaning down on its front paws in a predatory lunge.

"Stop, Tansy," I said, gritting my teeth.

"Daddy," she cried.

"It's okay, baby," Cam called back. "You just stay right there."

I couldn't bear to look away front Tansy and the wolf, so I didn't know how far away they were or if they were moving around behind us. The wolf stood up fully and veered its large head around, stretching its muscles.

I moved one step forward, then another when I went undetected. Soon, I was close enough to Tansy to grab her and push her behind me.

She yelped when I touched her and began crying. She ran to her father behind me as I was now the barrier between her and the unknown wolf. To my left, I saw Theo slidling around the trees, trying to catch the wolf by surprise when he decided to attack. He nodded to me, letting me know he was okay.

The wolf was massive, even more so when it was just in front of me. I faltered and stepped back. The wolf growled deeply in its chest, and its claws dug into the soft belly of the earth.

"Margo," Theo said warningly from my left. The three of us formed a triangle, and we looked back and forth between each other. "Take a step back," he ordered, his body already shaking to shift.

"I can't," I moaned.

"You can," he told me. "One step. Slowly."

I did as he asked, and the wolf bared its teeth to me. I stopped moving and an involuntary cry of helplessness. Theo growled back, low in his chest, and held his hand out towards me. I wanted to reach out and take it, but fear seized my chest, and I was paralyzed in it.

"Margo, get behind me."

"No." I shook my head quickly.

"Margo," he said sharply.

"I can't move," I whispered with tears coating my voice.

"Yes, you can. Just a few steps away."

I willed my foot to move, but I couldn't make any of my limbs go where I wanted them to. The wolf knew this and eerily smirked under its fur.

"Okay, I'm going to come to you. Can you take one step towards me?"

"No," I said honestly.

"Okay, just breathe." He nodded. Theo walked towards me with confidence, not faltering when the wolf's head whipped towards him and snarled. Theo grabbed my arm and swiftly pulled me behind him. "Leave," he ordered the wolf.

The wolf made no attempt to leave, though it did begin to pace back and forth in front of us. Its muscles rolled under its fur as it sashayed and growled.

"You need to leave this territory immediately."

Still, this did nothing to frighten or persuade the intruder. Tansy suddenly let out a cry from the other side of the trees where her father was holding her. That sparked something in the wolf, we could all sense it, and Theo pushed me forcefully behind him before shifting into his wolf form.

If I wasn't so terrified, I probably would have screamed as Theo's body exploded into a mass of gray and white fur. He was massive, far bigger than any other wolf I had seen. He stood his ground proudly, growling viciously at the other wolf. They moved around the small area, sizing each other up.

When the wolf got too close to me, Theo would change direction. They stayed like that for quite some time. I found it hard to look away.

The wolf leaned down, making itself small. They took a step closer and let out a howl so loud I had to cover my ears with my shaking hands. The wolf looked submissive, staring up at Theo with its amber eyes. Theo stood tall, glaring once more at the wolf before turning and moving closer to me.

He moved cautiously, gingerly taking a few steps and then allowing me to adjust to him. I tried to calm my breathing. When Theo had pushed me, I had fallen near a large pine tree, and I didn't get up.

Theo bowed his head to me, showing me that it was safe for me to approach him. I picked myself off the ground and brushed my arms off from the pine needles and dirt. He stayed still as I contemplated what I wanted to do.

His fur was a beautiful charcoal gray with white on his underbelly and face. The coloring suited him. Hesitantly, I took a step to the right, trying to make my way towards Tansy and Cam. Theo allowed this but took a step with me. I paused.

In their wolf form, shifters often acted on their instincts. Some shifters even had a notion that their wolf form had its own personality separate from their human form. Theo's wolf form seemed completely enamored by me. He moved each way I did, stepping close until he was near enough to rub his head along my legs and waist as he circled me.

I held my arms into my chest, fearfully keeping my fingers out of the reach of his incisors. Theo backed up and stared off into the distance, most likely getting a mind-link from someone. I turned my head to where the other wolf once was. I sighed, reassuring myself I was safe.

Cam had turned his back on Theo and me to pick Tansy up off the ground behind him where she had hidden. I blinked once, and things happened so quickly the only way my mind could make sense of it was to view it in slow motion.

As Cam stretched his arms out to reach for Tansy, the leaves on the other side of the clearing rustled and shifted. The intruder wolf from earlier darted from one side of the trees to the next, snarling loudly as it ran quickly, its muscles flexing and contorting as it raced towards Cam and his daughter.

Cam sensed the movement quickly and spun around with Tansy in his hands. The wolf moved with such speed and agility, I knew the only way Cam would be able to protect Tansy was to shift immediately, and with her that close, it could cause her harm.

Suddenly, I was moving. My body that seemed to be paralyzed in the face of the wolf was now running at full speed, trying to protect them or distract the wolf until help could arrive. Theo snapped out of his mind-link daze after a few seconds, and a ground-shaking growl erupted from him.

The wolf's head turned to see me, stalling it for a moment and slowing its speed. I don't know what I expected to happen when I faced the wolf, but seeing Tansy's large brown eyes filled with fearful tears propelled me into action. I stopped short of a few feet in front of the wolf and my arms stilled by my chest long enough to watch Theo barrel into the side of the wolf, knocking it off its feet.

As Theo's gray wolf and the tawny wolf fought, I tried to find the common sense to move. I knew I should have. I could hear Cam's voice calling to me, and after a few seconds, I finally found it in myself to turn my head. He held his arm up, gesturing for me to come closer to him. I took one step before Cam's eyes grew wider, and he opened his mouth to tell me something, but it fell on deaf ears.

Sharp, hot teeth sunk into my thigh, tearing straight through the muscles and bone. I don't remember the pain as it happened, but I remember the noise my bones made as they snapped. The wolf didn't remain on me long. Theo killed it instantly by tearing its throat out.

I don't know how long I was on the ground for or how long Theo dismembered my attacker. At some point, Theo came back in his human form, frantically yelling at me, but it sounded like I was underwater. I couldn't concentrate on anything other than the two birds that sat in the tree above us.

Cam appeared over me soon with three other males I didn't recognize. Theo gripped my thigh where the wolf bit, and I yelped as my body attempted to sit up and protect itself. Cam held my arms down, soothing me, and telling me it was going to be okay.

Theo tied a shirt around my leg, and I could feel my heartbeat echoing from the limb. I was lifted off the ground; Theo held my body close to him as Cam held my leg out steadily, putting pressure on the wound.

"Margo, just hold on, okay, love?" Theo told me as they rushed me as quickly as they could back to the house. "We're going to get you help. You're going to be just fine."

I moaned in response, my eyes rolling to the back of my head and then back around again.

"Margo, I need you to stay awake. Don't close your eyes, alright? I know it hurts, but I need you to be strong," I heard Cam order more assertively. "Bite Theo if it hurts."

"What happened?" Caddy's voice asked quickly as we arrived at the house. He ran over to us with shaking hands.

Dishes and placemats were thrown off the dining table, and Theo laid me gently on top. The shifters went to work immediately, handing Theo and Cam towels, a bowl of water, gauze, and bandage wraps. Theo brushed my hair away from my sweaty forehead. He leaned over me, trying to hold eye contact with me, although mine were wandering around the room feverishly.

"I promise you're going to be okay, Margo." He kissed my forehead, where his hand just was. "The doctors are going to be here at any moment, and they're going to fix you up. I'm so sorry, little one."

My hand shot up and touched him, trying to give him

some sort of response. He grabbed it firmly and squeezed be-fore placing hip lips on my knuckles. The warmth of his breath was the last thing I remember before waking up in the hospital eighteen hours later.

REMEDIES

I was awake before I could open my eyes. I tried to make a noise-ask someone for help-but it came out weak.

"Margo?" Theo's voice asked worriedly from next to me. I tried to speak again, and my voice cracked, its airy tone frustrating me. "Shh, shh, just relax."

I didn't listen to him and kept trying to speak. My eyes struggled to open, but eventually, they did, and I moved my body frantically. Theo grabbed my wounded leg near my ankle and held it to the bed and reached up to push my chest down.

"Margo, you're okay. Just relax, okay, love? I'm right here." He looked into my eyes; his were worried and serious.

I calmed my breathing and looked around. I was in a hospital room hooked up to machines and covered in a soft, cotton gown.

"How do you feel?" he asked while letting go of my leg and settling back into the chair he next to me.

"My leg hurts," I whimpered, my voice still cracking

from dryness.

"Okay, little one, I'll call the doctors, and we'll get you some more pain meds," he said. His voice was thick with remorse as well as his face. He mind-linked someone, and a man ran inside my room.

"She's awake," he noted, coming over to check all the machines I was connected to.

"She's in pain," Theo said angrily. "She needs more pain medication."

"I'll call the doctor. She'll have to see if it's time for that," the man said softly, bowing his head before leaving the room.

Theo ran his thumb over my hand, not making eye contact with me.

"Theo?" He didn't look up. "Theo," I said louder.

"Margo, I am so sorry I didn't protect you," he cried out. "I wasn't there when you needed me; I let you down."

I opened my mouth slowly, wanting to comfort him, but the doctor entered.

"Luna Regina, I'm Doctor Dernon, how are you feeling?" The woman was tall, skinny, her long limbs looked agile, and her face was kind. She had darker brown hair that was pulled up; she looked intelligent.

"Hurts," I said, not able to say anything more before I groaned in pain. My pulse throbbed in my leg hard.

"You had a lot of damage to your leg," she said, looking down at the chart. "Your femur was fractured by the force of the bite. We've placed a plate and four screws to secure the bone. The muscle was also torn around your upper thigh; we've repaired the blood vessels, but unfortunately, a portion of your skin on your thigh was torn off in the incident. We had to do a skin graft from your other leg. You may feel some discomfort, but that should be acute."

I tried to understand what she said to me. Theo saw my confusion and touched my head affectionately.

"Thank you, Doctor Dernon. I'm afraid my mate is in a lot of pain right now, I'm not sure how much of this she'll be able to understand or remember. Can we give her more medication?"

She pursed her lips and closed her chart. "Unfortunately, we don't have any pain medication for humans in this facility. The last of it was used when the doctors arrived at your home. I've sent someone to retrieve some from the closest pack, but until he gets back, there's not much I can do in terms of pain medication."

"She can't use the pain medication we use?" Theo asked. His voice rose louder and louder.

"The way our bodies metabolize medication is different from humans. If I were to give her even the lowest possible dosage, her body could reject it, she could slip into a comatose state, or her heart could slow down. None of these possibilities are worth trying that method right now."

"She's in pain!" Theo bellowed, leaning over me to yell at the doctor. I squeezed his hand and tried to tug it to tell him to sit down.

"I'm very sorry for your pain; I'm doing everything I can right now. The medicine should be here within the next two hours. There are other things you can do in terms of pain relief, though," she said cautiously. Theo looked at her, expectantly. "Many mated pairs use each other's blood as a natural pain reliever. The cells in mate's bodies are used to comfort each other so long as a marking bite is in place. A small cut on the wrist would suffice enough blood for her to ingest."

I shuddered visibly. The thought of drinking Theo's blood made me sick, and I vomited in the container Theo handed me when he saw me lurch. He grabbed my hair away from my face and whispered for me to relax.

When I sat back in the bed, I noticed the doctor left the room. Theo was already reaching for the small scalpel she had left on the bedside table.

"Theo, no," I panted, reaching for his arm. I had tasted his blood before when I marked him, but that was only a few drops, and even that was enough to make me wretch upon remembering it.

"You're in pain, Margo. This is all I can do for you, and I'm going to do it." He made a small incision on the side of his wrist near his thumb and brought it closer to my face. I turned away but couldn't do much to stop him since the pain immobilized me. He held my head forward on his wrist and kissed the top of my head.

"That's it, good girl," he muttered. "Just a little more."

When I swallowed the metallic, warm liquid, he sat back and let his wrist heal almost instantly. The taste of his blood lingered, and it made my stomach lurch again. Theo grabbed my shoulders and held me back.

"No, Margo, you've got to keep it down. I promise it'll help. Just give it a minute."

I groaned and shoved his arm away. He slumped back in his seat and just watched as I writhed in pain. I let out a small scream, and he grabbed my hand again, running his fingers over it, kissing my palm. After a few moments, the pain started to subside. My mind became foggy, and I found it hard to keep my eyes open.

"It's okay," Theo said as he smiled sadly at me. "You can sleep, love, and I'll be right here when you wake up. I'm not going anywhere."

My eyes closed, and I slumped into a sleep I didn't wake from for two days.

* * *

"I swear, only you could get a chunk of your leg taken out and still be worrying about other people," Caddy chuckled. He had come to visit me at the hospital and give Theo a break so he could go home and shower.

"I'm just worried about him," I admitted. "This is messing with his head, I can tell."

"Theo will be fine, he's a big boy," he laughed, taking a sip of his drink. He brought us food from a shop down the street. I rolled my eyes and bit into my sandwich.

"I know he'll be okay eventually, but you should've seen his face, Caddy. He looked like someone ripped his heart out."

"Well, they kind of did," he said, looking at me sympathetically. "You're his whole world now. That wolf almost took you away from him."

"I guess."

"But it'll work out," he said optimistically. "And in the meantime, I'll be here to provide you with plenty of entertainment until your prince returns."

"Shouldn't you be getting back to the pack?" He groaned and took a large bite of food. "They need you, Caddy. You're the Alpha now."

"I don't want to be the Alpha," he pouted. I giggled and threw a pickle towards him. "That was rude."

"You need to go back," I smiled sadly, not really wanting him to leave.

"Don't you want me here?" he asked, confused. I knew Caddy didn't have a lot of friends back in his pack. He was probably lonely.

140

"Of course, I do." I rested my hand on his arm. "But the pack deserves to have an Alpha like you. Theirs was just murdered, and their new one is MIA."

"I know, you're right," he grumbled, setting his sandwich down. "I'll go back soon."

"Good."

Theo came back from showering and in a new change of clothes. He didn't speak much. Caddy held most of the conversation until he left to go back to the packhouse and sleep.

"You know you can talk to me, right? If something's bothering you," I offered Theo. He sat in the corner of the small room, slumped against a cabinet. He didn't even move when I spoke. "Because I'm getting tired of this, Theo. I can't help if you don't tell me what's wrong, and you've barely said five words to me in the past week."

He moved around and stared down at his hands. I reached back and grabbed a pillow from my bed and threw it at him. He looked up, shocked. It was the first time his expression had changed in days.

"Will you just say something!" I yelled loudly. His eyes remained wide and unmoving.

A nurse came into the room. "Is everything okay?" she asked softly, looking between Theo and me rapidly.

"It's fine," Theo said softly.

"No, it's not fine," I called out, trying to hold back tears.

"Oh," the nurse said awkwardly.

"Just go if you want to go," I told him, crossing my arms over my chest. "But don't stay here and stare at me because you're upset."

"No," he said, too quietly for me to hear, but I saw his mouth move.

"Well then, get up out of that chair and talk to me! Do you think it makes me feel any better having you sit and sulk while I lay here? Because it doesn't." I didn't mean to be cruel, but if it got Theo to open up, it was worth it. Even if he was angry at me, that was better than this unimaginable silence.

The nurse left the room. Theo stayed where he was, and I pushed the button to adjust the bed so I was sitting up further.

"Theo, I'm serious."

"I'm not leaving you."

"You might as well. This isn't helping me at all."

"I'm the reason you have a broken leg!" he screamed back at me. I tucked myself inward. "If I had been more careful, you wouldn't be here."

"That's not true," I denied.

"You know it is, Margo. My job is to protect you, and I couldn't even do that. You needed me, and I wasn't careful enough. I'm trying to find a way to get over that and be the man you need me to be. And I don't know how to do that yet, so I'm going to sit here. And sulk. And not talk until I can do that."

I didn't have a response to him immediately. He settled back in his seat and his constant, unwavering gaze.

"You didn't let me down," I told him softly. "You could never let me down."

"Go to sleep, Margo."

"No," I shook my head. "We're going to have a conversation about this."

"I don't have anything else to say," he growled.

"Well, then listen to me. What happened last week was no one's fault. Did we say some mean things before that?

142

Yes. Should that conversation have waited? Probably. But that wasn't even the reason that all of this happened. Tansy was the one who ran out the door, and we're not going to sit here and blame a child for something that wasn't her fault. You would've done the same thing as I did, we all would have."

"That wolf shouldn't have been there." He shook his head.

"No," I sighed. "It shouldn't have."

"And where the hell were the guards? Why didn't the border catch them? There have got to be holes in our security, and I can't figure out who they are, and I don't know what to do."

"We can figure it out together," I suggested.

"Where the hell were the guards?" he asked, not paying attention to me.

"Theo."

"Was it a planned attack, or was it random?" he thought aloud.

"Theo!" His head snapped up. "Stop!"

"I can't!" he shouted, standing up. "I can't stop thinking about. I can't stop seeing it in my head over and over again like it's a rerun! All I see is that wolf's teeth sinking into your leg, and it's like I'm back there. Every time I close my eyes!"

"Will you just come and sit with me?" I asked.

He paused and dropped his shoulders.

"If that's what you want," he mumbled, walking over to me. He moved to take the chair next to the bed, but I grabbed his hand and tugged him towards me. He hesitantly moved onto the bed, one leg hanging off slightly. "You have to tell me," he began to say, but paused and swallowed the lump in his throat. "You have to tell me if you ever begin to resent me for not being there for you."

I opened my mouth to protest, the intention clearly on my face.

"No, Margo. Promise me." His eyes were serious.

"I promise," I said to soothe him. "I promise to tell you if I'm ever angry with you, even if it's just because you put mustard on my sandwich. I'm going to tell you so often that you're going to get sick of me and glue my mouth shut."

He cracked a smile.

"There he is," I greeted, grinning up at him.

"You're the best thing that's ever happened to me," he said sweetly, bending down to place a kiss on my forehead. I closed my eyes and reveled in the touch. It had been too long since I'd felt his warmth on my skin. He remained close to me, breathing in the smell of my hair.

"I probably don't smell too good," I told him, laughing. "The nurse helped me shower yesterday, but it was all of that scentless stuff."

"You smell like you." He smiled, ignoring my awkward comment.

"I can't wait to get out of this bed. I swear I'm going to lay in a bath for days."

Theo chuckled at me, sitting in the seat Caddy had previously inhabited.

"I can't wait to take you home," he said. I breathed in deeply, feeling like our bond was swelling with affection.

"Are you going to carry me over the threshold?" I joked, wiggling my eyebrows.

"Calm down, sweetheart." He smiled cheekily. "We've got to get you better first."

"I know," I pouted, sinking further into my nest of pillows and blankets.

"It shouldn't be long now." He shook his head. "Maybe a few days."

"A few days seems like a lifetime. I've been here for twelve days already."

"I know, but I'll make it up to you, little one," Theo said, smiling, a glint of mischief sparkled in his blue eyes. I narrowed my eyes at him, wondering what he was thinking about.

"How are you going to do that?"

Theo moved closer to me and set his hand on my hip, rubbing lightly with his fingers. A shiver ran up my back and settled in the nape of my neck. I closed my eyes at the feeling.

"I'm going to take care of you."

"That could mean so many different things," I whispered, trying to catch my breath. He smirked and rubbed my hip a little harder, dipping his finger into the soft flesh at the apex of my hip bone and stomach and what was below.

"I'm going to take care of you." His eyes left mine as he dipped his head, kissing my neck quickly, then my hand.

"Oh," I said breathlessly, twitching.

"Don't worry." He smiled sweetly. "I'll make it worth your while."

IF I TOUCH
YOU THERE

I was released from the hospital three days later when the slight infection in my leg had cleared. The doctor came in and gave Theo specific instructions on how to clean and properly cover my leg. We were sent home with gauze and bandages, disinfectant, anti-inflammatories, and most importantly-pain medication.

The stream of guarded cars came to escort us from the hospital to Theo's house. Theo didn't let me move an inch on my own, carrying me in and out of the car and to the wheelchair he acquired for me.

"The doctor gave me crutches, I don't need this," I told Theo as he placed me in the fancy wheelchair.

"You aren't going to be walking around on those crutches if I'm not here with you. I can just picture you falling down those stairs all too easily. Plus, Doctor Dernon said you were on bedrest for another two days to let the swelling go down." I cursed his good memory.

"Well, even if you aren't here with me, Caddy can help," I said happily, stroking the arms of the wheelchair lightly.

Theo looked down uncomfortably.

"What?" I asked.

"Caddy left three days ago. Don't you remember?"

"Oh," I said, recalling him telling me goodbye. "Those pain meds made my head so foggy."

"It's okay, love."

"I guess," I said absentmindedly.

"What's wrong?" Theo said down on a couch and pulled the chair closer to him, so our knees touched.

"It's just...I don't really have a lot of friends around here. I only know you and your family and friends...and they've been great! But it's just..."

"They're still 'my friends.'" Theo looked down guiltily. "I'm sorry, I didn't even think about that."

I reached over a placed a hand on his knee. "It's not your fault," I quickly said. Theo pursed his lips, and a stormy look came over his face. "What's wrong?"

"Hang on," he told me, holding up a hand. A distant look crossed his face, and I knew he was mind-linking someone. I waited and gently pushed his hand that was up to silence me back down and out of my face. He blinked a few times and looked back towards me.

"What is it?"

"It's nothing for you to worry about," he said, forcing himself to smile. I remained straight-faced, unamused. "I'm serious, Margo. The only thing you should be worried about is recovering. We all need you healthy again."

"Tell me what it is," I demanded. He groaned and ran his hand over his face, his arm muscles clenching. "Tell me."

"Alright." He gritted his teeth. His face became angry. "It's really nothing, but Cam finally tracked down where the wolf who attacked you was from. It wasn't the Forte Pack like we had thought, which is actually worse because that means our enemy base is growing. Porter is gaining allies, ones that have no problem dying for his cause."

I nodded, processing the information.

"But it's nothing for you to worry about, I've got this under control." He grabbed my hands, holding onto me tightly.

"I'm not worried. I trust you."

His smile grew.

Theo drew me a bath and allowed me to relax on my own for a while before we crawled into bed. The soft-cushions and blankets felt like a dream compared to the hospital bed I had laid in for two weeks. I was required to stay in bed, or at the least, not exert any energy for two days while the last fibers of skin and muscle repaired themselves from the infection.

Theo catered to my every whim, bringing me breakfast and lunch in bed, bringing me books from his library, watching movies with me through the afternoon. Halfway through one of his favorites, he began tracing his fingers up and down my arm. I shivered and tried not to move.

He brought his lips to mine, softly pressing them against my mouth. I sighed happily at the contact. His hand around my shoulders tightened and bunched my nightgown at my hip with his other hand.

I couldn't move much with the massive cast around my leg, so I touched him with my hands everywhere my fingers could reach. He shuddered as I trailed my fingers up and down his shoulders, across his chest, and up to his neck. He broke our kiss, feverishly burying his face in my neck, kissing and biting gently on his mark. I grabbed the back of his head to keep him there when he tried to move lower. I felt him smile against me.

His hand let go of my dress that had bundled around my hips, and he brushed his fingers along the side of my breast. His left hand followed, and before I could think, he was tugging my dress up and off my body.

We held eye contact as if he were asking if this was okay. I nodded ever so slightly and moved until my hands were straight above my head, begging him to slide my dress off. I already felt so naked before him; the thin piece of fabric hardly mattered anymore.

His hands tickled my skin as he took my dress off. His eyes never left mine. I could feel my heartbeat in my throat, and I tried to remind myself to breathe. When the dress was over my head, he threw it behind him carelessly. He took a deep, steadying breath, and then growled deeply in his chest. There was something primal about this side of him, something I didn't know I craved until that moment.

His fingers painted shapes over the upper curve of my breast, just along the lace at the top of my otherwise plain undergarments. I cursed Theo for not bringing me sexier lingerie when he helped me dress this morning, as if he hadn't planned this since breakfast. He planned everything. Slow, steady, planned movements were all he knew.

Theo didn't seem to mind the plainness; he was captivated by the curve of my chest, kissing, and nipping the skin. His right hand held my waist tensely like he was trying to hold himself back.

I didn't want him to. Everyone had been treating me with extra caution or weeks like I was a breakable piece of glass.

"Theo," I said breathlessly. He hummed a response, face buried in the valley between my breasts. "You don't have to be gentle."

"Trust me," he chuckled darkly, lifting his head only enough for me to see a rotten glint in his eye. "When we make love, I won't be gentle, but right now, you get to see the softer side."

"Well, then what are we doing?"

"Mmm," he moaned, placing a soft kiss on my lips. "Did you know the female orgasm is a natural pain reliever?" He smirked against my lips, eyes lighting up in mischief.

My thighs quivered as I tried to remain undisturbed by his question. I made a noise in the back of my throat as I tried to speak. I coughed and cleared it before answering, "No, I-I didn't."

"Mmm." He nodded, sliding my bra off my body swiftly and throwing it on the pile of my dress. "I had an eye-opening conversation with your doctor," he said while kissing down my chest taking small moments to lick the soft skin on my breasts and stomach. "Your brain releases all these endorphins." He kissed my belly button, squeezing my hips.

I choked on the saliva in my mouth. I tried to steady my breathing, not even bothering to answer Theo's mumbles.

"It's the world's most natural pain reliever." His voice got huskier the farther down my body he slid. "And I don't want my girl to be in pain."

I gulped as his nose skimmed my hip where my painfully boring cerulean panties were. He placed his nose and lips against my most intimate parts and exhaled a happy sigh.

No one had ever been this close to my body before. There was a time when a boy accidentally brushed his hand across my lower region in the pool, but his hand quickly retracted, and he apologized profusely as Caddy glared at him.

This was much more pleasurable.

He started tugging the fabric off my hips, and I began to tell him to be careful with my leg, but the sound of ripping fabric stopped me.

"Excuse me!" I cried in outrage.

"I'll buy you more," he said smirking.

Before I could even respond, I was thrust into a frenzy of tongues and fingers and panting breaths. The pool boy's hand felt naughty and forbidden. Theo's hands felt devilish, like he gave up his right to Heaven to be granted this power, and I thanked whatever devil or demon gave it to him.

My legs twitched. My stomach quivered. Theo rose from my thighs and came closer to breathe the air I was panting out. His scent, his eyes, his touch, his expertise; everything about him was magnified, almost to the point of overwhelming.

Having someone so close to me in such an intimate was nerve-racking, and terrifying, and anxiety-inducing, and absolutely the best feeling I had ever felt. The way he moved was so fluid and exact it made me wonder how much practice he had beforehand. No, I told myself, don't think about that. Focus on him. Focus on this feeling. Focus on-

Then it felt like every nerve in my body had somehow manifested legs and swam down to my belly where Theo's hand was holding me down to the bed. My body lurched forward, and I grabbed at his hand though he kept it steady and firm.

I swear I could see stars dancing around Theo's head as I floated back down to Earth from the Heaven I had obviously transported to. That might have been because I stopped breathing.

Theo crawled up to me, holding my face to his chest, stroking my cheek gently.

My mouth gaped like a fish, open, close, open, inhale, close.

Theo's boisterous laughter boomed and shook me as he held me to him. "I take it that was good for you?"

"Don't get cocky," I said while still trying to sit up. He didn't allow me to.

"Oh, no. You've got to wait for cocky. That comes later."

I groaned audibly and allowed my head to fall back on his chest comfortably. His fingers ran through my hair the best they could with all the tangles and curls. He placed a kiss on the top of my head as my eyes slid closed.

"I want to take care of you. Always."

REPETITION

Theo let me lay in bed until dinner when he forced me to come downstairs. He wouldn't allow me to walk yet and insisted on toting me around the house in his arms. When we arrived downstairs, I noticed Cam sitting at the dining table, shoveling food in his mouth with a large plate of tomato pasta.

"You couldn't wait two minutes until I got Margo? That's all I asked; you couldn't even do that?" Theo groaned. Cam paused and looked at us, caught, wide-eyed.

"Sorry," he mumbled with his mouth full of food. Theo pulled a chair out with his foot and settled me into it. I propped my leg on another chair and let out a heavy sigh. Even the smallest bits of effort wore my tired body out.

Theo walked back from the kitchen with two large plates of pasta. He set one down and sat in the chair next to me. I picked up my fork slowly and bowed my head to get closer to my fork, so I wouldn't need to lift my arm. Cam chuckled at me, and bits of food flew out of his mouth. Theo shot a look at him, wiping his forehead from pasta sauce Cam spat at him.

Theo grabbed my fork, gathered some food on it, and held it to my mouth. I glared at him, reaching up to grab it from him.

"Margo," he scolded, swatting my hand away. "Open your mouth."

"I'm not a child," I protested, reaching up once again. Theo dropped the fork noisily and walked out of the room. I followed him with my eyes, wondering what I had said wrong.

"Don't worry about him," Cam said more cheerfully than necessary. "It's just the mating bond and your injury, and you two...doing what you did."

I blushed a deep scarlet but didn't try to deny it. "What do you mean?"

"Our instincts tend to push us towards our mates to be fully bonded, especially if our mates are injured. His natural instinct is to keep you locked in his room, mate you, turn you, and never let another soul see you again." My eyes grew alarmingly wide. "Of course, he wouldn't do that. He's probably just fighting with himself.

"I was the same way with Gemma. She didn't really feel the mating bond as quickly as I did, believe it or not, but I was smitten the first moment I saw her. I couldn't fully bond with her, and I couldn't have her close to me always, so it took everything in my power to let her walk out of the door. I did everything I could to be close to her, I even saved her tissues. Not my finest moment," he cringed. "He's probably still upset that you got hurt, and his instincts keep telling him to mate with you, so he can protect you better."

"I don't want him to be mad at me," I said sadly, looking back where Theo's figure disappeared.

"He could never be mad at you, Margo," Cam soothed me, reaching over, resting his hand on top of mine.

I half grinned, thanking him for comforting me. Theo walked past us and left through the front door. I called his name, but he didn't acknowledge that he heard me. As he passed the window, I saw him transform into his wolf form and run into the woods. I closed my eyes and allowed my face to settle in my hands.

"Don't worry about him," Cam told me, standing up and taking our plates away. "He's just blowing off steam. Do you want to watch a movie or something?"

I nodded, looking down at my leg once again. "Would you mind?" I was embarrassed to ask Cam for help, but he happily obliged and swept me up in his arms. Once I was settled on the couch, he began searching through Theo's massive movie collection.

"Your mate has way too many movies," Cam scolded, shaking his head in disbelief. "He doesn't even watch some of these. He should give some to me."

"We'll get through them all one day." I smiled optimistically. Cam smirked and rolled his eyes. "What?"

"Look at you, talking about the future and stuff," he said laughing. "Planning to stick around for a while?"

I groaned and pursed my lips, not paying any attention to his teasing. It reminded me of Caddy, and my heart began to instantly miss him. I settled into the pillows, wanting to relax and enjoy a movie, but my mind started buzzing with questions. How was Caddy doing? Did he fit into his role as Alpha? Was anybody else hurt? Did he miss me? I knew he was only a call away, but a call seemed so distant and removed.

"Margo." Cam snapped. My eyes shot to his, confused and startled. "I've been talking to you for like five minutes, were you even listening?"

I frowned apologetically and shook my head.

"Theo just mind-linked me. He wants to know if you're angry at him or if he can come back to the house?"

"I'm not mad at him," I said sadly. Cam gave me a look but mind-linked Theo, nonetheless. Within two minutes, Theo was running back through the door, out of breath, and sweaty. I turned to peek at him over the top of the couch. He smiled at me hesitantly, wiping his face from the sweat that had pooled on his forehead.

"Come over and join us, Teddy!" Cam shouted from the floor where he was still sifting through films.

"Don't call me that," Theo growled. He sauntered over and slumped on the couch next to me. He grabbed my hand and squeezed it soothingly. Cam shoved a movie in the player and settled in the large chair next to us.

Theo's arm reached over and pulled my shoulder down until I was resting in his lap on a pillow. His hands began stroking my hair, lulling me to sleep. My eyes fluttered shut, not fully asleep, but too relaxed to move or pay attention to the film.

"Is she asleep?" Cam whispered loudly.

"Yeah, I think so," Theo said lovingly. His hands continued stroking my hair.

"You really do have to calm it down with all the overprotectiveness, or she's going to run the hell away like Gemma did."

Theo's hand paused and then resumed slowly.

"I don't know what I'm supposed to do. Every molecule in my body is telling me: protect her. Mate her. Never let her out of your sight. And I know I can't do that."

"Just try to tell her what's going on, so she doesn't feel like a child," Cam suggested. "Cause feeding her really isn't going to work."

"I know," Theo snorted. "I never thought having a mate would make me this crazy."

"It does something to ya, I'll tell you that."

The boys finished the movie, and Cam left shortly after. Theo held me in his arms, walking upstairs, and then he set me on the edge of the bed. He slipped off my sweatpants and took the socks off my feet. I grumbled and attempted to sit up as the crisp air hit my body, but Theo playfully pushed me down and slid my shirt off.

"Let me up," I all but whispered. He shushed me and slipped one of his large tee shirts over my head. Then, underneath the shirt, he changed my undergarments and tucked me under the sheets.

"I'm sorry for freaking you out earlier," he told me as he climbed into bed. I smiled tiredly and patted beside me.

"S'okay."

He kissed my ear and folded himself around me carefully. "My mom wants us to come visit soon." I hummed and nodded. "Do you want to go tomorrow? Thursday, I have a meeting with Alpha Sennia."

"That's fine." He heard how tired I was and didn't keep talking. I was asleep in minutes.

After a night of tossing and turning, I was exhausted in the morning. My night was filled with images of Theo constantly being attacked and killed while I was trapped somewhere I could not get to him. I clutched his arm for most of the night.

I told Theo I was fine and awake enough to go visit Sloane. He deserved to see his mother, and he wouldn't take us if I was tired. We loaded into the car after breakfast, and he drove us the short ten minutes to the packhouse.

It was the first time he had driven anywhere without the entourage of guards. Theo drove a lot faster than his drivers, and I clawed at the armrest to steady myself. Theo laughed freely and pressed the pedal down a little more.

"You better slow down, Theo, or so help me," I snarled, glaring at his boyish face. He opened his mouth and laughed harder.

"What are you going to do to me, little girl?" He said arrogantly.

I thought for a minute. "I'll tell your mom you were mean and scared your precious little mate." The car instantly slow, and Theo gave me a bored look.

"You'd tell my mom on me? I'm almost thirty, and you're going to tell my mother?" A cheeky grin crept on my face. "Wow, you're ruthless."

"What can I say? I was born evil." I poked his arm jokingly. He pulled away from me and pouted, mumbling something I couldn't make out. "What was that?"

"I said you couldn't even kill the spider in the bathroom last week, I doubt you're that evil."

I scoffed. "Excuse me, I'll have you know I once killed a centipede in Caddy's room because it scared him so much."

"Oh, wow, you proved me wrong," he said sarcastically. I huffed and scrunched my face at him. "Don't be pouty, it's a good thing you aren't that evil. You don't need to be killing things, that's why you've got me."

"Well, what about when you're not here?" I asked, mind still reeling from the intense dreams from the night before.

"That's never going to happen," he said seriously, reaching to grab my hand.

The words "already did" popped in my head, but I fought against the urge to speak them. He didn't need to be reminded of his guilt, and I didn't want to start a fight. Instead, I smiled and took his hand in both of mine.

FAMILY MATTERS

Theo's mother, Sloane, was beyond excited to see us again. As the current Luna of the pack, she was still residing in the packhouse with the other high-ranking pack members. Every pack must have an Alpha and Luna to survive, or Alpha and Solis, if the Alpha is female and the mate is male. Without both titles, the pack system falls apart, which is why a Luna will hold onto her title until her oldest son finds a mate; I remember when I was younger wolves would always say "Alpha's retire, Luna's don't."

As Gabriel hadn't found his mate, Sloane remained at the Luna position and accrued the wealth and luxuries that accompanied the title. She had her own wing in the packhouse known as the "Luna's Wing." Her personal maids and helpers resided there with her, much like a queen.

Sloane practically skipped towards us as we arrived at the front of the packhouse. Her hands were clasped together like a child, and she squealed as we got closer.

"Theo! It's about time you visited your mother," she scolded, grabbing his arms and pulling him into a quick hug. She pushed him away after a moment and turned towards me with sadness. "And my new, beautiful daughter Margo. With her poor little crutches." She hugged me the same as Theo.

"It's great to see you again, Mrs. Weston," I told her, smiling.

"Oh, call me Sloane or Mom. Misses makes me feel old." She brushed her hair back and smirked at Theo, who snorted.

"You are old, Mom."

She gasped and slapped his arm with some force. "Never say that again," she demanded and looked at me. "Especially in front of other people."

Theo smiled and nodded his head accordingly. She led us to her wing of the house and into a day room where she had lunch set up. Sloane began pestering Theo about every aspect of his life; work, me, his friends, his home, his health, his eating habits.

Theo babbled on, nodding his head, occasionally shoving a bit of food in his mouth.

"And this wonderful woman, how are you treating her?" Sloane kicked my good foot and smirked. I swallowed my food quickly and wiped my mouth.

"Margo's fine, Mom." He rolled his eyes and kept eating.

"Fine is not good enough! And she's got this huge injury I just feel awful about it. I would have Luna Pagan come over and try to help me heal you, but she's been on some binge lately, and it's making her insane." Her eyes got wide as she rolled them in the back of her head. "How is he, honey, honestly? You can tell me. I know he can be a bit demanding sometimes."

"He's great." I blushed, looking at Theo through my eyelashes. The afternoon light hit his eyes, and he looked back at me with glowing orbs. Sloane sunk back in her seat and watched us look at each other.

"You two remind me of your father and me," she doted, reminiscing somewhere in her memories.

"Where is your father?" I piped out, looking around the room for any signs of him. Sloane bit back her smile and looked down slightly. I turned to Theo, who was far away in his mind. The room itself was bright with sunshine, but it was a dark atmosphere.

"He passed away a few years ago, honey," Sloane told me, patting my hand to comfort the grief-stricken look on my face. I opened my mouth, trying to apologize or comfort her, but she just laughed softly and smiled. "You didn't know, Margo. There's no harm done."

"Why didn't you tell me?" I asked Theo. I was trying not to be hurt by his family's loss, but I couldn't help but feel out of the loop.

"It never came up." He shrugged halfheartedly. He pushed his food around with his fork, leaning over the table.

Sloane's giggle interrupted his moping. I looked at her as she got out of her chair and skirted over to a box on a bookshelf. She brought it back and set it on the table, brushing the dishes and silverware off towards Theo. He swallowed his anger and stacked the dishes and place settings.

"Ah," Sloane breathed out, grabbing a picture from inside the box. She held it over for me to look at. "This is Rush, Theo's father."

His sons were in perfect likeness to him. Sloane obviously had more to do with their personalities than their looks, although every now and then, I could catch her in Theo's smile. Rush Weston was a large man, tall, muscular, but also well-fed. The picture was of their entire family when the boys

162

were still fairly young; Theo was maybe thirteen.

Theo sat back, not bothering to look at the old picture with us.

"Oh," she cheered, holding up three different photos. "Look at this, this is Rush and Theo right after he was born."

Theo was barely born, still wrinkly and covered in pink, newborn, skin. He wasn't crying though; he was staring up at his father with doe-eyed wonder. Rush looked terrified.

"He's adorable," I complimented, handing her the photo. She looked at it again, smiling slightly before putting it back in the box.

"He was a good-looking boy," she admired, pushing the box back on the shelf.

"Still is," I told her. Theo's cheeks flushed with red, and he turned away. Sloane stopped and cocked her head at us, looking back and forth.

"Did you," she scrutinized. "Did you two...?"

My face was obliviously confused, looking at Theo to clarify. He scrunched his eyebrows together.

"Did we do what, Ma?"

Sloane shrunk further into her frame, looking down. "Nothing," she said quickly, biting her lower lip.

"Mom, what are you talking about?" Theo asked again.

"Nothing really, you two just haven't...you know, sealed the deal yet."

"Mother," Theo growled angrily. I sat back, covering my shocked mouth with my hand strategically.

"Don't use that tone with me," she scolded, narrowing her eyes at him.

"Our mating life is none of your business."

She scoffed, throwing her hair over her shoulders, and came to stand behind me. Her hands fluffed my hair. "I was just wondering," she drawled. She pulled my hair back around my shoulders, and I remained still in fear. "You know, with every-thing going on."

"We're fine, Mother, thank you," Theo said quickly and sternly. Sloane groaned loudly when Theo called her Mother.

"I heard talk of mating?" a laughing voice called as they walked into the room. Reese poked his cheeky face around the corner and wiggled his eyebrows suggestively.

Eli slapped the back of his head and walked into the room. "Hi, Mom," he greeted.

Sloane kissed and hugged her boys, fixing their shirts, and telling them to comb their hair. Eli tugged at his hair and pouted before hitting Theo on the shoulder and talking with him.

"What are you up to, Gimpy?" Reese teased, throwing himself carelessly in a chair next to me.

"I'm not a gimp, you ass."

Reese snorted and picked up a few pieces of leftover food from our plates, blowing imaginary dust from them, and shoving them in his mouth. I grimaced and fought the urge to smack the food from his hands.

"Theo, your mate really isn't as nice as I thought she would be," Reese noted, sarcastically surprised.

Theo coughed on his words and kissed his teeth. "Nope, she's really not nice to anyone. I'm not sure I should keep her around anymore. On the way here, she was threatening me and now this."

Sloane gasped dramatically and left her mouth hanging open. "How dare you. You know Margo is nothing but a gift to this family."

"Isn't a gift supposed to be something you want?" Reese's laughing instantly ceased as Sloane gripped his ear in her small hand. He let out whimpers of pain, curling towards his ear.

"See? You really should be nicer to me," I warned. "Cause Mama Sloane and I are going to team up, and you lot will be in a world of trouble."

"You're damn right," Sloane echoed, releasing Reese's ear.

"Theo, Gabriel said he wanted to talk to you about something before you leave. He's in his office," Eli said bored, getting up and looking at some knick-knacks on Sloane's shelf. Theo nodded and left the room.

"So, Margo." Sloane smiled mischievously, much like her son.

"Mom," Eli said warningly.

"What?" she asked innocently, batting her lashes.

"We all know that tone. Don't interrogate her just because Theo left."

"I was just going to ask her how she was liking the house," she harrumphed. I smiled my thanks to Eli. My eyes drooped, and I pinched my hand to keep myself awake. "Are you okay, sweetie?"

"I'm just tired. It's this medicine," I explained, closing my eyes tightly and then blinking them open. She cooed and stood up.

"I'll go get Theo to take you home, this is probably a lot of activity for you." I told her I was fine, but she gave me a pointed look, and I allowed her to go fetch Theo. Theo strode back into the room and kneeled next to me in concern.

"Are you alright?"

I nodded, stroking his scratchy cheek with my hand.

"Just tired."

He turned and told his mother that we were leaving. I said goodbye to her, thanking her for all the food and showing me pictures. She laughed exuberantly and hugged me close to her chest.

Theo helped me outside with the aid of my crutches, dodging all the other pack mates that tried to catch his eyes. He grunted as he helped me inside the car, rolling his eyes at the nosy pack members around us.

"Everyone just wants a piece of you," he said smirking, sending me a flirtatious look I shrugged and closed my eyes peacefully, letting the warm sun hit my face. Theo sighed, making me open my eyes, and I found him looking at me lustfully.

I shivered and sat up straighter in my seat. Theo started the car, speeding down the gravel road towards his house. I eventually slumped down again, tired and achy from moving around so much. As we got closer to the house, the trees condensed, and the sun rays became scarce.

Suddenly, my body was thrown forward and then held back by my seatbelt. I opened my eyes widely, looking around, looking towards Theo, who was shaking.

"What's wrong?" I heaved. My heart was pounding so hard I could feel it in my throat.

"There are wolves outside the car."

I shook my head, wondering what the issue was. His packmates had shifted around us before we left, checking to make sure we were safe and happy.

"They aren't from our pack."

DOPPLEGANGER

"Will you please, please, let me handle this alone?" Theo asked, his voice wavered with uncertainty. I gave him a pointed look and unbuckled my seatbelt. He nodded many times, bracing himself for what was outside.

He threw his door open, and it ricocheted back and closed on its own. Theo inhaled deeply and relaxed his muscles. He chuckled slightly and shook his head as exhaled, looking around like he couldn't imagine what was happening. He circled the car and helped me out before turning us towards the wolves. They were still, almost waiting for something.

"You need to be kept on your toes," a woman's voice called out from behind the trees. A girl stepped out, pulling a black shift down her torso.

"You scared me half to death, I hope you know that," Theo lamented. He let go of my arm and strolled over to where the woman was. As he threw his arms around her, she laughed, her voice as raspy as the tree bark, but it suited her.

He looked her up and down as she pulled away. I fought back the feeling of jealousy rising in my stomach. I couldn't move any closer without my crutches.

"Wow, you haven't changed a bit," Theo said in awe, shaking his head. The girl smirked and let go of Theo's hand, circling his body, trailing a hand along his shoulders.

"Funny," she drawled, licking her lips. "You have."

Their reuniting was quickly broken up by my sarcastic laughter. Theo turned, confused, and then he realized he had left me behind. He jogged over, wrapping an arm around my shoulders, kissing my head. I glared and shrugged him off me.

"Sorry," he apologized quietly, looking at me with boyish guilt. I huffed a little but leaned into him.

"And who is this?" The woman sauntered over, her long legs shaking the ground with every step.

"This is my mate, Margo. Margo, this is Bodhi Sennia, Alpha of the Nomad Pack."

Bodhi smiled, her lips curling up to her freckle covered nose. "So, this is the girl who has tamed our gentle beast?" she giggled. Her accent wasn't local, some sort of distant tone that was unknown to me.

"Nice to meet you," I tried to say honestly, reaching my hand out to meet hers. Bodhi took a step back and leaned down and bowed, holding her hand to her chest.

"Oh, the pleasure is all mine, Luna Regina." I blinked and looked to Theo, who was smiling and waiting for me to respond. "You are human?" Bodhi asked.

"Yes."

She nodded dramatically, and the dark, kinky curls on her head shimmied with her. I unconsciously tucked my own curls behind my ear.

"I was too, once," she flittered, rocking back and forth

on her bare heels. "In another life."

"Bodhi believes she was reincarnated," Theo told me. His voice was robust with amusement, and his breath tickled my ear.

"Don't act like that's so unbelievable." Bodhi's eyes tightened, looking at him. "Plenty of wolves believe in re-incarnation. You did at one point."

I forced a polite smile on my face as Bodhi turned and shook her head firmly at the wolves behind her. They shifted to their human forms. Many of them ran their fingers through their hair but remained naked. I averted my gaze, a warm blush coating my cheeks.

"Oh, please don't be embarrassed by my wolves. They feel more natural in their bare forms. It's nothing to be a prude about," Bodhi told me, her eyes lighting up with humor.

"I'm not," I denied, eyebrows furrowing. Theo's hand rubbed my shoulders and opened the car door for me. Bodhi crawled in the backseat and scooted to the middle. Her arms rested on the tops of our seats, forcing my lean towards the window. Theo didn't seem to mind.

"So, where are we going?" she asked, pressing a few buttons on the dashboard.

"To our house. Stop touching things." Theo brushed her hands back. She slumped back and folded her arms, unamused.

Theo drove us quickly and stopped in front of the steps, per usual. Bodhi climbed out and strolled up to the front doors, waiting for the guards to open them, and walked inside without us. Theo assisted me and carried me up the stairs behind her.

"You have no toilet paper," Bodhi called from the other room. Theo set me on the couch, taking my jacket off from around my arms. "I had to use a towel, but I threw it away when I was done." Bodhi walked back into the room, playing

with the hem of her large shirt that barely covered her underwear.

"Was she raised in the wild?" I hissed softly as I pulled
the collar of Theo's shirt down, so he was face to face with me.

"No," he choked out, taking the collar of his shirt out of
my hands. "She was raised by wolves."

"You think you're really funny, don't you?" I asked
blandly, shaking my head.

"Sometimes," he admitted.

"What's going on?" Bodhi asked.

"Nothing, don't worry about it." Theo threw my jacket
on the back of the couch and sat down on the edge of the cushion.

"So, tell me what this whole ordeal is about," Bodhi
ordered, crossing her arms.

"Reed Porter-"

"Ugh, Reed Porter," she interrupted, rolling her eyes.

"He wants to start a human genocide."

"Shit," she said, eyes widening. She glanced at me, and
her eyes grew wider still. "Shit! Well, that won't do."

"He's collecting allies, and we need to do the same,"
Theo insisted. Bodhi nodded seriously and stood up. "Where
are you going?"

"To find your phone," she said as if we should have
known better. She walked around aimlessly, opening drawers
and cabinets. "If we're getting an army together, that sort of
requires people."

Theo left me on the couch to lead Bodhi to the phone
in his office. Something about her didn't sit right with me. She
was too careless, too loud. I crossed my arms and sunk into the
plush cushions. Theo came back to me, but I could hear her

loudly talking to people on the phone in the other room.

"She's...different," I noted.

He laughed at my disinterest. "She's a good friend, a good ally. She knows a lot of people, and her wolves know how to fight." I knew he was right. The wolves needed allies if they were even going to make a stand against Reed, and humans needed wolves if we were going to survive.

"I just," I sighed, letting my words hand in the air.

"I know." Theo placed his hands around mine and kissed them. "She doesn't get along with other girls very well, but she told me she likes you. Can you at least try to get along?"

"Of course," I said optimistically, planting a fake smile on my face. Theo didn't buy it, but he let it go, and we made small talk until Bodhi strode back into the living room with her head chin tilted upwards.

"You may thank me." She grinned, placing her hands behind her back gracefully.

"For what?" Theo asked.

"I have a group of Alphas willing to fight alongside their great Enforcer." She smirked and leaned over the couch between us. "I'm waiting for my thank you." She chuckled huskily. "I will take it in the form of compliments or gifts."

"You're amazing!" Theo exclaimed loudly, jumping from the couch to pull her in an embrace. He looked down at me, pointedly, still smiling.

"Thanks, Bodhi," I mumbled, giving her my best impression of a smile. She paid no attention to my discomfort and pulled me off the couch by my wilted hands. I wobbled on my solitary leg and grabbed her for balance.

"We have to hold a gathering." Her eyes lit up with a mischievous glint of excitement, though they were off in a different place, lost in a memory or the future.

"That's not a bad idea," Theo mused.

"What's a gathering?" I wondered aloud.

"What's a gathering? What's a gathering?" She laughed low, looking at Theo is disbelief. "A gathering of wolves, Margo."

"It's an event where a pack hosts the Alphas, Betas, Head Warriors, and Lunas from each pack invited to take part. It's very diplomatic, strategic; it'd be a good thing to do so that we're all unified."

"It's not just about diplomacy," Bodhi said, her voice sharp. "It's about networking, communicating. Showing off your strengths so that other packs know how strong you are. It's about showing your allegiances."

Theo grabbed a pen and a short stack of envelopes on the coffee table. "Okay, so I need to meet with Gabriel, send an invitation to the packs, and we need to make the packhouse habitable for guests-though I suppose that's more of Gabriel's job." Theo scribbled some notes on the back of the mail. Bodhi told him a few other things he needed to do, and he wrote them down as well.

"Does this mean Caddy will be here?" I asked excitedly. Theo nodded, pausing from his writing to watch my face bounce from dread to delight. A soft smile graced his lips before he ducked his head down and resumed writing.

I hopped off the couch and wobbled over to Theo's office. I dialed the familiar number and sunk down into the plush chair.

"Hello?" a quiet voice answered.

"Mrs. Delphine?" I said.

"Yes, who is this?"

"It's Margo," I paused and was met with silence. "Is

Caddy there?"

"Oh, dear. He's not here right now," she breathed slowly. Someone grabbed the phone, and there was a short quarrel.

"Margo?" Caddy's voice asked after the brief jilt.

"Caddy!" I greeted happily.

"I'm so glad you called, I was just thinking about you," he admitted. A real smile appeared on my face for the first time since we met Bodhi.

"Good, because I was thinking about you, too. Guess what? Theo's holding a gathering for all the allied wolves, something about mingling and diplomacy, but that means you'll be here, right?"

"Of course, I'll be there." I could almost see the smirk on his face. We talked for a while more before Theo's silhouette shadowed the doorway. I continued talking as Theo sat down on the edge of his desk, looking at me, waiting for me to stop talking. I never did. This was Caddy, Theo could wait a few moments. He waited a couple more minutes, as long as he could, before he slipped the phone out of my hand.

"Hey, Caddy. It's Theo. I need to talk to Margo, but I'll send over the information soon. Yeah, you too, man. See you soon." He hung up.

"What was that for?"

"I need to talk to you about something." His face grew serious, and I knew that whatever he was going to tell me, I wasn't going to like it. I waited, looking at him through narrowed eyes. He fidgeted and ran a hand over his face. "Stop looking at me like that."

"I'm not looking at you like anything. Spit it out, Theo."

"Well, with the gathering taking place at the end of the week, I think it'd be silly to send Bodhi and her packmates back to their lands just to turn around and come back within a day."

"I agree," I said to his surprise. "So, we'll find them room in the packhouse. I'm sure Gabriel won't mind. He knows Bodhi, too, right?"

"That's the thing," he paused. "Bodhi doesn't feel comfortable staying in another Alpha's home."

"Where is she going to sleep?" I breathed a laugh, obliviously. "I know the air is mild this time of year, but it gets cold at night, even if she was in her wolf form."

"She's going to stay with us," he blurted abruptly.

"Why?" I shook my head. "If she's that uncomfortable with other Alpha's, what is she going to do next week? Plus, aren't you like the Alpha of Alphas? That doesn't make sense to me, why would she be comfortable here and not there?"

"Margo, it's a couple of days. She will hardly be in the way, and I think it'd be nice for you to have someone around. I know I'm quite busy these days, and you might grow to like having her here."

"I don't think I will."

"Why are you so adamant about not liking her? She hasn't done anything to you, and she'll be very helpful come gathering time."

"I just...don't like her," I whispered, looking down.

"Well, I'm sorry, but she's staying. You can either mope and stay in your room the whole time, or you can be friendly and maybe learn something from Bodhi. She's a great leader, and she would make a good friend to you."

"So, that's it?" I asked bitterly, a slow fire simmering in the pit of my stomach. "You get to make all the decisions, and I don't even get a say?"

"If you had a legitimate reason for Bodhi not staying here, I would take it into consideration," he paused, allowing me time to provide him with a reason. When I didn't, he stood up. "That's what I thought."

Theo left his office, leaving me to simmer in my displeasure. It wasn't that Bodhi had done anything significant to warrant my attitude. It wasn't that she had been rude or aggravating on purpose, or that she meant to stir my jealousy as she touched my mate. It wasn't even that she vaguely resembled me in a more confident, distinguished way.

Something didn't sit right about Bodhi, and I wasn't going to let that go to please Theo. I was allowed to feel what I was feeling, even if it wasn't deserved yet.

FESTER

The three days between Monday and Friday passed painfully slow. Theo was completely enamored by our house guest while I sat in the shadows, waiting until they finally grew tired of each other's perpetual presence. They never did.

She and Theo sparred outside with Bodhi's packmates while I watched from the porch sipping hot cocoa. Theo laughed as Bodhi hopped on his back and pulled on his hair. Her pack ran around them, pushing and tripping over each other.

A guard was standing close to me, and I reached my hand towards him for help. He looked shocked and flustered before he rushed to my side, helping me stand and giving me my crutches. Theo stopped playing long enough to see me go inside, and his face was no longer happy.

Bodhi continued to climb on his back, telling him to move forward like a racehorse. His eyes searched through the windows of the house to find me. We met eyes as I sat in my sanctuary.

It's not that I wanted to take him away from Bodhi. I knew he was mine, but the thought of Bodhi's hands on him made me itch. His skin should only know my touch. My fingers were supposed to be the only ones wrapped in his short hair. Only my breath should touch his neck.

I shook off his gaze and settled on my desk. I wanted to call Caddy, wanted to tell him all about Bodhi and Theo, and how he should do his best to ignore her, but he was already on his way to us. I tried to read my books and found that my eyes trailed over the words, but I wasn't actually reading. My mind was elsewhere.

I tried to remember a time my mind wasn't consumed with thoughts about Theo, where he was, what he was doing, if he was thinking about me, and if he wanted my touch as much as I wanted his. I couldn't pinpoint the exact moment I had begun to love him, but the fire in my lungs when his image danced across my mind confirmed it.

Theo shouted my name loudly from downstairs. I looked out the window and saw him with his hands cupped around his mouth, hollering my name. He motioned for me to come down, and I hobbled to the window in confusion. A car was pulling up, one from my old pack, and my heart leapt into my lungs.

Caddy was here.

I climbed down the stairs as fast as I could with crutches in my hands and flung the door open.

"Caddy!" I screamed happily as I walked quickly to the edge of the porch. I began down the steps, excitement filling me, but Caddy wasn't looking at me.

He was staring at Bodhi with the same twinkling look in his eyes that once filled Theo's.

I froze. Theo was looking back and forth between the two of them with realization and comfortable support.

"Are you kidding me?" I mumbled, forgetting I was in the presence of wolves with magnified hearing. Theo's eyes shot to me, and his lips pursed in disapproval. Everyone looked my way apart from Bodhi, who was staring at Caddy, trying to decide if she should smile or not. I hobbled forward, my crutches sinking into the soil. "Caddy!"

"Margo," Theo said in warning, ordering me back with his gaze.

"No," I breathed out sadly. This time Bodhi looked at me. "This isn't fair."

"Get in the house, Margo," Theo ordered, a mean look of disappointment glaring from his eyes.

Something broke within me; the last strand of will-power I had to stand on the sidelines while Bodhi took every comfort from me. She had taken the only home left for me. She had taken Theo's attention and admiration. She had even managed to take my clothes and the apples in the fridge. And now she had taken my best friend-my only friend.

"You can't take everything from me," I told her softly, though I knew she could hear me. I had meant it to sound harsh, but a sob from my throat coated it with anguish. "It's not fair."

Theo was immediately in front of me, holding me around the waist like a toddler. "That's enough," he hissed in my ear, walking us towards the house. Caddy reached a hand out to touch Bodhi's cheek, and she shivered at their first touch.

"Just go home," I wailed. My words echoed through the wolves' ears, and they watched me with disgust. I had insulted their Alpha; they were controlling their urge to attack me.

Caddy didn't even pay attention to me; Bodhi's eyes held him hostage.

A guard opened the door for us and closed it firmly behind as Theo stomped through the hallway. He threw me on the couch like a sack of flour and glared. He looked at me angrily, more angrily than I had ever seen.

"What were you thinking, Margo?"

I stared forward blankly. I wanted to soak in all the self-pity that had perfumed around me. I wanted to feel the hurt.

"That was a beautiful moment, Caddy just met his mate, and you're acting like a jealous, bratty, crazy-"

"Yeah, I get it," I nodded, cutting him short.

"I just don't understand." Theo shook his head. His eyes were clouded as he tried to piece together my actions.

"You're right, you *don't* understand."

"Stop shutting me out, just tell me what's going on."

"What's going on is that even since Bodhi arrived, you've been ignoring me and spending every moment with her. Don't give me that look, it's true. You didn't even come to bed 'til three in the morning because you were talking battle strategies with her, and then you were gone before I woke up."

Theo groaned and shook his head in disbelief, a small, sarcastic smile came onto his face.

"We've been talking about battle strategies to keep *you* safe, Margo. I have no interest in Bodhi other than her contacts and her expertise."

"You don't get it, Theo." I sat on the edge of the couch, reaching out to him with a dejected look. "You are the only one I have here. There is no one else for me. You and Caddy are it for me, and she shows up and takes you both away within minutes."

Theo slumped into the cushion next to me, rubbing his face with his right hand.

"I'm not leaving you, little one."

"But you did," I tried to clarify. "You left me all week. Hugging her and playing around with her, she's like this perfect, fun, Alpha she-wolf, and you eat it up."

Theo stiffened and dropped his head, looking at me through the corners of his eyes.

"It's not like that."

"Then why did you ignore me all week for her?" There was more hurt in my voice than I anticipated. I was trying to keep my stone exterior, but I was quickly breaking down those walls.

"I didn't mean to ignore you," he admitted, boyishly. "It's just...I haven't seen Bodhi in years. She was young when she became Alpha, maybe twenty? She was there for me when my dad died, nothing romantic, but she picked me off the ground." My heart reached for him, although my hands remained at my sides. "But you're right, that was no reason for me to ignore you."

"I just don't think you realize it sometimes," I breathed, brushing below my eyes.

"Then tell me." He rubbed the side of my leg.

"You want me to be a wolf so badly that I think sometimes you forget I'm still human."

"What does that mean?" He leaned back.

"Bodhi is everything I can't be," I said aloud for the first time. "She's loud and energetic, she's smart, she's strong, she's a leader, and she's a *wolf*, Theo."

"That's not true," Theo tried to fight back. It was a feeble attempt, even he didn't believe it.

"It is," I said sadly, though truthfully. "She is everything you want in a mate, and she comes wrapped in this beautiful package like she's this wild, gorgeous version of me, and I can't help it but feel insecure."

"I never meant to make you feel this way," he said, slumping to the ground in front of my feet. "I'm your mate, I should be making you feel beautiful and strong and loved, and instead I make you feel like this." His head was low, and he was searching for something within his own mind; maybe the moment he started treating me differently. I don't think he found it.

"I just want to be okay here," I told him, fiddling with my fingers in my lap.

"You are safe here," he said fiercely, looking up at me.

"Physically, yes." I stared back.

We stayed like that for a long time. Theo's fingers brushed against my thigh. It wasn't romantic, I think he just needed to be near me in some way.

"Do you think Caddy hates me?" I asked softly.

"No," he breathed with determination. "No, I don't think he hates you."

I nodded, brushing my fingers across his.

"Do you hate me?"

Theo's fingers stopped moving on my thigh, and his eyes settled to a soft close. He opened them, and he looked at me with a quiet reverence. His hand brushed my cheek.

"For you to even ask that question." He shook his head, his voice low and soft. "I feel like I've failed you."

I shook my head, tears pricking my eyes. That wasn't my intention. The question was innocently burning my tongue like cinnamon.

"I'll be nicer to her," I promised, biting my lip. "I'll try harder. It isn't her fault."

Theo rose to his knees and pulled the back of my head to meet his lips. As he kissed my forehead, I felt a surge in our bond for the first time in days. My hand found the valley of his chest, and I rested it there, feeling the heat from his skin sink into me.

"It isn't yours, either."

GATHER ME

Caddy and Bodhi stayed outside for a while, introducing themselves and getting to know one another. The sun was setting by the time they wandered back in the house. Theo was cooking dinner as I sat on a stool near the counter.

I made eye contact with Caddy first, waiting for him to show any kind of emotion before I unveiled mine. His face was blank, emotionless, cold, as he led Bodhi inside with his hand on the small of her back. Bodhi was looking down, a slight blush coating her neck and cheeks.

Theo stepped away from the stove to look at the pair entering. He smirked at Bodhi, who shot him a look that could make anyone want to crawl six feet underground.

"Look at you two lovebirds," Theo sang, stirring the pot on the stove wistfully. He cocked his head back to glance at me, nervously sitting at the counter. "Don't you think so, Margo?"

Caddy and Bodhi looked at me expectantly.

"Yes," I said, clearing my throat after speaking. "Yes, you're very sweet together."

"Really?" Caddy teased, raising his eyebrows. "You don't think we're terrible together and that we should leave right now before we ruin anything else?"

"No," I moaned in humiliation. "I'm sorry. I didn't mean what I said; I was just emotional and not thinking." I stared at Caddy, trying to show him how sorry I was. "I'm *really* sorry."

"Don't start crying," Caddy mumbled, nearly rolling his eyes as he walked toward me. He threw his arms around my shoulders and hugged me, softly whispering, "It's alright."

Over his shoulder, I could see Bodhi clenching her fists slowly, glaring at his back. Theo smirked and hit her on the arm. "Already feeling the bond, huh?" Theo smiled. Bodhi turned towards him and smacked his shoulder, hard. He winced.

Caddy reached for Bodhi as he released me, pulling her towards a set of two chairs next to me. She reluctantly followed, although she glared at me the entire way.

"Caddy, get your mate something to eat." Theo threw his head towards the stove and leaned on the counter to eat with me. Caddy quickly stood up and prepared two plates of food, eager to show his mate he could provide for her. She smiled at the gesture, her thin mouth curving around her fork as she ate.

Theo and I ate quietly, not wanting to interrupt the newly mated couple any more than we had already. Theo grabbed my dish when I was done with it and threw it in the sink. He came to my side of the counter and picked me up, climbing the stairs and setting me gently on the side of our bed. He knelt by my feet, peeling the thick socks I had on off my feet.

"What are you doing?" I giggled as his nose skimmed my

calf. He placed a firm kiss on my knee, looking me in the eyes as he did so.

"I haven't been giving my mate the attention she deserves," he pouted, feigning seriousness. I nodded along with him. "I think I need to make it up to her."

"I think you should," I agreed aloofly, looking off in the distance. A low growl brought me back to our bed and made me smile.

We didn't leave our bed for the rest of the night, giving Caddy and Bodhi plenty of time to get to know each other. I rolled over in the middle of the night and heard loud laughs from downstairs. My movement woke Theo up for a moment, and we smiled affectionately at the sound. He pulled me closer and kissed my forehead before we fell back asleep.

Early in the morning, Theo woke me up by tickling my sides. I groaned and swatted him away, but he threw the covers off and jumped back on the bed. The movement jostled me, and my arms quickly shot out to make sure I didn't fall.

"Wake up," Theo ordered. I grimaced and looked his way. I was not a morning person; he, however, was glowing with excitement.

"Why are we awake?"

"Because today is the gathering. You've never been to one, I'm excited to take you and show you off and see you all nervous and jittery around wolves again." I heard the humor in his voice but ignored it and frowned. "My mom picked out a dress for you to wear, it's hanging in the closet in a bag."

"I have to get dressed up?"

Theo nodded and touched my side again before hopping off the bed.

Theo's mother had picked out a structured, navy blue dress that ended just above my knees. It was a tight material that hugged my thin frame, and I struggled to get the dress on while sitting on the stool in the closet.

Upon sliding my injured leg in the dress, I toppled over the stool and fell to the ground. Within seconds, Theo was in front of me, frantically looking me over for injuries. I began laughing, loudly; eyes shut, tears leaking out, laughter. Theo froze and leaned back, confused.

I kept laughing, leaning my head back to lay flat on the ground. Theo was fighting a smile, still concerned for my well-being. I slapped his knee closest to me, reaching for him to help me up. He grabbed my arm and put his other around me to prop me up.

"I swear, you give me a heart attack every single day."

I smiled at the crinkles that appeared between his bright eyes. He shook his head and sat me back up on the bench, waiting until I was fully dressed and standing before walking away.

I followed Theo to the bathroom and brushed through my hair with my fingers. Theo got dressed and helped me downstairs when Caddy and Bodhi were waiting. Caddy was sitting at the dining table, listening to Bodhi teeter on about her pack.

"You both better get ready; we're going to leave soon." Bodhi's face scrunched up hearing Theo's words.

"You think I'm going to change?" Her eyebrow hitched up along with her pursed lips. Theo glanced at her outfit: a pair of tight black pants, a black, sleeveless top, and a long, green vest. She eyed my dress and choked back a snort. Caddy had on a casual pair of dark pants with a gray, long-sleeved shirt.

"You two have to look the part, we're just guests," Caddy reminded us in a teasing tone.

"See, I could totally wear pants."

Theo shook his head at my suggestion and tucked his arm around my waist.

"It's time to go," he said firmly and handed me the crutches that were leaning against him. We piled into the car, surrounded by the usual entourage of five other black vehicles. The time passed quickly, and we soon arrived at Gabriel's packhouse.

There were many other cars parked outside, intimidating men and women filing out of each and walking to the front door. There were guards stationed at the front of the building that allowed each pack entrance. It reminded me of the ball my old pack had when Dorian became Alpha.

As we entered, the other wolves bowed their heads to Theo, showing their respect. He kept a straight face but, unlike last time, he walked next to me with his hand at the small of my back.

Most of the furniture had been moved out of the main room to allow for extra space. The wolves in the room stayed towards the outer perimeter, leaving a large space in the middle. I kept glancing there, wondering what was going to happen.

Theo led us to the other side of the room where his brother Reese stood. I looked at him, confused.

"Bet you didn't know I'm the Beta of this pack, did you Gimpy?" Reese teased. Theo growled at him for disrespecting me around other people.

"I can't believe they'd let you oversee important things," I teased back. Reese just smiled and looked at Caddy and Bodhi behind us. A scowl painted itself on Reese's face.

"Why'd you bring her?" he asked Theo in disgust.

"What? You didn't miss me?" Bodhi sneered with a smile. Reese coughed in outrage but otherwise ignored her.

"Quiet," Theo ordered with a strong voice, startling the wolves around us. Gabriel entered the room and stood in the center. Theo began to move forward, gently guiding me along with him. I walked with him nervously, wondering why we were meeting Gabriel in the center of the room.

"Quiet." Gabriel echoed. Each wolf turned their attention towards us with hard eyes. "Thank you all for gathering here today. As many of you already know, a gathering is a time for us to communicate with other packs, share strategies and hardships. It's time for us to re-collect ourselves and remember what is important. Our noble Enforcer-" A thump surrounded the room as each wolf pounded their right fist over their chest. It was a sign of respect for Theo. "Has asked us here today to bring light to our present danger. An Alpha, Reed Porter, has declared a war against the remaining human population and those packs harboring them."

As he walked around the circle of wolves, I noticed they were soaking in his every word. The Weston's certainly had a way with words. They could control a room with one voice.

"Many of you are aware that Enforcer Weston's mate is human. So, this not only threatens good people and wolves, but it also threatens our rulers, our very way of life. We ask now that you evaluate where your allegiances lie because this battle won't be for the faint-hearted. It will not be for the weak or the easily persuaded. It will be for the brave, the ones willing to stand up and fight for what's just. So, if you are not willing to lay down your life for this cause, now is the time to leave. But, if you see a future like we do, a future of peace and prosperity, a future of progress, then you stand with your Enforcer and Luna Regina."

The same resounding thump echoed the room. I looked around at the wolves, wondering how so many people were willing to fight for a cause that didn't even affect them. Then the wolves lowered their heads and bent down on their right knee.

Theo tilted his head to whisper in my ear. "They cross their hearts for me, but they bow for you, Margo."

My heart swelled, and I wanted to thank them individually and promise them I wouldn't let them down. The wolves lifted their heads but didn't stand, looking to us for direction.

"Then let's get to work."

THE WAY WE
ARE BUILT

The wolves split into separate groups of Alphas, Lunas, Betas, and Warriors. Theo and I walked around to the different groups and observed the conversations.

The Alphas were predominantly concerned with strategies that would lead to the least casualties. Alpha wolves are protective of their pack members, and they didn't want to lose anyone if they had the choice. They were seated around a large circular table in one room while the Beta's met in an adjoining room.

The Beta's main job is to monitor security around the pack, along with supporting their Alpha. Their discussions focused mainly on how they would keep their borders secure. They had gone as far as using figurines to demonstrate their border formations. The wolves who guarded the territory, or Border Patrol as many called them, were the first line of defense against an intruder.

Warriors, as you can imagine, are constantly preparing and training for battle. The warriors that came to the gathering with their Alpha and Beta were predominantly Head Warriors who controlled the group of warriors. They had taken their place outside on the grass, sparring, and sharing tips and tricks they had learned in combat. Although the wolves looked fierce while fighting when they were done, they patted each other on the back and complimented each other.

The Lunas of each pack gathered in the main room where we had originally stood. They were all dressed similarly to me in dresses and classy shoes. Theo left me to speak to Gabriel when we came back inside, kissing my cheek as I stared at the group of women. I limped over the outer circle the women had formed. Although there were female Alphas, many still preferred to take the classic role of caring for the children of the pack.

As I approached, one wolf stepped back and let out a small gasp.

"Luna Regina, you shouldn't have to walk around on that leg of yours, it's simply dreadful. Let's get her a chair, shall we?" She waved her hands, and two other women looked around frantically.

"Don't worry about me." I gave them a small smile. "In fact, I'd rather like to stand, Theo has me sitting all day long. And please, call me Margo."

They chuckled strangely, probably perturbed by me referring to their Enforcer by his first name.

"I didn't mean to interrupt you all," I apologized quickly, seeing that their conversations stopped.

"You didn't," the woman with blonde hair next to me said kindly. "We couldn't be happier to have you with us."

"What were you all discussing?"

"Healing," the blonde woman smiled at me kindly.

"What do you mean?" I asked curiously.

"As a human, you may not know this, but when we become Lunas, things are passed down to us the same as Alphas. Some are tangible things like jewelry and dresses, but there are a few things that are given to us that you cannot see."

"Our mates are so concerned with our packs safety, sometimes they are too preoccupied to know how much power our bodies have," another woman stepped forward. She had red hair, braided, and pulled to the back of her head. She was older than me by some five years or so. "As leaders, our bodies were built to rule those around us."

"Our ancestors believe that our bodies were formed out of magic," the woman next to the red-haired woman came close to me and held out her wrist. "There are certain things our bodies can do that your human body cannot, apart from shifting."

I could see the veins on her wrist grow darker and darker as she spoke. She closed her small eyes and began to concentrate. I watched as the veins underneath her skin all became visible and dark purple. My wide eyes amused the Lunas around me, they giggled and came to circle around me.

"Our bodies can promote faster healing, our hands can heal a broken heart, our voices can soothe a child to stop crying. There's a reason most of us don't take Alpha positions. Our bodies were not built to protect, they were built to heal."

"In fact," the red-haired woman smirked coyly. The women around her smiled mischievously and gathered around me. I staggered back, and their smiles grew. "It usually takes a few of us to heal a wound this large, especially since you're human, but there are a lot of us here now."

"Do you trust us, Luna?"

I glanced at each of their faces, maybe fifty of them around me. I nodded sincerely, feeling my heart clench as their eyes filled with happiness. One woman gently took my crutches from me, and my arms shot out to grab onto something.

Two women held my arms up, and the other woman moved a small table over. They helped me onto the table, lifting my legs so that my back was flat. The red-haired woman and the brunette with small eyes stood on either side of me. They locked eyes and smiled before placing their hands on my ankles.

The woman behind them began placing their arms on the other's shoulders, forming a web of arms. I began wondering what they were doing, and while I was lost in thought, my injured leg began to tingle. I gasped and lifted my head, someone pushed it back gently. The tingles in my leg grew, it was now buzzing like it was numb.

I closed my eyes and tried to relax. One of the other Lunas took the cast off my leg and placed the pieces on the ground. My skin felt like it was moving, but it wasn't painful. A few moments later, the feeling stopped, and I opened my eyes. The Lunas lifted their heads and nodded their heads proudly.

I sat up and looked down where my scarred, mutilated, fleshy wound once lived. In its place was smooth skin. I ran my fingers over it, barely grazing my fingertips over it and yelped. It was as if the wound was never there.

I looked at the red-haired woman in awe. She looked at the other Lunas, nodding her head softly.

"How?" was the only word that left my mouth.

"Our bodies were built to heal, Luna," she said firmly, strongly, pleading with her eyes. "Please, please, do not forget this fact."

They helped me sit up, and I gradually put pressure on my legs. The bone was healed as well as the flesh, and I yipped in surprise.

I heard Theo's heavy footprints as he approached. The Lunas parted the crowd, and he made his way straight to me.

"I heard you yell, are you okay?" His face was stone, as it always was in public.

"Theo, look." I lifted the hem of my dress and showed him the pale skin that replaced the injury. He dropped to his knees and lifted his hand up to touch my leg. As he did, he had to hold in a gasp. His face was sad but joyful in a way. He was happy that his mistake wasn't causing me any more pain.

He stood up, and as he rose, he grabbed me around the waist and lifted me to his height. He kissed me twice, quickly, and turned with me in his arms. I laughed and threw my arms around him.

He looked around at the women. "Thank you," he said gratuitously.

"We may not always be on the front lines of battle, Enforcer, but we are useful."

"Absolutely," Theo said back with meaning. He set me on the ground and lowered his head slightly to thank the other Lunas. He began to lead me off, but I yanked my hand out of his and turned back.

The Lunas were watching us leave. I thanked them, trying to find each one of their eyes. Just as before, the Lunas sunk to one knee, bowing their heads to me. It was still such a strange feeling, but Theo pulled me along before I had time to comprehend.

I turned one more time as they raised their heads. Their eyes held fire behind them, the kindness still in their faces, but they were ready for this battle. Not every fight is physical.

NOOSE

The gathering continued for two more days after the first. The last day was more of a celebration than a meeting, and all of Gabriel's pack was invited. Familiar faces flashed in the crowd, Emily, Sloane, Eli, Albia.

The red-haired woman came and introduced herself to me formally. Joella and her mate, Felix, were from the Audacia Pack. They lived around ten hours to the south of us, high up in the mountains. They liked the solitude.

Many other Alphas, Lunas, Betas, and Warriors came and introduced themselves to me. They had met Theo when he visited their packs previously but were eager to make a good second impression. They shared stories of their pack, the landscapes around them, and past battles. A few of them had made it a game to see who could make me laugh first.

Theo smiled proudly as I met each one of the Alphas he oversaw. I stayed close to his side, although I felt comfortable being around these wolves.

Caddy and Bodhi found us after we met with another Alpha. I smiled widely as they approached, ignoring the scowl on Bodhi's face.

"Look at you, back on your feet and ready for some action," Caddy hollered. I gave him a twirl and showed him the spot where my bite used to be.

"Fully functional and everything." I smirked happily. Caddy clapped his hands dramatically and then placed them back around Bodhi's waist.

At the end of the day, the other packs left, and we returned home with Caddy and Bodhi. Caddy's Beta, Finn, insisted on leaving the same night instead of staying one more day like Caddy. Finn was strict and quiet, the opposite of Caddy.

We had a small dinner and careful conversation before bed. In the morning, Caddy was set to return to his pack with Bodhi and her fourteen other wolves in tow. They had agreed, on a trial basis, to integrate their packs and mutually oversee the wellbeing of all the wolves.

As Caddy said his goodbyes, I got emotional and held his hug longer than I should have. I sniffled and wiped my nose before I ruined his shirt.

"Margo, I'll probably see you in a few weeks," Caddy said, ruffling my hair. I nodded sullenly and shrank back to Theo's side. Each time Caddy left, I felt empty, like my past was gone with him.

Bodhi and I gave each other a polite smile and a short nod of our heads. We had tried to mend our differences, but it was only something time could heal.

Theo and I settled back into our lives; he was busy with work most of the day, and I read most of the time. I yearned for something to give me a purpose, some sort of work or hobby but I hadn't found it yet.

Time seemed to pass quickly after the gathering, one day into the next. Almost every week, an Alpha would visit our home to speak to Theo about some important manner. Theo claimed he didn't want to be like the previous Enforcer who was unapproachable and closed off. He wanted to be accessible and work together with the Alphas.

On days that we didn't have company, Theo and I would cook and take walks around his property. He made sure to have two guards following us at all times, although he thought I didn't know. Werewolves were not the quietest people.

Since Theo was more concerned with the protection of the border, he had the guards stationed at the front of his house to monitor the perimeter as well as the house. The guards would take turns, leaving the house to check in with the border guards every hour. This meant that Theo was super protective whenever I opened the door, and I had made it a game to see if I could beat him to it.

The doorbell rang on a Tuesday when Theo was in his office, talking to Alpha Trissur. I looked up from the book I was reading and marked my page before setting it near my feet. I crawled off the couch and tiptoed to the door. I peeked back and still heard Theo's steady voice on the phone. Theo told me Gabriel was going to stop by sometime in the next day, and I was excited to see someone I knew.

The door was heavy, and I had to lean with my entire body to pry it open. As I threw it open, I looked around curiously, no one was at the door. I went as far as stepping out on the porch and looking on either side of the house.

Theo wandered out from his office and met me at the door with a scowl on his face.

"Why did you open the door without me? What if something happened to you?"

"Oh, don't be such a baby," I teased, elevating my voice.

"No one's even here."

"Then who rang the bell, Margo?" he asked seriously. Before I could open my mouth to answer, Theo grabbed my hand and pulled me into the house. He flipped the two locks on the door and walked up the stairs quickly, nearly dragging me behind him.

He pushed me into the bedroom, locking that door behind us as well. I watched as his eyes glazed over, mind linking someone.

"Theo," I said softly. The situation was settling in over me as we stood there. His eyes came back to me, and he pulled me towards him, pressing me to his chest. "What's going on?"

"I don't know, little one," he breathed, kissing the top of my head. "But I'm going to keep you safe. Don't worry."

"I'm not worried about that," I admitted, pulling my head back from his chest. "I'm-"

"Margo," his voice was strained.

"I'm just confused," I continued, trying to step away. His arms surrounded my body and held me in a tight prison, forcing me to stay glued to his frame. "Theo?"

"Margo," he said again. The color of fear in his voice made me pause.

"What's wrong?" He didn't answer. "Theo, what's wrong?"

"If you trust me, I need you to face the door when I let go of you." My body clenched at his request. I slowly slid away from his body, his hands guiding me, and stood in front of him. His face was looking away from me, staring at the window.

I lowered my head and stepped to the side, walking the few steps towards the door. I heard his footsteps move to the other side of the room, and I tensed every second the room was silent.

"Theo?" I whispered.

"Close your eyes, Margo."

"What's going on?"

Theo's hand violently hit the window, and on instinct, though I knew I shouldn't have, I turned towards him. Theo stared out the window, his fist pressed against the glass, staring at something outside. I tilted my head as something pale stuck out from the dark, green leaves. I followed it up and saw it connected to something bigger.

I stepped towards Theo, and he turned around, mouth open to tell me to turn around again, but I couldn't hear him, because he had moved just enough to reveal the body that was strung up in the tree facing our window.

LITTLE WHITE ENVELOPES

My breath was knocked out of me, and I tried to swallow, but my mouth was too dry, and I just choked. My feet propelled themselves forward, not even hearing Theo as he called my name. I hit the window with enough force to shake it, arms beating the glass, nose pressed against the plane.

Theo pulled me from the window, but I fought him, kicking, and flailing my arms. I memorized the face; female, young, curly brown hair, completely naked. It was as if I was hanging there myself. Theo gained a better grip on me, one around my collarbone under my right arm, and the other around my waist.

He plucked me from the window, gently settling us on the ground. I fought against him weakly, pushing at his arms, trying to find out where the noise was coming from. Theo shushed me. So close to the sound, I realized it was me screaming. The noise was breathless and wavering.

His hand pushed my hair back from my clammy forehead multiple times, peeling the strands out of my vision. At some point, another body came into the room and began asking Theo questions. His hold on me didn't loosen while he was talking and tightened more when soft whimpers made their way through my lips.

I turned my head slightly, restrained by the cage of Theo's arms. Outside the window, wolves started lowering the body that was strung up with rope. When the body was on the ground, they undid the ropes and checked the body in a makeshift autopsy.

A man came and told Theo of something found on the body and wondered if it should be brought up to him. He said no and assured the guard he would be down shortly to look at the body. He said this in hushed tones with my ears covered by his body, as if he was hoping it would block the sound.

Slowly, my heart rate returned to normal, my breathing evened, and my body stopped shaking. I pushed gently on Theo's chest, and he loosened his grip, leaving just enough room for me to sit up on my own.

I couldn't look him in the eyes. Instead, I stared at a freckle on his arm that danced when he clenched his muscle. His face scrunched up and relaxed and moved as he had an internal battle with himself.

He stood up, grabbed my arms, and forced me to stand with him. I didn't know where we were going until I saw a warm bath.

Theo sat next to me on the stool, running his right hand over my curls; his left hand gripped his chin. The water continued to fill as I sat in the tub. When it was filled, Theo turned the water off and watched me sit for some five or six minutes.

He left me in the bathtub, most likely going to meet with the guards outside to look at the body. I didn't move until Theo came back in and unplugged the drain. I stood up, with assistance from Theo, and he wrapped a towel around me. He led me to the bed, slipped his shirt over my head, and sat next to me.

"Talk to me," he said roughly. I blinked twice and scratched my hand.

"About what?"

"You know what, Margo." He wasn't joking around.

"What do you want me to say?" My head remained bowed, unable to look at him still.

"I want you to say what's going on in your head. You haven't looked at me in two hours."

"Why did she look like me?"

"It was a threat from Porter's group, there was something carved into her back that made it clear," he said. I was glad he didn't try to sugar coat it for me.

"What was it?"

"It said 'lunam actio postulate.' It means 'the moon demands action.'" I shivered as his tongue grazed the Latin words.

"Action? Action as in killing humans," I said, understanding the meaning. Theo breathed out heavily and put his hand on my knee. I pulled my knees together, but he didn't remove his hand.

"Nothing is going to happen to you, Margo. We have more packs with us than he does; we have more Alphas, more wolves."

"That's not the problem. The problem is that the longer I stay here, the more people get hurt."

"That's not true, you can't think like that." Theo stood up and walked to the edge of the room before turning around.

"Theo, how many other people are going to be strung up in our trees? How many others are going to be left on our door-step? How many will die in that battle?" My voice rose higher and louder as I spoke. My hands frantically clutched the shirt around my thighs and pulled at the hem.

"Margo, that girl was a wolf, she wasn't human. This is not your fault. Reed Porter has been looking for a reason to attack for years, and he used his hatred of humans to rally his troops."

"Wolves, humans, it's all the same, Theo. It's all lives being taken away!"

He stormed over to me and grabbed my chin in his hand, forcing me to submit to him.

"You need to stop talking like this. This is my prob-lem, Margo. This is my battle to be fought, not yours. I need you healthy and happy and not worrying about bodies in our trees." His eyes were hard, it reminded me of the first time I met him, looking up into those cerulean gems. "Now, you're going to stay up here and get some rest. I'm going to go and make some phone calls. We need to be prepared, if these threats are coming, this battle is probably going to happen sooner rather than later."

I nodded and jerked my chin out of his grip, rubbing it slightly to make him feel guilty. He sighed and kneeled in front of me, turning my head towards him with his hand.

"What would I do without you?" he asked wistfully. I snorted at his cliché. "What?"

"You're corny," I told him, finally smiling a little at him.

"And you're smiling." I wiped it off my face, but he stood up happily anyways. "I'll be back in a little while, my love."

I nodded as he left and curled up on top of the sheets. I couldn't close my eyes, so I laid there for a while and listened to the gentle hum of Theo's voice through our vents.

We took it slow for the next few days. Theo doubled the number of guards outside our house and the ones around the border. The guards caught one wolf trying to sneak through the territory lines, but they ran off before the guards could question them.

A few of the other Alphas received threatening, ominous notes as well. Caddy called Theo and told him of the deer antlers he found on the pack's front entrance. It was derogatory to refer to humans as deer as if we were their prey.

Theo told me of each of these. I didn't have much to do, so I made a poster with all the items and packs, color-coordinated it, and hung it on the wall. Theo laughed at me when he saw it, but after the phone calls kept pouring in, day after day, he started using the chart as well.

Over the next two weeks, the progression of events accelerated; Reed Porter was ready for this battle, whether we were or not. Small skirmishes broke out on rogue land and the edges of pack borders, testing the waters to see how their aggressions would be matched.

Several human pack members had become the victims of violent crimes and murders; pack members wanting to protect their families by taking care of the issue themselves. It was what Reed Porter was hoping for, that this issue would turn pack members against each other.

On the first day of the month, Alpha Omar, the pack farthest away from us on the East coast, received a plain white card with the number "5". Alpha Horik received the same card with the number "4"; he lived slightly closer. A third card was sent to Alpha Trissur, only a few hours away from us, with the number "3". A bordering Alpha was given the number "2" a few days later.

Theo called the Alphas together when the third card was received. They decided to come to our territory and the neighboring packs when the number "1" was received to prepare for the battle. Hundreds of thousands of wolves from across the country camped in our territory, sleeping outside in their wolf forms, coming inside Gabriel's packhouse to eat and bathe.

Caddy and Bodhi came with their Warriors and wolves who volunteered to fight. I made up the guest room for them to stay inside, but they insisted on sleeping outside with their pack. I knew Theo wanted to do the same, but he wouldn't dare leave me by myself.

Packs across the continent were joining together, ready to fight for their own freedoms as they received threats from packs on their borders. We were not the only ones fighting this battle, and that somehow made it better and worse at the same time.

Two days after the wolves arrived, a Warrior from Gabriel's pack noticed a white envelope was hung on a tree at the edge of the territory. Theo brought me along when he went to open it. We trudged through the territory, nearly a mile and a half of the forest, and came to the tree. Alpha wolves stood behind us, waiting for Theo to open it.

I stood next to Caddy and Bodhi as he peeled the envelope and took out the last card. He took it out slowly. It was a plain white card like all the others, but there was no number inside. Instead, there was a smear of blood.

Theo lifted it and smelled it. He turned to us, confused.

"It's deer blood," he said, looking at the other Alphas and then locking eyes with me. The Alphas became tense and turned in fighting poses as footsteps quickly approached.

They relaxed when they noticed it was one of our wolves, but he was panting, shaking, and nervous. His Alpha barked out an order to tell them what was wrong.

"They're here."

Zero.

FATE

I didn't move an inch from Theo's side as we made our way back to the territory. His hand gripped mine too tightly. He walked faster than me, and I jogged to keep up with the wolves.

The Alphas were preparing for war, their faces like steel, bodies shaking on the verge of shifting. Caddy's face was dark, like nothing I've ever seen on him. Bodhi's expression matched his, and they grabbed each other's hands.

We broke the tree line and came into the clearing where the warrior led us. Our wolves had already shifted, a portion of them were in the clearing but most were still tucked back in the trees.

Reed Porter stood in the middle of the clearing, casually dressed, kicking his heel back and forth.

Theo pulled me along with him at the front of our group, walking towards Reed with disdain in every step. I trailed behind awkwardly, trying not to shrink away from

Reed's wolves. It was difficult.

"It's not too late to hand over your prey," Reed angrily yelled, narrowing his eyes. Theo growled low in his chest. "You really think one little human is worth all of this?"

"It's not about one little human," Theo growled.

"You're foolish, Theodore. Just like your father was, and where did it get him?" His eyes closed a little, and he tilted his head to the side, peeking over at me. Theo stepped in front of me and snarled, more beast than man.

"Don't look at her. And don't talk about my father."

"I don't know how you can even stand to look at her, let alone mate her. She's food, she's not a fucking Luna."

Theo didn't take kindly to that, and I had to give him a hard tug on his hand to keep him from starting the battle right then.

Theo mind-linked someone quickly as Reed glanced at all the wolves. From behind me, someone touched the top of my arms. I whipped my head around quickly and saw Eli and another guard.

"Go with them," Theo murmured. I stared at him for a moment too long, and he pushed my hip to encourage me. I stumbled a few steps with them. Theo grabbed my hand and stopped me just long enough for him to place a kiss on my palm.

We turned, and the wolves parted just enough to give us a walkway. I walked first; Eli and the guard flanked me from either side. Halfway down, someone stepped into the parted area, and we stopped moving.

I noticed Albia's blonde hair and looked at her, confused, trying to catch her eyes, but she was paying no attention to me. She walked fluidly, staring straight ahead at something behind us. We moved to either side of the pathway so she wouldn't walk straight into us and watched as she continued on her way.

Theo looked back to find where I was and turned fully around as Albia quickly approached. He grabbed her arm menacingly as she came up to him, but in one sharp shake, she broke free. He growled at her disobedience. She was unfazed.

She continued marching until she stood right in front of Reed Porter. He started breathing deeper and moved in towards her. His right hand reached out and touched her cheek gently. She shivered.

"Mate," Reed growled deeply. He then blinked rapidly, shaking his head, muttering the word, "No, no, no," over and over again.

Theo's growl could be heard for miles. He was halfway shifting, trying desperately to hold onto his human side, but it was a losing battle.

Reed stepped in front of Albia protectively at the new threat. His eyes darkened, and I knew he was fighting his own wolf. Theo shifted completely, lowering himself into a crouch, ready to attack. Reed pushed Albia back into the arms of his warriors and shifted as quickly as he could.

This snapped the other wolves into motion, and suddenly they were all shifting.

Eli pulled my arm harder, and we quickly ran to the back of our wolves. I knew very little about wolf fights, but I did know it was heavily dependent on strategy. With Reed and Albia as mates, it set both sides back. No one on our side wanted to hurt Albia, and no one on their side wanted to hurt their new Luna's family or friends.

It was an impasse. No one moved. They bared their teeth at each other, their fur stood up, making them look larger, and they looked to Theo and the other Alphas for an order to attack.

I didn't know what God to pray to, humans believed in many different gods, but wolves believed in the power of the moon. I prayed to both asking for protection and guidance. Eli placed his hands on my shoulders, standing almost a head taller than me. His grip was tight.

I knew he wanted to be fighting with his pack and family, but Theo needed someone he could trust to watch over me. There were a few others that stayed back near us when the other wolves moved forward.

"How can they be mates?" I murmured, more to myself than anyone else.

"Because fate is cruel," Eli responded, giving my shoulders a quick squeeze.

It became silent across the field. My blood began to chill me from the inside, my veins were frozen.

To the left, a wolf from Reed Porter's side jumped across the small barrier and launched itself at one of our wolves. That was enough to send wolves from either side into a cataclysmic fusillade.

It was impossible to see who was who, but the wolves knew each other's scents, they wouldn't attack someone from their own side. In the woods to either side of us, wolves from our packs created a system of lines that moved into Porter's group at different angles, forcing them straight into the group of Warriors.

I couldn't look away, as much as I wanted to. The battle entranced me. It was like a dance of sorts, wolves jumping over each other, rolling under others, bouncing off the trees for more power. My eyes sought out Theo's wolf; I scanned through the wolves I could see and became increasingly panicked when I didn't see him.

Eli's hand came over my shoulder, and he pointed to the left where Theo's large wolf was. He was tearing through other wolves like they were pillows, the tuffs of white and gray, and brown flying out from the attack.

"You would feel something if Theo was hurt," Eli told me. "The bond connects you both, you would feel it."

I took mild comfort in that while I followed Theo with my eyes. Reed's warriors formed a circle around Albia, who hadn't shifted yet. Her head whipped around, eyes glancing from wolf to wolf, not knowing who she was fighting for or against anymore.

Theo was searching for something, someone; Reed. He made his way through the wolves towards Albia, looking for the wolf he assumed would be close by. Albia shook as he got closer.

My eyes began searching through the wolves, wanting to find where Reed was. The trees provided cover, which was an advantage to us because we knew the woods better than our enemies, but it provided them as much coverage as it did us. Something glinted in the light, and my eyes narrowed in.

Two shifters, in human form, were dragging a wolf by its hind leg away from the fight. I knew in an instant it was Reese, bucking and trying to escape the silver chains that were wrapped around him. I could smell the burning flesh from fifty feet away.

"Eli," I barked out quickly. He was next to me in a second and looking around for danger. "Look." I pointed. His eyes narrowed in, and he was deciding his next move. "You have to go help him."

"I can't leave you." His orders were clear.

"You can't just let him die."

"Stay right here," he growled, checking to make sure the other guards were still close. He shifted mid-run and tore into the woods. He was gone behind the trees in seconds, but my eyes still watched his path, waiting for him to return.

Instead, someone else came into my line of vision that made my heart stop beating, Reed Porter, with a blade to Sloane's neck, staring directly at me, beckoning me.

His warning was clear, he would kill her without blinking his eyes. He planned this carefully; the other wolf had just been a distraction to get Eli away from me.

He held Sloane by her neck, cutting her air off just enough to keep her docile, but not kill her. She scowled, kicked, and jerked around, trying to break free. I knew what he wanted me to do, and I didn't see any other way around it. Maybe someone would get to me in time, but Sloane wasn't going to die in place of me.

The guards around me were faced outward from the small collection of trees we gathered around. I could squeeze right through the trees, and they wouldn't know I was gone.

So, that's what I did. I left the safety of my guards and walked straight towards Reed Porter, who smirked as I got closer. Sloane's eyes widened as I approached, realizing what was going on. Her eyes bulged, trying to give me a signal to stop moving, but I swallowed the fear building in my throat and stood right in front of them.

"I didn't know prey could be so brave," Reed mused, his face and voice lacking any kind of emotion.

"Let her go."

"You aren't in any position to be making demands," he sneered, clenching his hand tighter around her throat. The knife was down in his other hand, the one he kept pointing at me with.

His hand relaxed, and Sloane slumped halfway over, heaving her breaths in. While she was down, her arm shot out in line with Reed's groin and hit with more force than I thought she could muster.

He groaned in surprise and clenched his jaw but remained upright. One of his men grabbed Sloane by the arm and dragged her away from us. I held my breath and watched Reed saunter back and forth.

"It's just us now." His voice sent my mind reeling, trying to come up with escape routes. An arm came around my throat, holding me hostage until Reed came over and pointed the knife directly at my jugular. "And I intend to make this hurt."

INSTINCTUAL

Reed walked behind me, the knife just grazing the hairs on my neck. I couldn't think of anything other than the small nicks it was making against my skin. Three or four of his men followed us, and we met with a larger group of wolves.

They smiled wickedly at me, licking their lips, and yipping in excitement. I tried to keep the sneer on my face, but it was a losing battle; I was shaking, sweating, scared. It was cold outside, but it felt like I was standing right next to the sun.

"Ladies and gentlemen, please allow me to introduce the great Enforcer's mate." I stepped away from the knife and Reed grabbing my hair, pulling me back harshly. "Ah, ah, ah," he tutted, forcing me far enough back where he could put his face next to mine. "Please don't make me work for this, I'm really not in the mood after all the fighting."

I moved my face away from his, and he laughed once, lowly, leading me forward until we stood on a small cliff overlooking the clearing.

"See that?" Reed pointed the knife down to a wolf. "That's your mate down there. He has no idea that you're gone, and you can't mind link him. You are not the same as your mate, you are not the same as me. You are weak."

"You're an arrogant wolf," I noted quietly.

He paid me no attention.

"He doesn't even know you're gone," he hissed in my ear. I closed my eyes as he got closer to me and leaned down to inhale my scent. "Weak."

"Reed, what are we going to do with her?" another man asked.

"I haven't decided yet," he responded, casually looking sideways at the man. "I had this idea that I would cut her head off and sew a doe's head on top of her body and send it back to Theo but, skinning her also sounds sort of fun. Don't you think?"

A chorus of low approvals was muttered among them.

"What do you think we should do?" he asked me flatly.

"What will Albia think?" I asked, hoping to appeal to his human side.

"Who?"

"Your mate?" That angered him, and he smacked me across the face with the back of his hand. It stung the skin but with the surge of adrenaline, I didn't feel the underlying bruise.

"Don't say her name," he said as a warning.

"You don't even know her name yet, do you think this is the best first impression?" My words became increasingly quiet as his hand wound around my throat.

"You know, cutting your head off was the less painful option; once I cut through your neck, you would have bled out almost instantly. Now I'm kind of favoring the second option."

My breaths came in convulsions. I was going into shock, and I had to fight it if I was going to make any sort of attempt to live. I calmed my breathing while Reed was debating which part of me he would start slicing off.

"I think the face is a great place to start. We can make a mask with your skin," he whispered harshly, the air of his breath invaded my mouth.

He took his knife out of his pocket and touched the tip to the middle of my forehead. Methodically, his knife cut through my skin down to my skull and began to trace down the left side of my face just under my hairline.

I jerked and fought against him, crying out, screaming uncontrollably.

He stopped for half a second and flicked his knife behind him, shaking off the droplets of blood.

"Theo's going to kill you," I said weakly, blinking as a stream of blood cascaded over my eyes.

"Theo doesn't even know where you are. He's fighting with some other pack's wolves right now. By the time he realizes what happened to you, it'll be too late."

"He knows."

Reed stepped back, wiping a drop of sweat from his brow. "He can't even hear you." He called Theo's name loudly, glancing behind his shoulder. He called him again and then looked at me pointedly. "Here, I'll even give you a chance to get his attention."

He didn't move away from me at all, figuring there was nothing I could do. I wasn't a wolf, I couldn't mind-link him. I wasn't strong enough to fight Reed off or run for help.

The knife glinted in the sun again, and without even

thinking, I slipped it out of Reed's hand and brought it up to my neck.

"What? Are you going to do the honors yourself?"

Knowing there was no other option, I moved the knife to the side of my neck where Theo's mark was and pressed into it greedily. I screamed as the blade cut through my skin. Reed's eyes grew larger, and then he squinted, grabbing the knife from me and shoving me to the ground.

"I told you, you were arrogant," I whispered, quiet and hoarse.

From our position on the small cliff, we heard Theo's deafening howl that shook the birds from the trees. I grimaced, closing my eyes and praying he wouldn't get hurt.

After a moment, dozens of wolves were drawing in on us. Reed grabbed my arm roughly and hauled me up, moving my hair so that I was facing them. We waited until the wolves stormed into our line of vision. The Valkryie wolves had followed Theo along with Caddy, Bodhi, Theo's brothers, and a few other Warriors.

Theo shifted back as soon as he was close enough and growled so low I could barely hear it. He took in the sight of me, bleeding from my face and neck, bruised, barely able to stand up.

"Let her go," he demanded. The wolves around him shifted back and stepped into formation behind him.

"She's not going anywhere with you, isn't that right?" Reed tipped my chin up with the blade and moved us back. Theo stepped forward, and immediately the knife was pressed firmly into my jugular.

Theo stepped back and growled, snarling.

"That's really not a smart move," Reed advised, pursing his lips. Theo's eyes desperately searched for some way he could save me. Reed moved us farther back until we were in front of a large oak tree.

"Reed, I swear if you don't release her," Theo fumed, not bothering to finish his threat.

"I said," Reed bellowed. Theo's lack of submission angered him even more, and he started shouting. "She's not going anywhere." On the last word, he turned and shoved me against the bark of the tree.

His hand rose, clearly wielding the large blade. I tried to look at Theo's eyes as the knife came down and pierced through my right shoulder, just below my collarbone. The blade cut into the bark of the tree and pinned me there.

I gasped; my eyes widened. My breathing came in inconsistent pants.

Theo launched himself forward only to be pulled back by the Warriors. My life was at stake as well as his, but his instincts overpowered his rational thinking.

Reed was directly in front of me, shaking as if he was going to shift at any moment. Theo's eyes were clouded with black; he was not in control of his actions. In his distracted state, I feared he wouldn't be able to fight Reed and come out unharmed.

My body acted on its own volition; my mind was clouded with memories of Theo smiling at me. That was the only thing on my mind as my left hand came up and grabbed onto the handle of the knife. In two excruciating pulls, the knife was out of the tree and out of my shoulder. I could feel my skin shredding under the blade, bone chipping away.

I gave in to the shock of it all.

Everyone behind Theo stopped and watched me with open mouths.

I smiled softly, remembering the way Theo's hands felt

against my face, always brushing my hair from my eyes. I could feel the phantom touch on my skin as if he was right in front of me. He whispered to me in foreign words, and I breathed out in relief.

My feet took one step forward, and I lifted the blade. Before Reed was even aware of my presence, the knife was slicing from one side of his neck to the other, like a ripe tomato. He dropped to the ground with one loud thud, trying to reach for his throat, which was spewing blood like an uncorked fire hydrant.

All I could see were Theo's eyes, blue, so blue, impossibly blue. My body was falling.

Theo was running towards me, they all were. They were running and then they weren't. They were crouching in front of me, grabbing me, and trying to stop the bleeding. My hand raised slowly, shaking still, towards Theo's cheek.

He grabbed it with both of his hands and held it there, trying his hardest not to bear the weight of what he saw in front of him. He needed to be strong, even now, especially now.

I couldn't say the words I wanted to say. I couldn't form them on my lips though I tried so desperately. He needed to know. He needed to know that I was okay with dying if it meant saving him. He needed to know I wouldn't blame him. He needed to know that.

He needed to know that I loved him. And I didn't blame him. I could never blame him. He had shown me what love meant. But I couldn't say the words. I couldn't say them because everything went black, and I was gone.

PART 2

IN PURGATORY

I was drowning in the darkness; I was sure of it. It was
never-ending. It never faded. For so long, there was no light at
the end of the tunnel, no breath of fresh air, not one moment
when I believed I would wake up.

Then, in a burst, it was bright. It was too bright, blind-
ing, shimmering gold in every crevice of my mind. I squinted
and raised my arm to block the light. The world around me
was magical. It was a bright yellow; shimmers of sparkles and
iridescence bounced off each other.

Heaven. This surely had to be Heaven, it was too beautiful to be Hell unless that was the point of it all-to take away all
the beauty and be plunged into darkness once again.

In the distance, two people started walking towards
me. I couldn't see who they were; the light was too bright,
they were just silhouettes. When they got closer, I felt a familiar recognition. The woman smiled kindly at me, reached out,
and touched my cheek. The man reached for my hand and gave
it a gentle squeeze.

"Oh, honey," the woman's voice tinkered. "Look at how beautiful she is."

"And strong," the man added. They looked me up and down, trailing their hands over my hair and face and arms.

"Who are you?" I asked carefully. My voice was light as a harp, but it hurt to speak.

"Little one, you're our child," the man told me. They were changed from the memories in my mind; maybe it was age or the wear of time on my mind.

"Dad?" The man nodded. "Mom?" The woman smiled kindly. "Where are we?"

"Oh, little one, everything is going to be alright," my mom assured me. "We're going to be together now."

"Is this-" my question was cut off when the lights around us started to fade. My parents seemed frazzled and then panicked. I tried to reach out to them, but hands grasped at empty air.

"You're going to be okay," my father's disembodied voice assured me.

"What do you mean?" I gasped, trying to walk closer, but my feet were cemented in the same spot.

"Don't fight it, little one," my mother's voice was full of tears as she folded into her husband's arms.

"We'll always love you, no matter what."

Then all the lights were gone, and it was black again, darker somehow. I was pinned to the ground under an unknown pressure, and I struggled to get out from under it. I tried to touch it, but my arms would not move. Then, from my belly, I began to feel the burn. It was moving through my veins, my muscles, my heart.

It wasn't a hot burning. It felt like acid moving through me.

After a while, I grew used to the feeling. After a while, there was no feeling, just existing in the darkness. After a while, I started hearing something, *someone*, close to me.

After a while, I heard Theo's voice.

FIGHT FOR ME

I felt my feet first. Somehow, I could count every bone individually. I suppose when you have nothing to do but lay there, counting your bones is about all you can do.

My legs came next, all the way up to my knee, and then the cartilage underneath it tingled like pins and needles. My thighs and hips and lower back came alive a while after. Soon, I felt the tips of my fingers, my nails, my knuckles.

The rest of my body filtered in slowly. I didn't think I would be able to feel myself healing, but everywhere I felt pain, there was also a buzzing sensation, and the pain lessened by the minute.

Theo's voice hummed in my ear the entire time. His voice, along with Gabriel's, Cam's, Gemma's, and even Tansy's laughter, surrounded me.

I couldn't wake up, no matter how many times I tried. I heard another voice, presumably the doctor, who said I was on a medication that would make me sleep for a few more days.

"Hey there, little one," Theo breathed roughly, kissing my hand as he spoke. "I'm not really sure if you can even hear me or not, but I just want you to know that I'm never going to leave you ever again. I love you so much. Please, please just try to fight. I know it's hard and I know you must be tired but please. I can't lose you, Margo. I swear to you, when you wake up, you're going to be so spoiled. Anything you want, I'll get it for you. I'll never leave you again. Please, Margo. Please just try to fight, for me, for us."

Theo never left me, just like he said.

Gemma, Cam, and Tansy came in and sat and talked for a while. I was thankful that Theo wasn't alone. His brothers and Sloane came and made sure he was okay, although I don't think Eli ever entered the room.

I was poked and prodded and pinched all day long. There were two large bandages on either side of my neck that the nurse changed every few hours.

Another nurse came in and told Theo she was going to wash me; he didn't allow her to. Instead, he took the soft cloth and a basin of warm water and began cleaning me. He cleaned the dirt from my feet and fingertips, the dried blood on my arm, and some on my legs.

As he was dabbing the cloth around my forehead, I winced.

He froze and sucked his breath in.

"Margo?" he whispered gingerly. I practically moaned at his voice, it was breathless and barely noticeable. Theo huffed out a breath that sounded something like a laugh like he couldn't believe what was happening.

"Margo, can you hear me? Can you open your eyes?" I couldn't. I tried, but my eyes remained shut. "Okay, can you squeeze my hand?"

That I could do. It wasn't anything special, but I wiggled

my fingers in Theo's, and he cried out, picking my hand up in his and pressing his lips to every inch.

"Margo, I'm right here. I swear, I'm not going anywhere. You've just got to open your eyes, can you try?"

I wanted to glare at him, tell him, 'don't you think I would open my eyes if I could?' He would've given me a look and told me he was only trying to be encouraging.

Sometime later, maybe an hour or so, I could open my eyes. It was slow at first, but then my eyes snapped open all at once.

Everything was so crisp. I could see everything in the room at the same time. Theo was looking at me anxiously, my hand still in his grasp. I took a huge breath in and looked at him.

"Margo?" he said warily. His eyebrows were scrunched up, and he looked like he hadn't shaved in a week. I swallowed, and my ears popped. "Sweetheart?" This time his voice sounded much louder to me, clearer, stronger. I jumped a little in surprise.

When I looked at the rest of the room, I came to the realization that I could feel the blood pumping through me. I could feel each of my heartbeats, the beeps from the machines, the air coming through the vents, the click of someone's shoes down the hall, the wind from outside, a car door closing nearby.

I looked at Theo, and it was like I had never looked at him before. His eyes, which I never noticed, had little flecks of grey near his irises, watched me nervously.

I inhaled deeply and smelled something warm, like a wood-burning stove. Every noise around me got louder, and I started breathing faster, which made my heartbeats speed up.

I was hyperventilating before I could stop myself. Theo was immediately leaning over me, holding either side of my face, telling me to take deep breaths. He called for a nurse, and a woman ran in. She touched my arm, and I felt each nerve react where she touched.

My body threw itself forward, trying to get off the bed. Theo grabbed my arm as I swung my legs over the side. I shook him off and then stopped, how could I fight back so easily? I was human, but more than that, I was wounded it that arm.

There were no bandages on my shoulder, and I didn't feel any pain.

"Margo, please just relax. I can explain everything to you if you just lie back down." Theo tried to soothe me, but each new word sent me flying further into a frenzy.

I jumped off the bed and looked between them like a cornered animal. Theo held his hands out, showing me he wasn't going to hurt me. The nurse watched me with concern, her eyes were wide, and she had sweat on her forehead and upper lip.

"Margo," Theo said more aggressively.

I whimpered deep within my lungs and looked at the door in my peripheral vision. I dove for the door, leaping past the nurse, and scrambled to gain my bearings. When I was four steps down the hallway, Theo's arms circled my waist and held me to him.

I kicked and stretched my arms. He walked me back carefully and set me down on the bed. As I moved around violently, two thick straps were attached to my arms, strapping me down to the bed. The same straps were placed on my legs, I was trapped.

"Margo, listen to me, listen to my voice. I know you're scared, but I am right here. Let me explain this to you, please. I know your instincts are telling you to run, to fight me, but I need you to listen to me now." Theo's voice was hard, but there was a vulnerability in it.

Tears pooled in the corners of my eyes and leaked down my cheeks. Theo kissed them, although I turned my head away.

"Margo, after you passed out, we had to rush you here. You lost a lot of blood, and the damage to our mark wasn't allowing you to heal. The doctors were trying to save you, but there was a lot of damage," his voice broke. I calmed myself, but my breathing was still faster than normal. "You were stable for two days, but you didn't move at all. In the middle of the night, you started crashing. Your heart stopped. They tried to resuscitate you, but your heart wouldn't start beating again."

Theo placed his hand on my cheek and turned it to face him.

"I couldn't lose you, Margo. I know that it was selfish, and I know when you truly realize what I've done, you'll probably hate me, but I had to take that chance. I had to turn you."

It was like my heart stopped beating for the second time.

"Margo, please try to understand, I did it to save you. You would have died. I couldn't let you die, Margo, I couldn't let you down again. I failed to save you the first two times, and I couldn't let myself just sit there and let you be taken from me again."

Theo was crying. Three tears escaped his eyes, but he didn't brush them away. I tried to turn my head, but he pressed his hand more firmly.

"Little one, you are my entire world. I had to save you. I love you too much to let you go. I know that's mean and selfish; I know that. Please, Margo, try to understand why I did this."

I tried to sit up and was aggravated when the straps held me down. I jerked against them a few times, and then tried more violently. I was shaking, kicking, and punching the bed frame to get free. Theo leaned over my body and set his head on my thigh, crying gently.

When I stopped fighting the straps, Theo sat back up. "Margo, I know that this is scary for you. When wolves are turned for the first time, they have adrenaline pumping through them. Your strength is much greater than you think, that's why we have to keep you here until you've calmed down. I don't want you to hurt yourself."

"Get out," I croaked.

"Margo?" he said, surprised.

"Get out," I growled.

"Please just-"

"Get out! Get out! Get the fuck out of here!" My screams sounded psychotic, wild, rabid. Theo's shoulders drooped, and he hung his head. He placed his hand on the side of the bed and leaned towards me.

"Margo, I'm not going to leave you here alone."

"You said you'd give me anything I wanted when I woke up," I reminded him. He looked down, regretting his words. "I *want* you to get out."

"No." He continued to plead with me and tell me how sorry he was. I turned my head away and closed my eyes.

I didn't want to hear him.

My parents told me they would love me no matter what, but I couldn't.

STRANGER'S BODY

I was released from the hospital the next day and returned home on the condition that Theo stayed with Gabriel. He protested greatly, but when I told him I would go back to Caddy's pack, he promised he would not set foot in the house until I allowed him.

It felt different walking into the house alone. It felt emptier now, and not because Theo wasn't there to take up space, but because all the little nuances about the house were suddenly gone. The quiet clicking from the basement quickly became the sound of the radiator. The picture windows all had speckles of dust and grime across them, unnoticeable to my human eyes.

I walked slowly through the house, reacquainting myself with each fixture and crevice. The pantries smelled like sugary cereals. The kitchen table had a nick along the left side where Cam dropped his knife. My fingers trailed over the movie cases in the entertainment center. I could read all the titles in seconds.

The steps weren't as steep anymore.

The frosted glass door that entered to our bedroom had lost its luster, and I could see everything on the other side. Our bed was disheveled. The white comforter was bunched up on my side of the mattress, feathered out, and licking the rug under the bed.

I crawled from Theo's side of the bed to mine and moved languidly until the blankets covered me from my toes to my nose. The fabric smelled different.

This felt like a stranger's house.

This felt like a stranger's body.

I didn't understand how to move my arms. My legs felt lighter, or maybe it was that I was stronger, and it didn't cause as much strain to move them. My fingernails felt too long. My teeth felt foreign.

Nothing about this felt right.

I wanted to go back. I clenched my eyes tightly, hoping that in some alternate universe, I could be back to my old self. But there was nothing. When I opened my eyes again, I blinked away the frustrated tears and pulled the blankets closer.

The fabric felt softer.

I just wanted everything to go back to the way it was. But it couldn't. I wasn't human anymore.

I threw the covers off and ran to the bathroom where I turned on the water to the shower. I stepped in, shedding my clothes as they dampened around my skin. Tears blended with the water as they streamed down my face.

I cried out, knowing no one could hear me. Loudly, and without refrain. I cried to get the pain out from my chest.

My mark tingled on my neck, and I knew Theo could tell I was upset. I couldn't care about him right now, though. I couldn't fathom the pain he felt because my pain had filled up my entire threshold. There was nothing left for him at that moment.

I knew I was harsh when I yelled at him to leave the hospital room, and I meant to be. I was not worried about being demure and soothing when I screamed, I was worried about my own well-being. I was angry with him, a fit of anger I had never felt before, not even with Reed Porter.

Theo was my mate. He was supposed to protect me and love me and respect me above all else. This wasn't respect. This wasn't love. This might've been protection, but it was masked under the veil of selfishness. He was being selfish.

I had never made him promise me anything other than this. I hadn't asked for anything more. This was the only demand I ever made, and he ignored it when he placed his venom in my body.

I heard footsteps outside, and I could sense it was the guards switching their posts. Theo had increased the number of guards at our house and around the perimeter now that he wasn't in the house to protect me.

By the time I got out of the shower, my toes and fingers were pruned, and my hair had lost any sense of curl. I stepped raggedly over the edge of the shower, leaving my clothes on the tile floor.

I laid on top of the bed, letting all the water soak into the fabrics.

I didn't remember falling asleep, but I was woken hours later by Gemma entering the house. She called my name, and I could do little else but pull the blanket to cover my bare body. Gemma softly walked up the stairs and knocked on the door.

"M-Margo?" She whispered, cracking the door open. I didn't respond. "M-Margo, are you ok-kay?"

She walked to the other side of the bed, gently sitting on the edge near my knees. She looked over my blank face, and her eyes grew sad. "How are you feeling? D-Do you have any p-pain?" When she didn't hear an answer, she grabbed the covers surround my face. Her fingers pulled strands of wet hair from my cheeks and set them behind my head.

"Come on," she said, standing up. She held her hands out like she was waiting to help me. I didn't move. She took a deep breath and threw the covers back. I scrambled to pull something around my naked body, but she took my hands and hauled me off the bed. My hands lamely covered my flesh as she walked into our closet.

I was handed comfortable clothes, ones with Theo's scent on them. I pulled the pants on but glared at the sweatshirt. She sighed and handed me a shirt of my own.She made us sandwiches in the kitchen, and we sat on the same side of the counter, eating them silently.

Then, she started coming by the house every morning, and this became our routine. She would pull me out of bed or off the couch and make sure I ate.

I tried to cook something on the stove but found the smells were too overwhelming. I tried to read in the times I was alone, but the ink impurities on the pages were the only things my eyes caught. I walked around the house aimlessly, watching the guards outside the windows, and wondering how they could function so easily.

My muscles ached inside me, needing to be stretched out multiple times a day. It became difficult to sleep with the muscle aches, and I stayed up most nights, sleeping for a few hours during the day when I could. The cramps would hit me at all times of the day.

I was standing at the sink when my legs wavered so strongly, I had to hold myself up by my arms. Gemma watched from the kitchen table pitifully.

"You have t-to shift," she told me softly.

"No," I sniffled, closing my eyes and waiting for the muscle cramp to dissipate.

"It's the only way it's g-going to g-get b-better," she said stronger.

"No," I snapped.

"This isn't healthy."

My legs stopped cramping, and I tested my weight. I could stand on them again, and I took the opportunity to walk out of the room. Gemma followed me.

"We c-can help you shift," she explained. I didn't want to shift, nor did I want their help doing it.

"Go home," I told her softly, walking towards the stairs. "Go tell Theo what I did today."

Her footing faltered. "What are you t-talking about?"

"I know you've been reporting back to him," I confronted her, turning as I hovered on the first step. "That's why you've been visiting so much. He can't be here, so he sent you. I get it."

"M-margo, I'm here b-because I'm your friend," she shook her head, though her eyes held a little guilt. Both could be true.

"It's okay," I told her. "I'd do the same thing."

She groaned as I went back upstairs. "You c-can't j-just hide out for the rest of your life!"

"I'm not."

She made a noise of disbelief. "Really?"

"I just...I'm waiting until it goes back to normal," I murmured, crawling back into bed.

"Normal?"

"Human," I whispered into the pillow. She sunk into the

mattress next to me, laying where Theo normally did.

"You c-can't go b-back," Gemma said emphatically. "You're never g-going to b-be human again."

I ignored her and pulled the blanket closer to me.

"Is it really that b-bad?" she asked.

It took me longer to answer her than before. "It's not that."

"Then what?"

"It's the choice." She sucked in a breath and remained quiet. "I know not all wolves are bad, I know that," I said, sinking further into the pillows. "But it was my choice. Not his. It was my choice what to do with my body and what I wanted to be or not be, and he took that away. I don't want this body. I don't know what to do with it. I wasn't meant to be this."

"You would've d-died, M-margo," she returned.

"I know." I nodded into the blanket. My voice grew thicker. "I know that. But I can't help but think that would've been better than this."

"It's hard." She nodded against the sheets. Her lungs quivered as she sucked in a sharp breath. "B-but this life is b-better than that. You c-can't let that feeling win."

"I didn't get to choose," I told her, rolling over to look at her. Her eyes were filled with the same fat tears mine were. "I didn't choose this."

"I know." She nodded, wiping her tears away. "B-but, what was he supposed to d-do? Watch you d-die?"

"I don't know." I shook my head. She smiled sadly at me and took my hand in hers. That night, I didn't fall asleep alone in the house. And in the morning, I made the decision to call Theo over to the house. He smiled when I opened the door, but he didn't smile when he left that day.

CATCH22

Theo arrived at the house at 8:59 but waited outside the front door until I opened it at 9 a.m. He smiled when he first saw me and reached to touch me, but I stepped out of the way, giving him room to enter. He stepped around me and strolled into the house, taking note of things that were moved as he walked.

"You wanted to talk?" he announced, perching on the edge of the couch. I gingerly sat on the chair, nodding my head. "What did you want to talk about?"

"Why did you turn me?" I blurted out, looking straight into his eyes. He knew this question was coming.

He let out a small breath and said, "You were dying."

"Yes, and?"

His eyes narrowed. "And I needed to save your life. It was the only way."

"Are you sure?"

"What?"

"Are you sure?" I asked again. "That is was the only way?"

"Margo, you were flatlining. Your heart stopped."

"I know," I pressed on. "But was it the *only* way?"

"What are you trying to imply?" he said defensively.

"Did you change me because I was dying, and there was no other way or did you change me because I was dying?"

"You think if there was any other way, I would've done this to you? I know this isn't what you wanted," Theo fought. He was wringing his hands over and over again on his knees.

"When I said I didn't want to be a wolf, I meant it," I bit out, glaring at him. He paused to collect himself.

"You would have died," he said.

"And that should have been my choice."

"You don't mean-"

"Don't tell me what I mean or don't mean," I said pointedly but calm, looking away from his intense gaze. "I'm allowed to feel however I want to about this."

"I know that." He shuffled around, trying to seem calm. "But this isn't the worst thing that could have happened to you."

"You don't know that. You've never been a human, Theo."

"And you've never been a werewolf until now, and you're not even giving it a chance."

"Giving it a chance?" I chuckled, shaking my head in disbelief. "I shouldn't have to give it a chance. I shouldn't be this."

"But you are," he argued. "And I'm sorry that you hate it this much already, but you could also be dead and buried in the ground right now. So I'd say that's a victory."

"It's not," I sniffled. "It's not a victory. This," I gestured to my body. "Is not a victory. I don't know what this is. I don't know what I am anymore."

"You're still Margo," he breathed.

"I don't feel like myself." My voice was tight. "I feel like the last thing tying me to my parents is gone."

"I didn't mean to make you feel like that," Theo said, sitting beside me on the bed. We both stared down.

"You'll never understand what it's like to be a human," I said, shaking my head slightly. "You'll never get it. You were born this way."

"You're right," he said, surprising me. "But I know what it's like to lose a parent, and I can't imagine if my mom was gone, too. I don't know what I would do, but I know that I wouldn't want to die because of it."

"I don't want to die," I seethed. "I wanted to have the damn choice to my own body. This isn't you cutting my hair or changing my clothes. You took away everything about me that made me who I am. You changed the chemical makeup of my body, my genetics. I can never go back to being human. I don't care if I was dying, I should've had the right to choose, and you knew that."

"There wasn't a choice to be made," he snapped. "You were dying, Margo."

"I hoped you would respect me enough to let me go."

"And I hoped you loved me enough to fight."

"You hoped I loved you enough to fight for a life I don't want?" I stood up from the chair. "You hoped that my love for you outweighed everything else I liked about myself? You hoped my love for you would make up for the fact that you took this from me?"

"I didn't take anything from you!" he yelled, his face growing red. "I saved your life! What part of that don't you get?"

"I didn't want to be saved!" My body shook under the weight of my anger. Theo recoiled. "I didn't want to be saved, Theo, and you're selfish to think that this is some kind of gift you've given me. You're being selfish."

"Me?" he questioned. "I'm the one being selfish? Can you take one minute to understand that being alive and a werewolf is better than being dead? Can you at least acknowledge that?"

"No." I shook my head firmly.

He closed his eyes and took a deep breath. "We're not going to agree on this."

"Then get out."

"What?" he asked, stepping closer to me.

"I said get out," I growled. "This isn't something we get to agree to disagree on. If you don't think that taking away my choice to my own body is a mistake, then you need to leave. This isn't something I can live with."

"I'm not leaving you here alone," he vowed.

"You're not. You sent Gemma, and I'm sure you can send Sloane and Gabriel and Cam and Reese and Eli and anyone else you can think of to check on me. And they'll report back to you because you're their Enforcer. But you aren't mine. I don't care if I'm a werewolf now. You aren't in charge of me. And I don't care if this is your house," I pushed against his chest roughly with both of my hands. "I want you out. I want you to leave! Get out! Now!"

"Margo," Theo pleaded. He allowed me to push him back but stopped firmly near the front door.

"Can't you see that you're hurting me?"

His jaw quivered, and he closed his eyes, stilling briefly before he threw the door open and walked out of it quickly. My chest tightened, and I placed my hand over my heart to make sure it was still beating correctly.

I stumbled back to the couch, where I spent the remainder of the day staring at the wall until late afternoon when Gemma came back for her evening routine. She brought a pre-made dish over that she finished off in our oven as I sat at the kitchen counter.

"How d-did it go?" she mumbled while slicing a loaf of bread.

"Fine," I breathed.

"That's not what I heard."

"He doesn't understand."

She pursed her lips. "D-did he try to?"

"I'm not even sure," I sighed. A muscle cramp surged in my stomach, and I tried to ignore it until the pain felt like it was twisted around all the organs in my belly. I made a small noise of discomfort, and Gemma's head snapped toward me immediately. My hand clutched at my stomach, and I heaved in deep breaths, wincing again.

"M-margo, you need to shift," she snapped, slamming everything down on the counter.

"No." Another ripple of pain rushed through me, and I stumbled out of the stool I was sitting on, leaning against the nearby fridge for support. This time, a louder cry broke free from my mouth, and it sounded more animalistic than human.

"G-go outside." Her eyes glazed over, and I knew she was mind-linking someone. It was an expression I had grown accustomed to.

"Don't tell him," I pleaded, staggering toward the back

door. The cool wind touched my skin, and I felt like I wanted to leap out of my body. My whimpers turned to bellows and bellows to screams as muscle cramps took over nearly every inch of my body. I dropped to the ground and let my head fall in the grass.

I should've been able to smell Theo before I saw him, but my mind was clouded. He dropped on the ground next to me and moved my arms away from their position clutching around the middle of my body.

"Margo," he said sternly, trying to make eye contact with me. I blinked rapidly but looked back at him. "You're going to shift."

"No," I whimpered, trying to break free from his hold. He placed my hands on the ground and moved my feet, so they were laying out away from me. "No, please."

"Margo, your body is readying for a shift, whether you want it or not. It's happening, but I am right here, and I'm not going to leave you."

"No, I don't want-"

"I know this is not what you want." He nodded, stroking my cheek sadly. "I wish I could take it all away for you." He paused for a minute, petting my hair back from my sweaty forehead. "Do you want to let it happen naturally, or do you want the pain to be over now?"

"Make it stop," I pleaded softly, closing my eyes as another wave rippled through me.

"*Shift.*" It was an Alpha tone. I had heard him use it on others before, and it sounded only mildly gruffer than his normal voice, but now in this form, I felt an undeniable need to submit.

My body began contorting, and violently, I was thrown from one set of bones and muscles to another. The pain was pinpointed to a mere moment, but it felt like I was shattering into dust on the ground.

I groaned, and when I heard the animalistic noise that came out, I whimpered. My eyes opened, and I saw that I was lying in the same position, but Theo was now in front of me, kneeling before me, stroking my head softly. I couldn't speak. That was the most alarming thing. I kept trying to form words, but they came out as terrible, sad, whines.

"Shh, you're okay," Theo said, touching the side of my face with his hand. "You're alright, little one. Just relax. I'm here. It's over."

I slithered around on the ground before I tried to stand up on four legs. It felt foreign to me, but I moved naturally into the correct position. My limbs were still weak, and they shook under me. I felt over onto Theo, who ran his hand down my back. My feet kicked out from underneath me, but it only propelled me further into his body.

"Margo, you're doing great. Just relax. Breathe. Let your body adjust." His hand continued to stroke from the top of my head down my back and up again. I huffed and released my body. "Do you want me to shift too?" he offered.

I quickly started whimpering and whining in protest, wiggling in his hold to get away from him.

"Okay, okay, I won't. It's alright. It's okay. We're okay. I'm not going anywhere."

He continued to lay with me in the grass, petting me, and holding me. After I completely relaxed in his arms, he gave me another command to shift back to help me.

His shirt was shed from his body and wrapped around me instantly as I traded forms. I tried to push myself up from the ground, but Theo's arms pulled me up into his chest before I could attempt it. My eyes remained closed until I was laid gently on our bed.

Theo grabbed the covers and replaced his shirt for the

soft cotton. He brushed my hair from my face, and it was that moment my eyes opened.

It was the first moment after shifting that I had made eye contact with him, and immediately something moved inside me. All the molecules in my body somehow solidified themselves to him, and I was no longer just part of myself; I was now one half of this man. I don't know how to explain it in any other way than I understood why he did what he did. In that quiet moment, I knew why he turned me.

I reached out softly and placed my hand on his hand. The soft smile on his face grew.

"I understand," I whispered, trying to fight the sleep that was trying to overcome me.

"You do?" There was uncertainty in his voice as his hand hovered over my cheek.

"I understand now." And I did. More than I knew was possible.

At that moment, it wasn't about human or werewolf. It wasn't about my choice or his. It wasn't about any of the little things that were suddenly changed in my world.

It was about him and me.

And I knew I would do absolutely everything in my power for a future between the two of us to exist. I would do anything to keep him safe. I would do anything to protect him. Half of my heart, half of me, existed in him, and I knew the same existed in me.

I understood.

PROVOCATION

I slept next to Theo for a few hours and thought it was short, it was the best sleep I'd gotten in weeks. When I woke up, it was dark outside, and Theo was asleep with his head slumped back, propped up by his neck uncomfortably.

I nudged him and caressed his cheek as he sleepily opened his eyes. He smiled tiredly and leaned his face further into my hand. With his eyes closed, he looked younger. He opened his eyes as my hand moved up and down his cheek, gently brushing against his skin.

His eyes trailed from my face down to my waist and back up to stare at my lower lip that I was biting. He lifted his hand and pulled my lip from my teeth, and it lingered there for a moment. My body was getting hotter like there was a fire burning in the pit of my belly, and the flames were licking out.

I leaned my head down and pressed my lips to his. He grabbed the back of my hair; the little tug he gave sent a shiver down my spine. I pulled myself closer to him, hungrily kissing the lips I hadn't touched for so long.

He let out a small grunt from the back of his throat when my lips left his and moved to his cheek, to his chin, to his neck.

"Margo," he murmured with gentle remonstrance. My left hand popped the first button apart of the shirt he had put on and touched the skin underneath. He had a small smattering of hair on his chest that my fingers drifted through. His hand slowly rose and pressed my shoulder away. I sat up and looked at him in confusion.

"We shouldn't do this right now." He smiled sadly and rubbed his thumb against my collar bone.

"Why not?" I asked, plucking his hand from my chest and moving it to my lips.

"You've just been turned. Your emotions are going to be heightened, and your...sex drive is going to be a lot greater." His voice dipped when I opened my mouth and sucked the tip of his index finger. He looked flustered, which I thought was sweet, and I moved so I was sitting on his lap with my legs on either side of his.

"I feel fine, Theo. I just want you." Our faces were millimeters away. Foreheads touching, lips open in anticipation.

"Trust me, I want to. I wish we could, but I want to do this when you're ready and willing and not just because your hormones are making you horny. You'll regret doing this later."

I didn't listen to him and nipped his upper lip.

"Margo, no. We need to stop." I pulled away at his serious tone and looked at him. He had a hard look on his face, and his hands had captured both of my roaming wrists.

"Okay," I gulped, trying to hide the fact that I felt rejected. I clambered off the bed and started walking towards the bathroom. Theo groaned and said my name like he was cursing. He followed me and stood in front of the doorway, blocking me.

"It's not that I don't want to. I just want to wait until you know you're ready."

"I do know I'm ready," I said earnestly, putting my hands on his waist, my thumbs brushing the thick muscles underneath.

"Margo, there is nothing I want more than to throw you on my bed and ravish you, but I know you aren't ready for that, and I'm trying really hard to control myself. You affect every part of me just by touching me, just by looking at me. But I want to be together when we're both in the right mindset. This is the first time you've touched me in weeks. and I know some small part of you knows this isn't the right time."

I blushed, a warm heat filling my face and neck at his words. His arm wrapped around my shoulder as I hid my face in his chest.

"Now, why don't we go downstairs and get something to eat?" he suggested. I nodded, and we walked downstairs, me before him.

Reese and Cam were sitting downstairs on the couches while Gemma was bustling around, trying to clean up after my destructive state.

"Why are you all in my house?" Theo asked amusingly. Gemma stopped moving, un unfolded blanket and pillow hung in her grasp. Reese snorted loudly, and his head shot back in laughter.

"We wanted to see how your little wolf was holding up." Reese smirked. I glared but blushed nonetheless.

"I'm fine," I grumbled, holding onto Theo's forearm.

Reese shook his head and pushed himself off the couch. "That's not what I heard. I heard you were a little cranky these past few days," he cooed to me as he passed, ruffling my hair with one hand while the other stayed tucked in his pocket.

I pushed his hand off me and growled. I understood what Theo mean when he said my emotions would be heightened; one moment, I'm trying to seduce my mate, the next, I'm almost in tears, and then I'm ready to rip his brother's hand clear off his body for touching me.

"Oh." Reese's eyebrows shot up, and he gave me a sarcastic look of fear. "Pup's got claws."

"Reese, quit it. You remember what it was like to be newly shifted." Theo gave his brother a stern look and pushed me forward gently.

"I was just teasing, sis, no need to bite my hand off." I ignored him and went into the kitchen. Theo was close behind me, his hand never leaving the small of my back.

"Just ignore him," he murmured.

"I usually do," I joked.

* * *

After a week of doting on me, Theo was immediately launched back into his work. Claims of misconduct and unfair treatment surfaced, and he spent most of the day in his office. I made him snacks and brought him a cup of coffee every so often. He would cover his phone on his chest and kiss me before returning to his call.

Theo put Reese and Eli in charge of training me in self-defense, both in my human and wolf forms. Eli took his job more seriously than his brother, going as far as to create a point system with rewards and punishments for how well I performed.

Reese mostly sat on the grass next to us, eating the snacks meant for Eli and me and giving me snarky comments about my feeble attacks.

I collapsed on the ground, exhausted after our tenth training session. Eli made me run two miles before practicing my retaliations from being grabbed or attacked from behind. Every time, he got his arms around me and held me still while I kicked and bit and cursed, claiming that once I got free, he was going to be in a world of trouble.

Reese patted my shoulder as I laid next to him.

"Come on, get up, you think your enemy is going to wait until you're well-rested?" Eli called provocatively. I groaned and told him to leave me alone. "Margo, Theo's going to be mad if he comes out here and finds you on the ground instead of learning how to fight."

"Theo will be mad at you, he'll tell me I'm doing wonderful," I teased, sticking my tongue out.

"I'm going to tell him that you and Reese were sitting over there flirting the entire time," he said flatly. I sat up immediately, flipping myself over to look at him in outrage.

"You wouldn't," I denied, still concerned that he would.

He shrugged his shoulders. "You never know," he smirked, kicking his heel.

I snarled but stood up nonetheless and pushed Reese over. He slumped to the ground and opened his mouth in surprise.

"How dare you," he said, brushing the grass from his shoulders.

"What are you even doing here?"

"I'm here for moral support," he claimed, peeling another orange open and throwing the scraps behind him.

"You're just taking up space," I said, walking back over to Eli.

He growled and pushed himself off the ground. "I'll show you a waste of space, sis." He grabbed my arm and pinned it behind my back. I turned and jerked my arm out of his grasp. He cocked his head and took a fighting stance.

I glanced at Eli, and he nodded at me encouragingly. I took a stance like Reese, and he lunged. I stayed out of his arms for most of the time though I realized he was going easy on me. He turned, and I took the opportunity to stick my foot out and kick his legs out from under him.

He landed on the ground with a bang, and his breath was knocked out of him. Eli laughed loudly and clapped his hands. I took a big bow and wiped the sweat from my forehead.

"Very nice," Theo's booming voice called as he exited the house. "I'm kind of worried that my own brother can't protect himself from the wrath of this little minx."

"Oh, give it a rest," Reese grumbled, standing up and walking towards Eli, who wiped an imaginary tear from his cheek.

"I wonder if you'd like to test your skills against someone a little more, *qualified*." Theo smiled as he walked towards me, rubbing his hands together.

"Oh, no," I backed up, shaking my head. "I'm not going to fight you."

"Why?" His smile was kind compared to the threat behind his joking words. "Afraid to be knocked on your cute, little, butt, just like Reese?"

"Yes." I looked away and frowned. Theo came closer and grabbed my arms, which were crossed over my chest.

"I promise I'll be gentle," he whispered huskily.

Reese let out a loud noise of disgust.

"Come on, Theo, she's not going to be humiliated in front of her mate's family," Eli said, his words irked me, and I uncrossed my arms.

"I am not going to be humiliated," I promised. "Let's do this."

"Alright," Reese clapped his hands and hollered.

Theo smiled at me and backed up; I followed him. He took the same sort of stance that Reese did and flexed his arm muscles. I rolled my eyes and walked toward him casually. He narrowed his eyes and stood up straight. I stepped behind him and launched myself, jumping on his back childishly.

He grabbed onto my legs and laughed.

"Do you really think this is going to work?" he chuckled, turning his head to look at me.

"Isn't it?" I joked, wrapping my arms tighter around his neck.

"I could literally have you on the ground in seconds, little one."

"Oh, please-"

Before I could even finish my sentence, Theo had grabbed my arms and flipped my body over his shoulder. I was flat on my back with Theo above me, eyes twinkling, mouth pursed.

"Looks like I win," he poked. I laughed and brought his face even closer to mine, pressing a firm kiss to his lips. He groaned and lowered himself until he was resting on his elbows. I lifted my legs and wrapped them around his waist.

"Ew, guys, stop," Eli called.

Without warning, I torqued my body and flipped Theo onto his back. He released my lips, stunned, and moved his hands to my hips as I sat on top of him.

"I'll have you know that I am a very deadly werewolf now," I teased, leaning down to lay one more kiss on his lips.

"It's going to be harder to take me down now."

Theo sat up, forcing me to lean back, but he wrapped his arms around my waist.

"That was the first time you've called yourself a wolf," he breathed happily. I looked down and tried to fight the grin that was trying to come on my face.

"Yeah, well," I mumbled non-committedly.

"Margo, you don't know how happy that just made me." His voice was serious. I peeked back, and Eli and Reese, who were trying their best to look like they weren't eavesdropping.

"I'm still getting used to it, but..." I shrugged my shoulders.

"I know you are, and you're doing great."

He moved me off his body, and we stood up, grabbing each other's hands before walking towards Eli and Reese.

"I think we'll just be going right about now," Reese badgered us, talking large steps backward, hitting Eli's shoulder to follow him. "Leave you two to your hanky-panky nonsense."

"Reese," I yelped. He wiggled his eyebrows and skipped away. Eli followed him with half the enthusiasm.

"Come on." Theo put his hand on the small of my back, and we went back inside. Theo had already picked up dinner from Emily's bakery. There were a few sandwiches on the table along with raspberry scones, the same thing I ordered when we first went.

I beamed and bounced over to the table.

"I thought you might be hungry," Theo said. "I didn't want you to have to cook."

"Thank you," I said through the bite of sandwich I had

just bitten off. Theo sat next to me, not eating, just watching me devour my food. I stopped and looked over at him, awkwardly with a piece of lettuce poking out of my mouth. "Aren't you going to eat?"

"I'm not really hungry for that," he mused, crinkling the wax wrapper from my sandwich.

"Then why did you get it, you should've gotten something else," I told him guiltily. I set my food down, noticing I had already eaten half of the large portion.

"I'm hungry for something else." His eyes were lowered.

"What it is? We can go pick something else up, I can take this in the car with us," I insisted, beginning to wrap the wax paper around my food. He chuckled and pinched his nose between his eyes.

"Margo," he relented. "I'm not hungry for food."

I was confused for a moment until I saw the dark glint in his eyes. He continued to stare at me as realization coated my features, and I blushed a dark crimson.

"Oh," I said stupidly and let my food sit on the table.

"God, you don't even know what you do to me," he groaned, pulling the base of my chair towards him. I jumped a little in surprise. "How hungry I am for you, I've been trying to hold myself off, to give you time to adjust, but I don't know how much longer I can wait. Now that you've turned, it's like my instincts are so much stronger." He continued kissing and nipping the fabric near my neck.

"I know, I feel it too," I admitted.

"Then why don't we do something about it. I don't want my girl to go *unsatisfied*," he teased, flicking his tongue out to touch the very edge of his mark on my neck.

"Theo, I'm all sweaty still." I blushed, a shiver erupted through my body when he touched his mark.

"I don't care, you're about to get sweatier, what does it matter?"

"Theo," I said softly. His hand wove into my hair, forcing me to look at him. His eyes were honest, breath hitched, longing coating his skin.

"I know you're nervous, but I promise you this will be amazing. I adore everything about you, from the way your eyes crinkle in the corners when I make you laugh, to the way your skin flushes when I touch you. I love that you're shy but bold, and so damn strong. I love every hair on your head, Margo. Let me worship you."

AS MUCH AS
WE COULD

Theo kicked the door open. I had wrapped my legs around his waist and was hungrily kissing mouth, neck, any part of him I could. We tumbled onto the bed, and I was pressed against the soft covers as he hovered above me.

His breath was labored and frantic like he didn't know when he would get another breath. I took just a second to notice the way his lips curved and dipped. I lifted my hand, bringing it to the back of his neck.

He lowered himself, and his lips melded with mine softly. The taste of him invaded my senses, and I knew I was lost to this man. He had every part of me, and I wanted to give everything to him. His nose touched mine, and his fingers grabbed at my hip, almost too harshly, but the sting only excited me further.

His eyebrows clenched angrily like he was angry he

could only feel so much of me at once. I tugged his shoulder down to the bed and moved so that I was leaning over him. He lifted his head as I backed away, trying to keep us connected, but I left his lips and nipped at his jaw with a quick bite.

My hands grazed his chest, still covered in his gray, long-sleeved shirt. My hands drifted down to his waist, and I lifted the fabric, my fingers skimmed his taut stomach. He clenched his muscles, trying to control the urge to move and take over dominance, but I wasn't ready to give up yet.

I tugged the shirt up as far as I could, and Theo grabbed the bottom and lifted it over himself. He took my head between his hands and placed a searing kiss on my lips, keeping me over him.

I broke our kiss when I needed to breathe and lifted my leg to move it over his waist. Sitting on top of him was liberating for someone so used to being held down by muscular arms. I leaned down again, lips lathing onto one another.

His hands didn't hold my face this time. Instead, they pawed at my waist, going lower and touching the curve of my backside. My breath hitched as he grabbed more firmly, and I tried to calm my racing heart.

My hands latched onto his hair, pulling at the roots, trying to tell him that I was just as much a part of this as he was.

He groaned low in his chest, blowing hot breath onto my lips.

"I love you," I told him hastily as soon as our lips stopped touching. He smiled, mouth still parted and breathing heavy.

"I love you, too," he assured me, sitting up, so he was level with me. We didn't kiss for a few moments.

We took each other in.

Memorized each other's features.

Breathed in the same breath.

He slowly peeled the sleeveless top off me as I held my arms up. He kissed my cheekbone as he trailed his fingers, sown my spine, and back up, stopping as he reached my bra. I swore the next time we were intimate, I would wear something more alluring. He didn't seem to mind the tight fabric pressed over my chest and lifted that up next.

I pulled myself closer to him, trying to hide my naked chest against his. He sighed and closed his eyes, leaning his head down to kiss my exposed shoulder.

His arms encased me.

We continued to kiss, fingers grazing skin, legs tangled, hair ruffled.

He laid me down on the bed, sliding himself off the edge. I lifted my head and gently bit my bottom lip, watching him. He was like a work of art as he undid the buckle of his belt, sliding it off as he looked in my eyes. His pants slid down his legs, and he kicked them off with his feet.

The only thing covering him was his boxers, and soon I was left in the same position. My thin, spandex pants were ripped from my body, threads snapping as he stretched them. I silently giggled as he growled, annoyed with the fabric.

His eyes met my laughing ones, and he smiled lustfully. His hands moved with him as he took his place on top of me once again. His fingers found their way beneath my underwear, gently stroking the fire that was burning. I gasped and pushed myself closer to him.

The evening light flooded through the window, hitting Theo's eyes and lips. He was a painting, stuck forever in my mind, that orange glow around such crystal eyes.

His fingers found their way inside of me, stretching me. I had never known such a feeling, and I felt my eyebrows raise in surprise. Theo bent down and kissed my forehead. My legs practically slithered around him.

Soon, I was a shaking, mumbling mess of anticipation. He let me go, looking me in the eyes as he licked his fingers. I shuddered when I felt him move the last piece of clothing down the rest of the way.

He climbed back on the bed, and before he could guide me again, I turned over and pushed his back flat on the bed. He watched me curiously as I pressed kisses down his chest to the waistband of his boxers. I lifted them and gulped.

I promised myself when the time came, I was going to give myself to this fully, even if I embarrassed myself. I wanted to give Theo the same pleasures that he gave me.

This wasn't a one-sided affair.

As I tugged the boxers down, I tried to keep my eyes on his. He watched me as my eyes trailed from his to his chest and down below.

I was nervous, inexperienced, fingers shaking.

"It's okay," he whispered encouragingly. "You don't have to do anything you're not comfortable with."

"Just let me do this," I told him, smirking. I don't know where the sudden confidence came from, but I was determined to try.

"It's not going to hurt you," he joked. I wanted to retaliate, but I was too focused on keeping my newly found courage.

My fingers gently touched him, and Theo sucked in a breath, taking all the uncertainty out of the room. I continued to explore, all the while, Theo groaned and clenched his eyes, bucking his hips into my hold.

I lowered myself further and, in some moment of dauntless wanting, touched my tongue to him. The moan that erupted from his chest was enough to fill me for days. Without warning, Theo was lunging towards me, taking a fistful of hair in his hands to pull me to him. His kisses were frantic, hungry, needy.

His legs moved mine and pinned them down, capturing me body under his. Our hands flew over each other, no inquisition other than needing to touch as much as we could. He dipped closer to the bed and, in one upward motion, licked me and kneeled.

I shivered, my eyes closed until I felt him against me. My eyes sought his, and he didn't break our line.

Slowly, he began to push into me. He watched me for any sign of pain, and even the twitch of my lip was enough for him to pause and wait for me to adjust. He pushed my knees up and opened, holding them to control himself.

When he was in me fully, he lowered his head.

We kissed. Not frantic. No rush. Just one kiss, telling me he loved me.

He began to move faster and then slower when I lifted my hand to press against his thigh. Being filled so completely, physically, and emotionally by this man was more than my body could handle. Our bond hummed against our necks.

My breath was coming hotter and faster as he changed his pace. He moved and held himself up on his fists, our foreheads just barely touching. I moaned and panted, each noise fueling Theo's resolve. A shiver wove its way from my toes to my core, and I pulled my legs tighter around him.

He took my breast in his hand, and at the sensation of being stimulated so completely, I shattered against him. My scream dissipated to a breathless moan as my vision swirled with black. He watched as my body trembled against him, grabbing at his shoulders and chest for some kind of reprieve from the pleasure.

Not long after, he threw his head back in reckless abandon, hands clenching my waist, bruising the soft skin.

He left me and laid beside me, grabbing my face and guiding it to his. He kissed me again, quickly, and then pressed his lips on my forehead. The cool air in the room drifted over our bodies on top of the bed.

"Theo," I painted, noticing a drop of sweat slipping down his forehead.

"I love you so much," he vowed. My heart swelled, and his mark burned like a fading flame.

"I don't say this nearly enough," I admitted, curling myself further into his chest. "But I'm really glad you're my mate." I pressed a kiss to his chest, laying my head there as exhaustion and residual pleasure coursed through my veins. His hand wove into my hair and held me against him.

"You are my entire world, Margo."

DOUBLE VISION

Evening came, and hours passed, but we did not move. Naked and warm, curled up between Theo's arms, I allowed time to pass without any plan to leave. Theo didn't say anything as he played with my hair, messy and tangled from the sheets.

He chuckled suddenly, and I crooned my head up to look at him. He smiled down at me, eyes still laughing.

"What?" I asked nervously.

"I've been trying to fix your hair, and it just keeps getting bigger and bigger," he said. I moved and sat up, reaching up to touch my hair that was frizzy and sticking up. I groaned and tried to pull my fingers through it like a comb, but they got stuck after a few inches.

"This is all your fault," I teased, sliding off the bed to grab my brush from the bathroom. "If you hadn't been pulling my hair, this wouldn't've happened."

"Don't act like you didn't like it." His eyes narrowed,

grinning at me like a snake. I scoffed and set the brush down. I ran into the room quickly, jumping onto the bed near Theo, and sat in his lap.

"Yes, how could someone resist this?" I asked, pulling on the roots of his hair. He grunted and lifted his head to kiss me.

"Don't tease me, little one," he breathed hoarsely. I giggled and climbed off his lap.

"Come on, let's go make something to eat."

He followed me reluctantly, groaning the entire time about how we should have stayed in bed.

"Can't we eat this in bed?" he grumbled.

"No, you're going to get crumbs everywhere." He rolled his eyes and continued shoveling slices of pizza in his mouth.

The phone in his office began ringing loudly, startling us both. Theo pushed the last piece of crust into his mouth, brushed his hands off, and jogged into the other room. I turned around on my stool and watched him answer the phone, smiling warmly when the voice on the other end answered him.

He sat on the corner of his desk, rubbing his hand over the stubble on his chin. He looked up and caught me watching him through the doorway; he smiled gently and looked down as if he were embarrassed.

It wasn't until I shifted that I felt the attraction to Theo like he described. Now every inch of him attracted me, like a siren song luring me to his ocean.

He took the phone away from his ear, pressed it to his chest, and motioned for me to come into the room.

"Do you know a woman named Saskia?" he asked as I was walking toward him. I shook my head, no, and my eyebrows were tugging together in confusion. He nodded and lifted the phone to his ear again. "No, she doesn't know either."

I sat and listened to the rest of his call, wondering who

Saskia was and why Theo looked so concerned. Hung up and ran his hand through his hair.

"Who's Saskia?" I bombarded him curiously.

"I don't really know." He slumped against the desk, brushing his leg against mine. "The Alpha from the Audacia Pack just called me. Felix, he's Joella's mate, he said something about a woman named Saskia who was on the edge of their territory asking for refuge, but she wouldn't say what she needed refuge from. Apparently, the pack next to them heard the same when she tried to pass through their territory."

"Maybe she's just scared," I offered. I felt bad for the woman; this world wasn't always an easy one to live in for a woman.

"Possibly, but I have to look into it. If there's something in her pack that made her run, then I need to figure out what it is."

"Well, can't you do that tomorrow?" My hand drifted up to his leg, where it touched mine. Childishly, I walked two fingers up his pants, drifting over his lap. He shuttered and blinked his eyes slowly.

"What did you have in mind, little one?" His voice was husky, he already knew what I was suggesting, but he wanted to hear me say it.

"I thought maybe this time we could try it in that giant shower of yours." Theo grabbed my wrist and dragged me behind him excitedly, pulling me up the stairs and into the bathroom.

I giggled while pulling his shirt off my body. He struggled to get his pants off around his ankles.

We stumbled into the shower, slipping into each other.

❋ ❋ ❋

Theo's mother called in the evening, wondering what our plans were for the rest of the week. She insisted on spending time with her family after all the chaos, making it known that she would be crushed if we couldn't come. The next day we woke up in the late morning and headed over to the pack-house.

"Oh my gosh," Sloane gasped. I stopped walking towards her and glanced at Theo beside me. He huffed a laugh and looked at his mother, confused. "You two have mated."

My face erupted in a dark blush, and I wanted nothing more than to crawl under the table.

"Aye, there you go, man," Reese hooted, strolling into the room with a cold beer, cracking the tab.

"Reese shut your mouth right now and apologize," Sloane scolded, narrowing her eyes.

Reese looked down in fake remorse. "So sorry," he said placatingly, winking at me, bumping his fist to Theo's shoulder as he walked past. Theo ignored him and greeted his mother with a hug and kiss on her cheek. Sloane pushed him away after a moment and rushed to hug me.

"So, any grandbabies in our future?" she squealed. I shook my head. I knew wolves couldn't get pregnant unless they were in heat. She slumped and nodded understandingly.

"It'll happen in time, mom," Theo assured her.

"You really want a bunch of little Theo's running around here, sis?" Reese asked, face scrunching up at the thought.

"Better than a bunch of little Reese's." I grinned widely.

"You know, I don't like you as a wolf, you're meaner this way." Reese looked down, distraught, and took another gulp of his beer.

"I think you don't like that she laid you out flat on your

ass during training," Eli noted from his spot on the doorframe. Theo told me he had already forgiven Eli for what happened during the battle, but I don't think Eli was so sure.

"You probably don't like that she calls you on your shit now either," Gabriel grinned from behind Eli, shoving his shoulder, so he was forced to walk in.

"Well, I just adore Margo. So, I'm sorry, son, but it looks like you need to grow up a little and get over yourself," Sloane said fiercely. Reese chuckled and finished off his drink.

"I'm just kidding," he told Sloane. "See, I like Margo. We have this love-hate relationship." He came and wrapped his arm around my shoulder, grinning wildly.

"It's hard to tell where the hate ends, and the love begins, *bro*," I teased back, shoving two fingers into the side of his stomach. He jumped back and put a hand on his side, protecting himself from me.

"Not that I don't enjoy all of your company, but is there a reason we're all here?" Gabriel asked. Sloane whipped her head to the side and glowered.

"I just wanted to have my family all together, is that so much to ask?" she said with a warning in her voice. Gabriel shook his head, not fighting her. "I feel like I never see you all anymore, what has been happening in your lives, come, tell me."

We all reluctantly settled into the chairs and couches in Sloane's living room. I glanced at Eli, who was looking at me, wondering what we were supposed to talk about.

"Alright, so let's talk." She grinned. "Theo and Margo are completely mated now; I could smell it the second they walked in."

"We don't need to talk about that," I rushed out, fiddling awkwardly with my hands.

"What would you like to talk about then?" Reese said, eagerly waiting for me to speak.

"We could talk about how you hooked up with January Evers in the pantry during the last pack meeting," Eli suggested, smiling wickedly.

Gabriel growled lowly. "That's where you went?" Reese smiled sheepishly and scratched the back of his head.

"I needed something to amuse me, that meeting went on forever and ever," he droned, faking falling asleep to solidify his excuse.

"You're the Beta of this pack, Reese. You need to start taking more responsibility for your actions."

Reese rested his head on his fist in boredom, mimicking Gabriel's never-ending speech with his other hand like a puppet. Gabriel stopped and smacked Reese's hand.

"Boys," Sloane called. "This is not the time for all your pack nonsense."

"Nonsense?" Gabriel nearly growled. "Mother, you were Luna of this pack for nearly twenty-six years, and you think this is nonsense?"

"Don't talk down to me Gabriel, I know how this pack works better than all of you combined. I'm tired of you speaking to everyone like you're the only important one in the room. Rush would never want you to use your power this way." Gabriel lowered his eyes at the mention of his father. "I just wanted one nice afternoon with my family."

"And that's what you'll get," Eli insisted, urging the rest of us with his pitying eyes.

"Of course," Reese murmured. Theo and I nodded our heads.

"Alright, so tell me what has been going on with you all."

"Well, I passed the written test to be a Pack Warrior," Eli

said softly, fighting the proud smile on his face.

"That's amazing honey, I'm so proud of you," Sloane gushed. Eli shrugged his narrow shoulders, and I wondered how he would ever pass the physical portion of the test. He wasn't small by any standard, but he was lanky and still covered in his lean, boyish muscle. He wouldn't stand a chance against the hulking Warriors who guarded Valkyrie pack land.

"I know I've still got a lot of work to do, but at least I'm making an effort," he said to spite Reese. Reese rolled his eyes and scoffed.

"Enough about Reese," Theo declared. "What's been going on with you, Gabe, apart from Alpha business." Gabriel looked deep in thought for a few moments, deciphering the parts of his life we wanted to hear.

"Well, um," he stammered. The usual fluid confidence from his voice was lost. "I met a woman last week." Sloane perked up and leaned towards him.

"A woman?" The bewilderment in her voice was almost rude.

"Yes, a woman, mother. She wasn't my mate, but I don't know. I'm twenty-eight. I'm beginning to think I'm never going to meet my mate."

Theo was instantly offended, opening his arms in a display, shouting, "What am I, roadkill? I was twenty-nine when I met Margo."

"You never thought you'd meet your mate either, Theo. In fact, weren't you thinking of asking Albia-" he was cut short by Theo's murderous gaze.

"Thinking of asking Albia what?" I voiced, looking between Theo and Gabriel.

"Nothing," Theo assured me.

"He was thinking of asking her to step in," Reese said in annoyance. He got up and grabbed another beer from the table.

"Step in? You mean like step in as your mate?"

"Margo, it was before I met you," Theo said regretfully.

"We can talk about it later," I whispered, lowering my head.

The room fell silent for a few awkward moments.

"So, what was this woman's name?" Sloane said slowly in the silence.

"Saskia."

ON THE RUN

"Saskia?" Theo asked to clarify.

"Yes, Saskia," Gabriel answered, his lip tugged upward as he looked down.

"I just got a call about a 'Saskia,' apparently she was looking for refuge in another pack. Wouldn't say what she was running from."

"Is she okay?" Gabriel asked quickly. Theo's head tilted to the side peculiarly.

"Why don't you tell me," he challenged.

"She left here almost a week ago now, she was visiting here with some other women. They were traveling to different packs hoping to meet their mates, but Saskia was the only one that crossed our border. They were unharmed when they left," he assured Theo, fighting back the dominance that wanted to take over.

I shrunk back on the loveseat. Eli glanced at me, pursing his lips. Somehow every gathering ended in a show of dominance one way or another.

"I'm sure Gabriel treated them with nothing but respect," I said, suspiciously looking at Theo, wondering what he was trying to accuse his brother of.

"I don't doubt that," he said, not looking at me. "But it's my job to figure out what happened to her. Felix said she was terrified and crying."

"Well then something happened between here and the Audacia Pack," Gabriel spat, his upper lip curling.

"Yeah, well, we'll see," Theo promised, standing up. "It was great seeing you all."

Theo walked past his family and out of the room. I sat still, stunned, and slightly angry at Theo's behavior. His family turned and looked at me for an explanation.

"Apparently, that was my cue to leave," I said jokingly.

"He's probably just stressed, dear," Sloane told me lovingly. "You should have seen him when he was an Alpha, he was that uptight all the time. This is a much better job for him."

I'm sure Margo also had some part to play in that," Eli yipped from behind Sloane.

"We'll see you soon, Margo. Take care of my son, won't you?"

I nodded and hugged her close to me. I waved goodbye to Gabriel and Reese as I skittered past Eli, patting his shoulder as I left.

My shoes clicked against the linoleum floors, and there was no other sound to drown it out. I tried to remember the way back down to the foyer, but even Sloane's wing in the packhouse was massive and winding.

I eventually found Theo standing in the ballroom, hands tucked in his pockets, staring out a large window.

"Are you okay?" I asked softly behind him. My hand reached up and touched the space between his shoulders. He flinched.

"I'm fine, Margo," he said blandly. I moved around him; his answer didn't satisfy me.

"What's wrong? You were so tense in there, and then you just got up and left." He looked down like a little boy and avoided eye contact with me.

"I just miss it, I guess," he confessed.

"Miss what?"

"Being an Alpha." I nodded my head understandingly. "I love what I do now, but I just miss being in charge of a pack. This used to be mine. I knew everybody in my pack, I kept them safe, they trusted me. The Alpha blood inside of me just likes to oversee people."

"Theo, you're in charge of all the other Alphas," I pointed out, reaching my right up to cup his cheek. "That's the most important thing. You keep everyone else safe."

"Most Alpha's can take care of themselves. I'm needed for a few days, and then they're back on their own. I know it's silly, I just miss it sometimes," he smiled fondly, the gesture not fully reaching his eyes.

I stepped closer. "It's not silly at all."

"Do you want to go home?" He asked, hand reaching out to rest on my waist.

"Sure, do we have to drive, though?" I asked hesitantly.

"No," Theo drawled, confused.

"I thought maybe we could run back, you know, shift." I gulped and looking down at our feet.

"You want to run back?" he asked unbelievingly. "Because you'll lose this race, little one."

My head snapped up. He was laughing silently, smirking.

"I may be new, but I'm still faster than you." He took my challenge, and we walked outside to the front of the house. He let go of my hand and bent down in a sprinting pose. I followed him and waited cautiously for him to move. He shifted in half a second and took off into the woods.

It took me a moment longer to shift and start running. Being on four feet instead of two still felt strange, like my body was off-center. I didn't let that stop me though and trailed after Theo's large wolf.

He wasn't running as fast as he could, obviously waiting for me to catch up. I scoffed, he thought I needed a head start?

As I gained on him, I bit the end of his tail playfully. He whined and skidded in the dirt, trying to fight back. I outmaneuvered him and ran ahead.

He growled and ran next to me, brushing his fur against mine. I waited for him to push me out of the way, but he stayed next to me.

We stopped in front of the house, panting, leaning against each other. After we shifted, we went inside the house, not bothering to cover ourselves from each other.

"What did your brother mean when he said you were going to ask Albia to step in?" I asked insecurely. We had moved up to lay in our bed on top of the covers.

"I was hoping you'd forget about that," he evaded, jokingly. When I didn't laugh, he let out a deep breath and put his hand over his face. "I never thought I would meet you, Margo. Dorian's pack was my last stop, and I'd pretty much given up hope before that. It was just an idea, really."

"But why Albia?" I couldn't hide the jealousy in my tone.

"Because she was a nice girl, and I knew we got along. I mean, she's pretty, but I wasn't attracted to her," he offered.

His thumb gently moved across the skin on my hip, little circles, soothing me.

"I get it," I said even though I didn't. For most of my life, I thought I would end up alone. A small part of me thought I would eventually be with Caddy, but I knew he would meet his mate, and I would be left behind.

He turned on his side, resting his forehead on mine. His eyes still held a sad glint from earlier, but he hid it well.

"I know you said you missed being in charge of something earlier," I muttered, gazing up at him through my lashes. He smiled a little. I offered him my wrists slyly. "I'll let you be in charge of me for a little while."

He laughed loudly, boomingly, and threw his head back. When he came back to look at me, he noticed I was serious. His happy exterior quickly melted into groaning seduction.

"You really want me to be in charge of this little body of yours?" he asked, voice heavy. His left hand trailed down the curve of my stomach and hips, drawing little shapes on the beginning curve of my backside.

"Yes. Only if you reciprocate the favor later," I smirked. He tried not to chuckle but leaned in and kissed me nonetheless.

* * *

When Theo finally released me, I wrapped myself up in a sheet and waddled down the steps for a glass of water. I held the sheet up to my skin, but it was so large I kept tripping on the ends of it.

"Be careful," I head Theo yell as I made a loud thud from missing a step.

"Thanks," I said sarcastically. I made it down to the sink

and filled up one glass of water and drank it all in one large swoop.

Theo's office phone started ringing loudly as I set the glass down.

"Can you get that? I'm in the bathroom?" his loud voice came from upstairs. I nodded before I realized he couldn't see me.

I slumped down into the large office chair and reached over his desk for the phone.

"Hello, this is Margo," I answered.

"Margo?" a woman's voice said, surprised. "It's Joella."

"Hi," I said confused. "Is everything okay? Not that I wouldn't like to talk to you, but I'm sure you need to talk to Theo, I'll go get him." I rambled on.

"No, actually, you're the person I wanted to talk to," she paused, and I waited for her to continue. "I just can't get that woman out of my mind. That Saskia, something just sits wrong with me. She needs help, and she ran off before we could offer her any."

"She just left?"

"Felix kept asking her what she was running from, and she wouldn't say. He wasn't comfortable letting her in our territory without knowing what was after her. When she came onto our lands, she came in from the south, and one of our wolves said he caught her scent on the north end, so we think that's where she went, but Margo...I can't get her out of my head." I scribbled that down on a piece of paper.

"She's headed towards Caddy's pack," I noted aloud.

"Cadence? Your friend? Maybe he could help her, or at least keep her there until Theo can question her, and you both can help her," she suggested. Joella sounded worried and exhausted.

"I'll give him a call, thank you, Joella. I can't imagine how worried you are."

"Just, please find her. I don't know what kind of trouble she's in, but she might end up seeking help from the wrong kind of people. You and Theo need to find her," she told me desperately.

"We will," I agreed, halfway certain we could never find a lone wolf running across the continent.

"We'll talk soon, okay?" she promised.

As I hung up, I noticed Theo standing near the door. I smiled nervously.

"How would you feel about going on a scavenger hunt?"

INTERRUPTION

My legs were shaking, knees clacking together, as Theo drove us towards Caddy's pack. I bit my lip to hide my excitement and stared out the window. Theo's warm hand reached over and landed on my thigh just above my knee.

"You a little excited there?" he teased. I snickered, and my cheeks blushed a faint pink.

"I just haven't seen Caddy since the fight, and he left so quickly after." Theo nodded. We hardly spoke about the fight or anything about that day.

"Well then, this will be a nice visit." He bobbed his head. I tucked my hand under his on my knee and fiddled with the stereo until the cd player turned on.

The drive was long. The last time we had driven this far was when Theo first took me from the pack. I never realized how long it was, probably because I was trying not to look up from my muddy shoes.

We stopped a few times along the way, for the bathroom, and for our growing appetites. By the time we reached Caddy's pack, it was the middle of the night.

Caddy stood at the entrance to the packhouse with Bodhi and his mother behind him. I threw the door open in excitement and tried to stop myself from running over to them.

Caddy's boyish laughter greeted me, and I launched myself into his open arms. I let go after I heard a soft but palpable growl from Bodhi. I looked down sheepishly and searched for Theo, who was approaching with our bags.

"Good to see you again." Caddy stuck out his arm. Theo set a bag down and clasped arms with him.

"Likewise," he said formally.

"Come on in," Caddy invited us, and we walked into the packhouse I grew up in. "Margo, you remember my mother and Jax; he's the Beta now."

I peeked at Jax through the corner of my eye. He was one of the bigger wolves, always glaring at me when I walked around the house. I didn't know how to talk to him now that I was a wolf, too.

"Margo," Mrs. Delphine bit out painfully. "Nice to see you, dear. And your mate, as well." Caddy had mentioned she blamed Theo and me for the death of her brother, Dorian. Apart from that, Mrs. Delphine never held much room in her heart for me.

"Thank you, Mrs. Delphine," I said with a fond smile.

"We'll talk more in the morning, but for now, I'll let you get settled in." Caddy left us at the door of a guest room, pinching my arm as he walked toward his mate. I grimaced and rubbed where he pinched me.

I opened the door to the large room. It was nothing like my old room, that was another floor up. I set my bag on the bed and fished out some pajamas.

Theo found the bathroom and retrieved our tooth-brushes. We both collapsed on the soft bed from exhaustion.

"Do you think Saskia is in any real trouble?" I wondered out loud. I felt Theo shrug.

"She's been running from pack to pack, no one does that if they're just looking for their mate. The correct protocol would be to inform all the packs you're planning on visiting and wait for consent from the Alpha. And what about the sup-posed women she was traveling with; where are they?"

I nodded and began thinking of dozens of possibilities.

"Theo, what if she already knows who her mate is, but she doesn't know where he is," I pondered. "She said she was looking for her mate, not that she hadn't found him yet. And maybe the other women found their mates and are with them."

Theo rolled onto his side and settled his hand in the crook of my neck.

"How'd you get to be so smart?" His tone was teasing, but also complimenting me at the same time. I blushed and pursed my lips.

"It's a natural gift." I smirked, leaning into the warmth of his hand.

"I guess we'll see tomorrow. If our calculations are cor-rect, she should be passing through mid-morning."

"Well then, we better get some sleep," I concluded. He agreed though we stayed up for a while talking. Each time my eyes closed, he tickled the back of my neck, and my eyes shot open again.

"Go to sleep," I said through gritted teeth. I had turned away from Theo, scooting to the edge of the bed, trying to fall asleep.

"No, I like bugging you," he said chuckling. His hands

pulled the warm covers off my body. I held onto them and was pulled upward.

"Come on, Theo, please?" I begged, looking at him with sad eyes.

"Fine," he grumbled and released the covers. I curled up in them once again, and Theo curled around me.

* * *

Caddy knocked on our door promptly at 8 am; he had always been a morning person.

"Wake up, sleepyheads! It's time for breakfast!" His fist pounded on the door. Theo sat up happily while I remained hidden under the thick quilt.

"Margo," he laughed, peeling back the sheets.

"No," I whimpered as the cold hit my skin. I hated being woken up early, even if it was by Theo. The covers were ripped from my body, and I curled into Theo's warmth to shelter myself. His arm wrapped around my waist and pulled me to him tightly. "Don't let go."

"Margo, we have to get ready. Saskia will be here soon. Don't you want to see if any of your theories are true?" He nudged me. I frowned deeply but nodded.

"You're right," I sighed. "You usually are."

He looked at me surprised and furrowed his eyebrows. "You're unusually agreeable this morning."

"I'm an agreeable person," I whined, mouth gaping in offense.

"Margo, you are many things, but compliant and agreeable are not on that list," he chortled, grabbing a shirt from his bag. I continued to stare at him with my mouth open, trying to come up with a retort. He walked past me to get to the bathroom but stopped and held my chin for a moment and muttered, "You should close your mouth, or I'll put it to good use," before leaving me.

"Theo!" I yelped, banging on the bathroom door that he locked. "Open this door right now!"

"There's the Margo I know and love," he said loudly from the other side of the door.

"You're going to get it one of these days," I vowed when he finally opened the door.

"I can get *it* anytime I want, mate."

I hit him with my hip as he walked past. "Is that all you think about?" I asked. He shrugged, pulling his shirt over his head.

"Most of the time, yeah."

I chuckled and looked down, shaking my head.

We met Caddy downstairs, seated with Bodhi, Jax, and a few other wolves I remembered vaguely.

"Hey, Margo," Caddy smiled. I smiled back and then stopped as Bodhi glared at me. "Bodhi quit it."

His voice wasn't the same loving tone I remembered him using the first time they met. I froze in confusion but decided to leave it alone until I could talk to Caddy.

"I'm going to eat in my room," Bodhi grumbled, picking up her plate. "Or would his highness like to protest," she spat bitterly.

"You can go wherever you like; I'm not keeping you here," he answered, raising his eyebrows.

Bodhi grumbled and stormed past Theo, barely missing the collision of their arms. No one said anything as the awkward silence in the room resonated.

"Sit down, guys," Caddy jutted out, smiling nervously.

We sat and spooned some food onto our plates. I kicked Caddy's foot under the table, and he looked up.

"Later, okay?" I whispered. He nodded, looking down at his food again.

"Alpha," a Warrior called from the end of the table. "Kendrick just mind-linked me; he said yours was blocked. They caught the scent of a female wolf not far from our borders."

"There's our girl. She's fast," Caddy noted, pushing his seat away from the table. We all pushed our seats back, breakfast forgotten, and followed Caddy as he walked towards the back of the packhouse.

We filed out the back door and walked quickly to the tree line 500 feet ahead. The packhouse was located along the southern border or the grounds; we weren't far from the edge.

"Alpha," the Warrior called again. "They have the girl; they've cornered her a quarter-mile south-west."

We started off in that direction, quickening our steps when we heard the feral growl of a wolf. The backs of the warriors were all we could see as we approached. Caddy touched the shoulder of one, and he stepped back, giving us access to the girl.

She wasn't a girl though, she was a woman, probably a few years older than Theo. She bared her teeth as she moved around, trying to keep her eyes on all the warriors.

I lifted Theo's arm over my head and moved under him. The girl had tan, glowing, skin, and straight, brown hair that swished around her waist as she circled.

She noticed us and stood up straight, taking us all in.

"Saskia?" Caddy addressed her firmly. She didn't even flinch at his voice; her eyes were fixed on me.

A small, meaningless smile can onto her lips, just under

her sharp, thin nose. "I was wondering when you'd show up."

RANSOM

Everyone seemed to stop what they were doing to look at me, confusion and suspicion filling their eyes.

"Me?" I asked incredulously.

"Margo, right?" She smiled, tilting her head to the side.

"Yes, and who are you?"

She smiled, mouth open, revealing a perfect set of white teeth. "I'm Saskia Rechovnik," she said proudly. "You're a wolf now."

An unsettling cramp started in my stomach. I leaned back an inch until I felt Theo's presence, calming me.

"How do you know her?" Theo asked. Saskia lifted her eyes and looked at him, her lip twitching.

"How do I know any of you, Theodore? It's kind of an urban legend where I'm from. A small human girl is mated to an Enforcer, and they kill hundreds of wolves to save her humanity, only for her to lose it the same day."

"I don't appreciate you speaking about my mate like this," Theo growled, pushing an arm over my chest to move me back.

"Speaking like what?" She smirked. "The truth? Oh, you Weston's really do have a problem with the truth, don't you?"

"What is your business with my brother?"

She scoffed, hair falling over her slender shoulders as her body shrugged forward. "He told you, did he? I don't want anything with your brother, he was simply something to mind my time while I was traveling. Although, he was very curious about my thoughts on him choosing a mate to step in."

"Why would he do that?" Theo asked through gritted teeth.

"Because he's never going to find his mate."

"Oh, and you're an expert?" Theo asked, smiling in humor.

"You don't know me, Theodore. You don't know what I'm capable of."

"Why don't you tell me," Theo offered, gesturing a hand. "You've been running onto different pack lands claiming to be looking for your mate or needing refuge, which story is it going to be this time?"

She pouted slightly, looking down like she wasn't surprised he knew. "I was helping my friends search for their mates," she paused and gulped. "But I ran into a little trouble along the way."

"And where are these other friends of yours?"

"I want to talk to her." Saskia pointed a fragile finger at me and closed her mouth.

"Why do you need to speak to my mate?"

"Because this is a sensitive topic," she pressed, glaring at Theo. "And in case you haven't noticed, she is the only other woman here. I'd feel more comfortable talking to her."

"You aren't-"

"That's fine," I interrupted Theo. He gave me a stern look, but I nodded my head, telling him I could do this.

"Fine," he bit.

"Let's go back to the packhouse, and we can discuss this further," Caddy suggested. Theo nodded in agreement and placed a hand on my shoulder. Caddy led us back to the packhouse and into the only conference room towards the east end of the house. Caddy sat at the head of the table, Theo and I to one side, and Saskia settled on the other.

"What were the names of the other girls you were traveling with?" Theo reached over and pulled a thick pad of paper from the end of the table.

"That's classified, Theodore," Saskia said, placing both hands on the table in a folded pile.

"Why is that?"

"Because." She smiled. "I don't want to tell you."

Theo set the pen on top of the pad of paper and stared at Saskia. "Why don't you want to tell me? We can help them if they are in trouble."

"You don't help anyone in trouble."

Theo's calm façade shifted into one of offense, and he took three deep breaths before continuing. "That is my job, Saskia, to help people. If you or these girls are in danger or some sort of trouble, I can help you."

"Just like you helped Reed Porter?"

The name sent shocks of ice into my bones.

"What do you know of Reed Porter?"

Saskia chuckled and unfolded her hands, placing them on her lap. "I know a lot more than you might think. I know that you murder people in cold blood and call it self-defense."

"Reed Porter declared war and died defending his beliefs," Theo claimed.

"Reed Porter was fighting for what he believed in, and his Enforcer did not facilitate a safe compromise. He contacted you in hopes you could help him, and you denied him that right."

"If that's what you think, then so be it." Theo nodded noncommittally. "Now, what are the names of the women you were traveling with?"

"I won't tell you."

"Then you won't leave."

"I won't tell you," she repeated. "I'll tell her."

Theo and Caddy's heads snapped to me as my eyes grew wider, and my mouth parted, ready to decline the offer.

"Fine," Caddy spoke quickly. Theo angrily glared at him. "We will be right outside the door. If you need anything, just say so." Caddy stood up and waited for Theo to do the same. Theo rose uneasily in his chair and touched my shoulder before walking out of the room.

Saskia released a nervous laugh and tucked some hair behind her ear.

"So, what are the names?" I asked, trying to have the same confidence as Theo.

She smiled at my attempt and shook her head. "You don't have to be like them, you know?"

"Like what?"

"Ridiculously masculine and straight to the point." Her head tilted right. "I like that you're softer."

"I'm not soft."

Her eyes didn't believe the words I said, but she nodded, nevertheless. "You remind me of me many years ago."

"In what way?" I was curious to see if she would open up to me now that Theo and Caddy were on the other side of the door.

"Skittish," she said, pursing her lips to one side. "Skittish and looking to man to guide you."

"What makes you think I'm skittish?"

"You flinch every time I move my hands." She laughed under her breath. "You're scared. Of me. Of Reed Porter; when I mentioned his name, the blood drained from your face. But you're trying to put on some persona of cockiness, and it just doesn't suit you."

"I can't imagine you'd ever be skittish," I told her.

Her eyebrow lifted, and her eyes melted away to another time and place. "I was quiet when I was younger," she said nodding, recalling some memory. "My parents, they didn't give me much room to speak. They were so tough on my brother and I. They would make us train for eight hours a day and then we'd be sent to our rooms for the rest of the night. They wanted my brother to become a pack warrior when he got older, and they wanted me to be strong enough for an Alpha to mate me."

"They didn't want you to find your mate?" The notion was foreign to me. All the wolves I'd ever met held mates sacred above all else; I couldn't imagine parents trying to ignore that sanctity.

"My parents were Betas before my brother and I were born. My father made some mistakes, but they were trying to make up for it. They hoped with my brother in a warrior position and me mated to an Alpha or Beta, it would put them in a better position in our pack." She allowed a false grin to cover the wobble of her lips. "But I met my mate before they could find an unmated Alpha and I was marked the same day. He wasn't an Alpha, he was a Warrior in our pack, which they were sated with. They pushed my brother to become a Warrior as well, telling him to be like my mate.

"He died the week he became a Warrior. They both did. An Alpha ordered the kill, and they were gone," she grimaced, gritting her jaw. "It wasn't their fault, and the Alpha just killed them without asking him any questions. They were both innocent."

"I'm so sorry," I said. My chest became heavy as I watched her eyes well with tears.

"It took a while for me to get over it." Her falsetto grin flashed on her lips once again, and all the negative emotion filtered out of her façade. "And I wanted to do something with my pain and my anger, so I helped some women find their mates."

"They why were you running?"

"Because right as another girl joined us, we were attacked."

"By who?" she sighed at my question.

"Some men I owe money to."

"Who are they?" I was hoping if I spoke loud enough, Theo and Caddy would be able to hear on the other side of the door.

"Men I hired to look into the death of my mate and my brother." She placed her elbows on the table and let her forehead fall into her hands. "I didn't have the finances to pay them at the time, and I told them I would pay them back when I had the money. As you can imagine, they didn't like that answer very much. So, they took the girls. And they're holding them until I can come up with the money."

"Do you have the money?"

She laughed. "Do I look like I have the money, Margo?"

"So, what do you plan to do?"

"That's where I need your help," she said seriously. I flinched back slightly in my seat. "I need you to find those girls and bring them to me."

"Why?"

"Because I was the one that got them into this mess, and I need to make sure their plans come to fruition. I know what it's like to love a mate, and I just want these girls and their mates to experience that, too. I promised them."

"Why didn't you want to tell Theo about this?"

Her eyes turned darker at the sound of his name. "Because I don't trust him. But I trust you. You're like me, I can see that in you, you'll do the right thing."

"I'll need Theo's help to find them. I can't do it on my own," I warned her.

"As long as you return those girls safely to me, I don't care if you need every wolf on this continent to help you."

"Fine," I leered apprehensively, grabbing the pad of paper and pen Theo had left in the room. "Where are they?"

"They're in a cabin in the south end of the mountains. I don't know any other way of directing you there. But five men are keeping them captive."

"Okay, and who are these women? What are their names?"

"Olympia Trent, Pilar Aisles, and Verona Avery." She didn't make eye contact with me as she jutted out the names. I scribble the names down quickly and set the pen aside.

"That's really helpful, Saskia," I praised her. "We'll do everything we can to find your friends."

"They aren't my friends," she clarified, looking at me with her caramel eyes through a mess of dark eyelashes. "If anything happens to them, this on you now."

Her words made me unsettled like she was loading a gun on the table in front of me. I nodded and folded the paper in half, rising from my seat slowly. She stayed sitting, looking over at the table angrily.

I opened the door and walked towards Theo and Caddy, handing them the sheet of paper.

"It's a long story that I'll explain on the way. But we need to go to the south end of the mountains to save these girls from a group of men who are holding them hostage."

"Well, that's not how I thought this conversation would go," Caddy admitted, rubbing his thumb over his eyebrow.

"You're brilliant." Theo wrapped his arms around my midsection and hauled me up. Our chests pressed together, and I buried my head in his neck.

Theo set me down, and I steadied myself on my feet. The small smile I had didn't reach my eyes, and Theo asked what was wrong. "Nothing," I said softly, reaching up to rub his cheek with my thumb. His stubble tickled my skin. "I just-"

My words were interrupted by a shattering sound from the conference room. I stilled as Caddy tried to throw the door open, only to be blocked by furniture stacked up on the other side of the door. With Theo's help, they pushed the door open completely and saw the remnants of a shattered window.

"She's gone. She's fucking gone."

IN THE BRUSH

"Caddy, sit down," I urged, pushing a chair out from the table with my foot, motioning for him to sit. He slammed the chair back in roughly and hit the table with his fist.

"Caddy." Theo's voice cut through the room. Bodhi had peeked through the door, watching Caddy with cautious eyes.

"What, Theo?" he practically shouted, throwing his arms into the air.

"You need to calm down," Theo said softer, eyes motioning to the seat that I had pushed out previously.

"I need to calm down?" He laughed. His eyes were wild. "I don't need to calm down. I need to get a grip on my pack. I don't know what I'm doing," he gritted out, enunciating each word individually. "And it's not like *she* cares enough to help."

Bodhi threw the door closed as she left. Caddy leaned over the table, exhausted, and his head dropped down to his chest.

"I don't know what I'm doing," he said again.

"You're doing the best you can," I tried to soothe him.

"Well, it's not good enough." He stood up and turned his back to us. I looked at Theo.

"He just needs time to adjust," Theo promised me quietly, setting his band on my knee that was bouncing rapidly. I folded over and set my forehead on his shoulder.

"I want to help him."

Theo placed his hand under my chin and pulled me up. His lips pressed against my forehead, and then his forehead touched mine.

"I know you do, but the most you can do is just be there for him. Every Alpha has a hard time fitting himself in with his role and the expectations that come along with it. He's doing a fine job."

"You should tell him that."

"He won't hear it from me right now." I knew Theo was right. "You should talk to him. I'll leave you two alone."

Theo got up and snuck out the door before Caddy noticed. I stood up and walked over to Caddy, placing my hand flat on his back. He flinched and then settled himself.

"Caddy, what's going on?"

"Everyone thinks I'm a joke," he said sadly, gazing out the window to the front grounds. "Even my own mother doesn't believe that I can be an Alpha."

"Caddy, you're already a great Alpha, despite what anyone may think."

"Jax rolls his eyes at everything I tell him," he chuckled, tucking his thumbs into the pockets of his jeans. "My warriors hesitate when I give them an order."

"It takes time to build that trust up." I removed my hand from his shoulder.

"When my uncle became Alpha, he had control over this pack almost immediately."

"Your uncle was also thirty when he took over for his father," I pointed out.

"My age shouldn't have anything to do with it. Everyone in this pack knew I would take over for Dorian one day, why should it matter if it was now or in another six years?"

I couldn't answer him. I didn't know what to say.

"What about Bodhi?" I asked, watching his eyes glaze over at the sound of her name.

"What about her?" he said indifferently.

"You two don't seem like you're on the best of terms."

"What gave it away?" he chuckled. He noticed I didn't laugh and then grew serious. "She and I got into a fight right after we got here. She wanted to be introduced to the pack as another Alpha, and I thought it was too dangerous for the pack to be introduced to another Alpha before they were used to the first one. She took that as me telling her she didn't have as much claim to be an Alpha as I did. It's been a power struggle ever since."

"Have you tried explaining to her what's been going on?"

"Multiple times, but as you can imagine, if it's not something Bodhi wants to hear..."

"She doesn't listen." I finished, nodding.

"I just don't know what to do."

"Just keep trying." He turned and looked down at me through his overgrown hair. "And get a haircut, no wonder Bodhi won't talk to you."

He laughed loudly and grabbed my shoulder to hug me. My face was squashed to his chest, cheeks smashed together.

"We need to find out what packs those girls are in," Caddy said as he released me.

"Already got it," Theo announced as he walked back into the conference room. He laid out a map of the packs surrounding us, pointing to which three packs the girls were from. They were from packs far west of us, leading all the way to Gabriel's pack.

Olympia was training to be a Pack Warrior, Pilar was a chef, and Verona was barely out of school. None of the women resided in the pack Saskia was from, nor did they have any similar characteristics. They were various ages, from nineteen to twenty-six, various skill levels, and interests.

It made no sense to me, which I voiced to Caddy and Theo. They ignored the inconsistency and tried to locate placed near the mountains where the girls could be held. Three places immediately came to mind.

They decided that in the morning, we would head down to the mountains to search the area. Caddy sent six warriors with us since he could not leave his pack but promised to help if needed.

I woke up to the sound of Theo packing our bags again, shoving things haphazardly inside. I yawned and rubbed my hand over my face.

He looked up and smiled at me, sending a flock of butterflies to my stomach.

We got back into Theo's car and started on the eight-hour trip down to the bottom of the mountain range. It was five hours before the mountains came into view, and every minute we drove closer, the more daunting they became.

"Have you ever seen the mountains?" Theo broke the silence.

"No," I said, face pressed against the glass in wonder. "I was never allowed to go, Caddy always said it was too dangerous for me."

"They are dangerous, I want you to stay close to me. I don't know anything about the wolves that took these girls."

I nearly rolled my eyes at the protectiveness in his voice. It was endearing, but also frustrating because I knew I could hold my own.

"I will," I agreed.

It was starting to get dark as we drove through the winding roads on the outside of the mountains. Theo had his headlights on, and along with the two other cars behind us, the dark woods and rocky terrain were illuminated. I stared out the window, hoping to see something through the trees.

It began to rain lightly, drizzling down the windows, and Theo slowed down to stay safe. I wiped my hand on the glass as it began to fog from my breath. Something moved in the brush, and I screamed for Theo to stop the car.

He pressed his foot on the break and put the car in park, looking over at me worriedly.

"What's wrong?" he asked frantically. I didn't answer him. I opened the car door and walked to the side of the road.

My hair clung to my face from the rain. I brushed it out of the way and steadied myself on the slippery mud.

"Margo, what are you doing? It's cold and rainy, come back in the car," Theo insisted, reaching for my hand that was stretched out to give me balance.

"You go back in the car, then," I said loudly over the pounding rain.

"Margo," he started again.

"Just...shush!"

He stayed nearby as I lowered myself further into the trees. It was hard to see with the rain and darkness. I crouched down, hoping to see better.

Something moved to my left, and I bolted over to the leaves that moved. I lifted them cautiously.

A hand twitched underneath them. I threw the branch out of the way and yelled for Theo to help me. We cleared the twigs and dirt off her and turned her onto her back.

She was a small girl, pale, with short blonde hair that was stained from the mud. She gasped for breath, the obvious trauma that her body was put through made it difficult. Theo held her head off the ground.

"Can you hear me?" I asked loudly, reaching over to press my hand on the girl's cheek. Her eyelids fluttered open and closed and then stayed open.

"Help them," she ground out, her raspy voice cutting through the air.

"Where are they?" Theo asked her. We huddled in closer to her, trying to share our body heat.

"North, about two miles." Her voice was weak, and her split lip wobbled terribly. "There's a cabin."

Theo carefully lifted her in his arms and brought her over to the cars. The Warriors from Caddy's pack were waiting outside their cars. Theo settled the girl into one of their cars and told one to stay with her. The others followed us as we shifted into our wolves and dove into the forest.

I trailed behind Theo closely, paws slightly squishing into the ground. There was a small cabin in front of us, lights off, no smoke from the chimney.

We slowed down as we got closer, listening to see how many people were inside. I counted three heartbeats. Either the girls were in there along with another man or the girls weren't there at all, both possibilities equally terrifying.

"*Around back,*" Theo said through our mind-link. We

snuck to the backside and found a window. Theo shifted back first, and the Warriors followed him. There were no clothes left on their bodies, but at that moment, it was the least of our concerns.

I shifted back, slipping slightly as I got my balance against the dirt. Theo stepped in front of me, hiding my body from the gaze of the Warriors.

"Margo, shift back," he ordered.

"Theo, you need me. Those girls are probably scared to death. What are they going to think when six, large, men burst in, and you tell them to come with you?"

He growled and bit his lip, trying not to admit I was right. "Fine, but you go in last, right before me." I nodded.

The Warriors shattered the window with one kick and leaped through the opening. Theo lifted me through since I wasn't tall enough to enter without cutting myself on the glass. He jumped in after me and immediately searched for the women.

A muffled cry came from the room next to us. Theo tried to open the door, but it was locked. He twisted the knob farther, causing the fixture to break, and threw the door open.

Two women were huddled in the corner; their hands were tied to a pole, and thick, black tape was over their mouths. I pushed past Theo and knelt next to them. After I untied their hands, they carefully peeled the tape off their mouths.

"Pilar? Olympia?" I searched their faces.

"How do you know our names?" one asked. She had tanned brown skin, long black hair, and pink lips. The other had darker skin, shorter black hair, and bright hazel eyes.

"Saskia," I said in explanation. The one with darker skin spat blood out of her mouth at the mention of her name.

"Tell me that bitch isn't here," she barked.

"No, she isn't." They relaxed visibly, sinking down. "Why?"

"Because I'm going to kill her the next time I see her."

THREE FOR THREE

The man that was in the cabin fled when he heard the glass break. Two of the warriors left to track the scent and the others stayed to help us transport the injured girls to the car. Olympia refused to let us help her, tearing herself out of our grasp.

Pilar's ankle was cracked and twisted, healing quickly from her wolf genes, but healing improperly. She had various bruises and lacerations covering her arms and abdomen. Olympia's arm was hanging weakly from her body, her shoulder stretched too far. The rest of her body was in the same condition as Pilar's, injured but treatable.

The girl in the car, Verona, was the worst of them. Her face was mangled, lip split, cheek busted open, eyes were swollen, and popping out of the socket. The rest of her body was as badly hurt as her face.

Verona remained lying across the backseat of the warriors' car. Pilar and Olympia sat in the back of our car, watching our surroundings like they expected someone to jump out.

I called Joella from Theo's phone; she picked up on the third ring.

"Hello?"

"Joella? It's Margo. I need your help."

"Anything. What is it?" she said fiercely.

"I need to bring three injured women to your pack, and I need your help to treat them."

"When will you be here?" she asked immediately.

"About thirty minutes," I guessed. We were already headed towards her pack.

"I'll be ready. I'll have Felix alert the borders. Bring them straight to the packhouse."

We hung up, and Theo sped up slightly as we got out of the mountains. Pilar was whimpering softly in the backseat, tears streaming silently down her face. Olympia was stone.

We entered the Audacia pack safely, pulling the cars up along the walkway near the entrance. Joella, Felix, and a few others rushed out to help us. They carried Verona into the building first, and Joella ran in after her. She was the one that needed the most attention.

Two Warriors assisted Pilar, limping up the few steps into the house. Theo attempted to help Olympia, but she jerked out of his arms and walked towards the door, determined. She held up arm close to her body, shaking with each step. When she nearly collapsed hallway there, she allowed Theo to put his arm around her waist.

I pushed my wet hair off my face and hurriedly jogged inside. Joella had a small triage set up in the main room. Three long tables had been brought in, draped with sheets, and equipped with medical supplies in red bags.

Joella rested her hands on Verona's stomach, closing her eyes. I moved to the other side of the table and watched Joella. She growled, and her eyes opened.

"I need you," she said. She grabbed my hands and placed them on Verona's stomach. "I need you to help me heal her."

"Jo, I don't know how," I rushed out.

"Just close your eyes and focus all of your energy on her. Think of healing her. Picture every cell in your body being transferred to hers. You're a Luna, too, Margo. I can't do this alone."

I closed my eyes and tried to concentrate on what Joella told me. I waited for something to happen and grunted when nothing did.

"Just relax. Focus." Joella snapped. I moved a strand of hair and placed the hand back on Verona's stomach. My hands started to tingle, and I cautiously opened one of my eyes to look at it. I shut my eyes again and imagined giving all my strength to Verona.

After a few minutes, I opened my eyes to see Joella checking Verona's body. Her skin wasn't as pale, and her breathing had evened out.

"She'll be fine," Joella said thankfully, grabbing a needle and some type of thread. She began to suture a gash along Verona's arm.

I backed away, looking for Theo, who was arguing with Olympia.

"I don't need any help," she said sternly, smiling despite her anger.

"Your shoulder is out of the socket, if you leave it to heal like that, you could lose function of your arm," Theo explained like he was talking to a child. Olympia smiled sarcastically.

"That seems like something I should worry about, huh?"

Joella brushed past me, grabbed Olympia's shoulder firmly from behind, and before she could protest, pulled her arm back into the socket.

Olympia screamed loudly, sending chills down my arms. Theo looked pleased and left her side.

"Are you alright?" I asked her, leaning over the table. She turned her head and glared.

"Do I look like I'm okay? If it wasn't for that bitch Saskia, I wouldn't even be in this position. Fucking witch woman."

"Witch?"

She grimaced, holding her shoulder tightly. "She came into our packs with scraps of fabric, claiming that they were from rogues who killed her family. She asked us if we recognized the scents. One smelled familiar to me, in a weird way. She told me they were probably my mate and that I needed to follow her to make sure he wasn't in trouble.

"We visited a few packs, even my supposed mate's brother's pack. She made us wait outside, and we left as quickly as we got there. Went to a few more packs, and the next thing you know, we're grabbed from the middle of the forest muzzled and shoved in crates. They brought us to that cabin and held us there for five days."

"And Pilar and Verona, Saskia told them the same thing?" She nodded. I thanked her and walked over to Theo.

"This makes me sick," he murmured, staring at Verona.

"It's Saskia's fault," I told him, tugging on his arm to follow me a few steps away. "She's the one that told the girls to follow her. She said their mates were in danger."

"I thought they weren't mated yet?"

"They aren't, they recognized them by scents from

clothes Saskia had."

Theo looked over my head.

"Theo, she's not lying," I insisted. His blue eyes looked back down.

"I know. I just don't know what Saskia's end game is. Why would she tell us blatant lies only for us to save the girls?"

Joella set a roll of gauze down and walked toward us. We shifted to be facing her, bracing ourselves for any other news.

"What the hell happened to these girls? That one can't stop crying." She pointed towards Pilar.

"They were led into an ambush by Saskia," I said lightly. "They were muzzled, crated, and held in a cabin for five days." Sadness took over Joella's expression, and she sighed. Felix walked up behind her and wrapped his arm around her waist.

"Joella, you should sit," Felix said in her ear.

"I have to finish Pilar's ankle first," she told him, leaving his embrace but pulling his hang to follow her.

"You should rest," Theo whispered to me. His hand wove into my hair, and he looked at me like he already knew I wouldn't comply. I gave him a look.

"I'll rest when Verona is healed."

He sighed and let my hair go, bending down to kiss the top of my head.

I picked up a damp cloth and started wiping blood and dirt off Verona. She was caked in layers of filth. okmSuddenly, her eyes flashed open, and she gasped for air. I reached for her arms to press her back on the table.

"Verona, you're okay. You're safe." I soothed. She thrashed against me, eyes rapidly searching the room. Olympia hopped off the table and came to the other side of Verona.

"You're fine," she said firmly. "V, it's okay. She's a friend."

Verona settled back, resting her eyes for a moment.

"Verona?" I said softly. Her eyes opened again. "How did you get outside."

"They tried to rape me," she wheezed, looking off into the distance. I became stiff. "Dragged me out to the woods and started to tear my clothes off when your cars scared them off. They ran."

"You're safe now," I assured her, grabbing onto her hand. She relaxed back on the table momentarily before her body started convulsing. "Joella!"

She ran over, placing her hands on either side of the girl's head.

"She's having a seizure," she spat out angrily. "Help me turn her on her side." We picked her up and held her steady until her body settled. Joella heaved out a breath.

"We need to find out who her mate is," Joella stated.

"Why?"

"Because she might not last much longer, and his blood could help her. She should at least meet him," she said sadly, rubbing her thumb over Verona's pale cheek.

"We need to get the clothing scraps." I stood up and paced the floor.

"The scraps?" Pilar yelped softly. I nodded, looking over at her in pity. "We have them."

Joella's head snapped to her. "What?"

"We have them," she said again, leaning over to reach something from her back pocket. She pulled a piece of black fabric out, bringing it to her nose before she held it out for me to take.

I took it, smelled it, and handed it to Theo. He inhaled the scent and looked at me, I nodded.

"This is my brother Gabriel's scent," Theo told Pilar. Pilar looked confused and then whispered Gabriel's name, smiling. Her tan skin filled with color for the first time since we met. "Where are the others?"

Olympia pulled a white piece of fabric from her pocket, handing it to us.

"Reese," Theo confirmed.

Joella reached into Verona's pocket's, finding a blue scrap.

"Eli."

STUCK TOGETHER

Theo lifted both of his arms and pulled on the roots of his hair.

"Why the hell did she gather all of my brother's mates and lead them into an ambush?" he fumed. "How the hell could she even know who all of you were mated to before they did?"

"Mates can sense each other through smell," Joella said.

"But they visited Gabriel's pack, how did my brothers not recognize their scents?"

"We waited outside pack lines," Olympia told us. "Saskia told us it was safer this way."

"So, she drags you on a hunt for your mates, brings you to them, but then doesn't allow you to meet them."

"Verona wasn't with us yet," Pilar said softly, glancing over at the younger girl. "Maybe that's why we couldn't go in. Maybe she needed all three of us for something."

I could tell Theo's mind was reeling, moving too fast to put the pieces together.

"Maybe we shouldn't be focusing so much on the mate thing, but what about the ambush? If she was going to hold you for ransom or something, there would be no reason to do that." I continued to pace the room as I talked.

"Do you know who took you?" Theo asked Olympia. She snorted.

"No." She rolled her eyes. "I didn't recognize them, but they knew Saskia, they called her by her name."

"Listen, this is great and dandy," Joella cut in. "But we need to get Verona to Eli if she wants to have a chance at surviving. This girl has been through a lot. She needs him right now."

"How are we going to do that?" Pilar softly asked, her eyebrows curling up in worry. She would be a good Luna. "Will she be okay on the drive?"

Felix came into the room, a hand covering the voicepiece of the phone in his hand. "I just got off the phone with Alpha Horik, he said you're more than welcome to use his plane. They live only twenty minutes west of us. You'll be there in about an hour. It's the safest way."

"I'm going with you," Joella announced, packing up the things in her medical kit. Felix grabbed her hand to stop her.

"Jo," he said softly.

"Felix, this girl needs me." Felix didn't let her hand go.

"Jo, our baby needs you. You need to stay here."

"You're pregnant?" I asked her. She looked over at me and, after a few moments, nodded. Her shirt pressed up against a small bump of her belly that I hadn't noticed in the

"It's not safe for you to fly." Felix pushed her back into her seat.

"Felix, I'm fine to fly. It's not close to my due date," She grabbed his hand and pressed a kiss to the back of it. "I could never forgive myself if this girl didn't make it to her mate safely before she even met him."

"I can't come with you, I can't leave the pack," Felix said sadly. She nodded and pulled him closer to her.

"I love you," she said lovingly in his ear.

We waited for them to part, looking down to give them a moment alone. As they let each other go, Joella looked at us expectantly.

"What are you doing? Get the cars ready," she snapped. We moved quickly into action. Theo and Joella lifted Verona carefully into one of the cars. Felix and I helped Pilar and Olympia into another vehicle.

Felix stood at Joella's door, whispering something to her. She blushed and kissed him once before he closed her door.

Theo led us to Alpha Horik's pack, where we were greeted at the border by Drax Horik himself. He led us to an airstrip with a sizeable plane, prepped, and waiting for us to board.

"Thank you," Theo said as they clasped arms.

"Mates are a gift," he said happily. "Plus, I hate crazy she-wolves."

"You and me both," Theo said, chuckling darkly. I stood on the steps of the plane, waiting for Theo. He jogged up behind me, and we found two seats.

I had never been on a plane before, which was evident to Theo as I gripped the armrest so tightly my hands turned white.

"Nervous?" he teased. I ignored him, trying to take deep breaths as the plane jolted into motion. "You're going to be fine."

"Hold my hand?" I asked him, my eyes still closed. His warm hand came under mine and squeezed back just as tightly.

I didn't let go of Theo's hand the entire flight, even when he tried to pull away. Olympia and Pilar sat next to each other, speaking quietly about their future mates. Joella was next to Verona, who was strapped down to a gurney, with the rest of Caddy's warriors.

We landed on a flat strip of the road south of the pack-house. Gabriel, Reese, Eli, Sloane, along with multiple warriors and medics stood waiting for us. When the plane was secure, the door to the steps opened.

Theo was the first one out, helping a limping Pilar down the steps. I waited until they were down the steps to leave with Olympia. I stood in front of her, halfway turned around to assist her, but she continued to push me front-ways and tell me she was fine, over and over.

Gabriel immediately was at Pilar's side before she even got off the last step. His usual steel exterior was gone and in its place was concern, love, and longing. He took Pilar's arm from Theo and helped her down. She took one step before Gabriel leaned down and lifted her off her injured ankle. She gasped girlishly and held onto his neck.

Reese was too busy looking at Gabriel and Pilar happily to notice Olympia right away. She was at the end of the stairs before Reese's face wrinkled in confusion, not expecting his own mate to reveal herself immediately after Gabriel's.

Theo hadn't disclosed to Gabriel that the girls were their mates, only said that they were needed when we landed.

Reese's eyes lit up, and for once, he didn't look like he was laughing at someone else's expense. I had only known Olympia for a short time, but I knew she was extremely strong-willed. The moment she saw Reese, her warm skin filled with a deep pink blush.

Theo and I waited as Pilar and Olympia were united with their mates. Joella coughed loudly, getting our attention. Theo jogged up the stairs and grabbed one corner of Verona's stretcher. Joella, Theo, and two warriors carefully brought her down.

I watched Eli's face turn from utter joy to devastation in seconds. He pushed past everyone else and gripped the stair rail. As soon as she was down, Eli was leaning over her battered body, tears filling his eyes.

"What happened?" he trembled.

"We will explain later. She needs you right now," Joella soothed, placing her hand on his shoulder.

"What can I do?" he asked quickly. His hand grazed her forehead, cheek, and then gripped her hand.

"She needs your blood."

Without hesitation, Eli's fangs descended, and he ripped his wrist open. Joella helped him prop her head up and funnel his blood into her mouth.

Verona's pale skin became stained with dark red, but almost instantly, her heartbeat strengthened.

Eli wiped a drop of blood from her lips.

"You did good," Joella told him. They lifted the stretcher once again, and Eli gripped her hand, walking beside her as they brought her to the packhouse.

Sloane rushed over to Theo and me the only ones still standing by the plane. She threw her arms around him, reaching out to pull me closer to their hug. She let us go and wiped the fat tears from her cheeks.

"This was supposed to be the happiest day of their lives," she wailed.

"It still is," Theo told her. I nodded and curled into his side. Sloane looked at us before grabbing us in another constricting embrace. We laughed and held onto her tightly.

We followed everyone else to the packhouse, but before we went in, Theo pulled me back. I was about to ask him what was wrong as he gripped my face tightly and kissed me. I was startled, but love quickly spread throughout my body and our bond. He leaned back, and I kept my eyes closed, leaning up, trying to stay connected.

"Margo," he said seriously. I opened my eyes and listened. "I love you so much."

"I love you, too, Theo," I said honestly, still confused.

"Please, don't ever leave my side," he said, smiling at the ridiculousness.

"Never," I said anyway.

Joella called our names from inside, and we hurried in. Verona was in the medical room; there wasn't much they would do for her there other than monitor her. If anything went wrong, they would have to transfer her over to the hospital building I had woken up in twice. Eli refused to leave her side, annoying the doctors who had to work around him.

Gabriel, Reese, and their mates waited out in the main room, huddled closely. They held each other close, inhaling scents, touching skin.

"Is that what we looked like?" I asked Theo, looking up at him at my side.

"Not at all." He laughed. "I'm pretty sure you looked like you wanted to kill me for the first few days." I looked down, ashamed. I couldn't even think about hurting Theo now.

"Sorry," I mumbled. I felt his hand reach down and hold mine.

"It's okay, you make up for it now." I could hear the teasing in his voice, and I bumped him lightly with my hip.

Joella walked over to us. She was tying her long hair up in a ponytail as she approached.

"We should get some rest, we've been up all night," she grinned tiredly, running a hand over her belly. "This little pebble's making me tired."

"You're more than welcome to stay here with us," Gabriel said behind her. She turned around and faced them; Gabriel had his arm around Pilar's shoulder, and the other held her hand.

"Thank you," she accepted.

"We should get home, we'll be back later," Theo told his brother. We said our goodbyes and shifted, running home. It was a slow run, more of a fast walk. We collapsed on the porch as soon as we got there.

"We should have taken the car," Theo whined. I shuffled to my feet and tugged Theo's arm, pulling him through the doorway. "What are you doing?"

"Taking you to bed," I bent down and kissed his head before standing up again. I had to use all my strength to drag his body. He laid on his back, allowing me to scoot him across the hardwood floors. I came to the steps and stopped, stuck.

He closed his eyes and raised his eyebrows like he was waiting for me to come up with something. I sat down on the first step and wrapped my arms around his waist from behind. He turned his head, close to my face, and kissed my cheek.

I attempted to pull him up a step but failing and slammed back down into the step painfully. I let out a high-pitched whine.

"Oh, no," Theo said dramatically, turning over, so he was hovering over me. I laughed tiredly and rubbed my hand over my bottom. "Come here and let me look at it."

"Theo," I said happily, hiding my face behind my hands.

"What?" He looked at me innocently. I shook my head at him and kissed him quickly. He skootched back and grabbed a blanket from the edge of the couch and covered us with it. He set his arm out on the ground to put my head on.

We laid on the ground, too tired and lazy to make it up to bed. We slept there, sunlight streaming in through the windows, curled up on the hard floor, my head on his arm, and his hand on my backside.

It was dark outside when I was woken up as Theo shifted his body, apologetically looking at me while he moved his arm. I grumbled incoherent words and shook off the sleepiness.

"Come on, you can go up to bed," he said, blinking heavily.

"You aren't coming?" I wiped my mouth, hoping I didn't drool on him while I slept.

"Gabriel just mind-linked me." He shook his head. "Albia just came to him and said she knows where Saskia is." I stood up and fixed my clothes.

"I'm coming with you," I said, following him to the kitchen.

"You don't have to," he said, smiling, as he grabbed an apple from the fridge. I closed the door and got his attention.

"Hey." I reached up and grabbed his chin. "We're a team, you and me. We stick together, alright? Everywhere you go, I go."

"Everywhere you go, I go," he repeated, kissing my head.

WOLFSBANE

When we arrived at Gabriel's packhouse, it was deadly silent. Theo opened the door hesitantly and stuck his head in before me. We wandered in slowly.

"Theo," Reese greeted. We turned and noticed him coming out of the kitchen with a glass of water.

"Hey man, where is everyone?" Theo asked.

We trailed after Reese, who took us to the hospital wing where Verona was sleeping. Eli was in the same place, in a chair next to his mate, holding onto her hand. Everyone looked up as we entered, nodding a silent greeting.

Reese handed the glass of water to Olympia and stood next to her shyly. Pilar was sitting on a windowsill behind Gabriel, arms wrapped around his shoulders. Sloane sat in the corner, violently knitting something that unraveled every time she moved her fingers.

"Where's Albia?" I asked quietly.

"In the pack cells," Gabriel said, not looking up from his

stare with Reese.

"The cells?" Theo asked in outrage. "Why is she in the cells?"

"When you hear her story, you'll understand," Eli spat. His face was murderous, but he kept the same gentle grip on Verona's hand.

"Will you take us?" Theo asked his younger brother. Gabriel nodded, turned and kissed Pilar, and then led us out. We climbed down two sets of stairs into the basement and then through another dark corridor.

I clutched Theo's hand in mine.

"Through here," Gabriel told us. He pushed through a set of doors. Two warriors stood guard, allowing us to pass freely. There were cells along the walls; classic metal bars and cement floors held only Albia.

She was curled in the corner, tears wetting her cheeks. Her hair was messy like she ran her hands through it multiple times, and she was scratching her wrist incessantly. Her head snapped up as we entered. She bolted to the bars, grabbing onto them before hissing and dropping her hands, burning from the silver.

"Theo, please," she begged, wiping her cheeks. "You've got to believe me. I never wanted any of this to happen."

"What did you do, Albia?" he asked softly. She looked down, scratching her wrist again.

"I was only trying to help at first," she began. "Saskia came to me and told me she wanted to help people find their mates because she had lost hers. She told me, 'the Weston's deserve to have their mates.' Then she asked me to get clothes with their scents on them and bring them to her."

"When was this?" I prodded.

"Just after the war. I met her outside pack grounds and

gave her the bag of their clothes."

"And?" Gabriel prompted angrily. She looked down again, breathing heavily.

"And then she called me. She said that it wasn't right that we lost our mates." She stopped and looked up at me, her jaw jutting forward. "She said we never got a chance to be happy. So, she wanted me to help her get revenge."

"On?" Gabriel prompted again.

"All your mates."

Theo growled loudly and instinctually put his hand in front of me, pulling me back behind him. I allowed him to.

"It isn't fair," she shrieked. "You get your mate, and you kill mine before I even get to say two words to him!"

"Albia, Reed was insane."

She growled lowly at Gabriel.

"He was my mate," she growled again. Then she paused and looked down sadly. "But then she said she wanted to get revenge on Gabriel and Reese and Eli, too, and I didn't want to do that!"

"Why?" Theo asked.

"Because Rush was the one who gave the order to kill her mate and brother."

"Rush was the Alpha?" I whispered under my breath.

"So, she tries to kill our mates?" Theo asked, stepping closer.

"She said 'if we can't have our mates, they don't deserve to have theirs.'"

Theo was fuming. I rubbed his back gently, trying to keep myself calm as well.

"I realized she was crazy," Albia said frantically, grabbing fistfuls of her hair. "She came back to the packhouse two weeks ago and threatened to kill me if I told anyone what we did."

"So, where is she?" Theo asked.

"Her plan was to bring all the girls back here once she found the third one but those men, they were in on her plan to get revenge on you all, and she owed them money. They took the girls hostage until Saskia could pay them. Saskia said they could do whatever they wanted to those girls until she got back, and that would pay her debt."

"Then why did she need us?" I said stupidly.

"You gathered them all up and brought them back here. So, she fulfilled her debt to those rogues, and she still gets to plan how she's going to kill all of you."

"The games over," Theo told her, stepping away from me. He walked up to the bars, breaths away from the silver. "No more tricks. You're going to die in here, Albia."

Albia whimpered, and a fresh set of tears cascaded down her face.

"Where is Saskia?" Theo asked darkly.

"She's here," Albia said so softly only Theo could hear.

"She's here?" he asked louder. Gabriel and I were immediately on guard.

"This was my last task," Albia breathed out. "She was going to kill me."

"Well, now I'm going to kill you," Theo hissed lowly. "So, I wonder who you should be more afraid of. Saskia? Or *me*."

The few dim lights on the ceiling sputtered and went black as Theo talked. We left the cells quickly, ascending the steps, moving faster when we heard loud noises coming from upstairs.

As we came to the ground level, we were plunged into darkness again. All the lights in the packhouse were out.

Gabriel led us slowly to the medical wing, listening carefully for any suspicious sounds. As we opened the door again, everyone in the room tensed until they smelled our scents.

"The power's off," Eli said frantically. The machine that recorded Verona's heartbeat and administered her medicine and oxygen was off. "We need to get her out of here."

"Albia told us Saskia was here. That's what she wants, she wants to flush us out of the packhouse, and that's when she'll attack." Gabriel rushed to where Pilar stood.

"We can't just sit here!" Eli exclaimed. Theo shut and locked the door behind us, leaning up against the metal surface.

"We need to get the power turned on, that's the first thing," Gabriel ordered. In our human forms, our eyesight was better than a normal human's, but it wasn't pristine. I could make out shapes and shadows, but it wasn't much help.

"The power box is in the basement," Sloane noted. "I'll go."

"Mom, you aren't going," Theo nearly spat. Sloane came to his side and put her hand on his cheek.

"Sweetheart, you all need to stay here and protect your mates. Let me do this," she insisted.

"Mother," Gabriel called. "Saskia is somewhere here, either in this house or outside of it, but either way, you aren't going to wander around here by yourself. I'll go with you."

"Gabriel, with all due respect, you don't order me around. You said it yourself, I was the Luna of this pack for twenty-six years. I know this house better than any of you. If Saskia wants revenge for something Rush did, let her get revenge on me-not my babies."

Before anyone could protest, she threw the door open, hitting Theo in the process, and left the room. Theo's chest rumbled, and he reached for the door. I grabbed his outstretched hand and pulled it close to me.

"Theo, let her go." He wrenched his hand out of mine. "Theo."

"That's my mother," he said softer. I sighed and let go of his hand.

"We can't just sit here," Reese declared. "We're a pack of werewolves, and we're going to let one person keep us prisoner in our own house? Let's go show her exactly who she's messed with."

"Easy," Gabriel warned. "Saskia is dangerous. She's manipulative and a liar. We don't know what else she's capable of. We have more than just us to think about now."

The air grew thick as everyone clutched their mates close to them. Theo's hand curled around the curve of my neck and brought me to his chest. I wrapped my arms around him, grabbing onto the thick muscle of his back, not caring if I left nail marks.

"We need to get Verona out of here," I said, speaking the thoughts of everyone else.

"If we can get Eli and Verona out of here, the rest of us should be enough incentive for her to stay here," Gabriel said, plans reeling in his mind. "The cars should still be out front, I'll mind-link the guards in the prison to come and escort them out. We need to keep her inside the house, if she goes after Verona, I don't know how much longer she'll be able to hang on."

Eli took the cords and needles off his mate carefully. He lifted her to his chest, and Pilar covered her with the soft blanket on her bed.

"Let's go," Eli said. Theo opened the door and led us outside, looking down every hallway, and peeking into every corner as he walked. We got to the front door and hesitated. We breathed, almost synchronously, as Theo unlocked and opened the door.

The black SUV was running, a guard in the driver's seat, another waiting near the door to open it. Eli stepped forward with Verona.

Before they exited, Gabriel and Reese stepped back, moving into the open area of the room. Gabriel reached out and grabbed a lamp from the corner before turned and smashing it loudly against the wall.

Reese began doing the same thing with anything breakable. The loud noise was enough of a distraction for Eli to get Verona to the car. He looked back as he climbed in. Theo nodded to him, assuring him we would be okay.

The car started, and Theo closed the door quietly before locking it again. Gabriel and Reese came, and we walked together into the middle of the room.

"Quiet," Gabriel said, holding up a hand to silence us. We waited and listened closely. There are a few rumbling noises that come from below us and then a few light tapping noises. I could hear the prison bars rattling even though they were two floors under, and I wished my eyesight was as good as my hearing

Someone started clapping behind us. My body tensed. Theo's grip on my hand tightened to a bruising degree.

Collectively we turned; Gabriel, Reese, and Theo stepped in front of their mates on instinct.

"That was a great distraction you made," Saskia drawled, lips curving sinisterly. "Too bad it's not going to save you."

"Saskia," Theo said sternly, no fear in his voice. "It's

over."

"Oh, you think it's over?" Her voice rose as she talked. "That's so...*cute.*"

The lights flickered on slowly, illuminating the half-destroyed room in front of us. I sent a silent thanks to Sloane and braced myself for Saskia. She stood in front of us, holding a small sphere in her hands.

"What is that?" Gabriel asked.

"This?" She lifted the ball and her eyebrows raised, almost innocently. "I had it developed by a couple of people who owed me a favor. It's a silver gas bomb."

She stepped forward, crossing her ankles as she strolled inches ahead.

"When my finger pulls this pin, this entire house will fill up with silver and wolfsbane in seconds. It's funny that you think this is over."

TO THE NEXT

"Saskia, I need you to think about this," Theo warned, holding his hand out, cautioning her. We knew the moment she pulled the pin, we would be dead in a matter of seconds.

"Theodore, you aren't in control here."

"Saskia, if you let this off right now, you and Albia are going to die, too," Reese pointed out, uncharacteristically serious.

"You honestly think I care about that? That little bitch is too weak to even think for herself. She wouldn't've lasted a day with Reed." She shook her head.

"You knew Reed?" Theo asked. I knew he was stalling for something; I didn't know what, but I figured we needed to keep her talking.

"Knew him? He loved me," she said smiling. She looked happy for once, but it was short-lived. "I told him I despised humans, how else was I going to get him to kill the Enforcer's mate?"

"You were behind the attack?" I asked, already knowing the answer.

"Did you think Reed was smart enough to plan all of that on his own? I mean, he is diabolical-that idea of hanging the girl in your tree was all his idea. He messed everything up, though, wanted to make it something personal with Theodore for getting the Enforcer position over him."

She played with the pin in her bomb, clanking the metals against each other.

"The original plan was to start with Margo and work my way down although, I must admit, Reed's mistakes sure made for a more...dramatic ending, wouldn't you say?" Her words were mischievous, but her voice held a tone of absolute control.

None of us moved.

"You know, Eli and Verona escaped, you can't kill all of us," Pilar said, voice wavering.

"And them living in a world where they know they left their family to be murdered is enough revenge for me." She moved closer towards us.

"Saskia, this has nothing to do with us," Theo told her, stepping forward. She took a step back and put her finger in the pin for good measure. "What our father did is on him. If you want to get revenge, then get revenge on us, but leave our mates out of this."

"You're sweet," she told him, nothing teasing in her voice. "You all want to protect your mates, and I think that's really noble of you. But I know what it's like to live in a world without your mate; I'm really just putting them out of their misery early."

"We can all walk out of this room right now." Theo stepped further. We all heard the click as she pulled the pin to its taut end; the next move she made would detonate the device.

"Yeah? And do what? We can all live happily ever after? You know the second I put this bomb down, you either kill me or throw me in a jail cell to rot."

"That's not true," Gabriel stepped forward.

"No? Then what's going to happen?"

"We can figure it out together if you just hand Theo the bomb," Gabriel smiled nervously.

Reese put his arm out and pushed us backward, Saskia didn't notice, she was too busy paying attention to Theo and Gabriel.

"*Margo, get out of here,*" Theo told me through our mind-link.

"*No, I'm not leaving.*"

"*This isn't time to play around, you need to get yourself out of here. Take Olympia and Pilar with you. Grab my mother if you can, but get yourself out of here safely.*"

"*Theo, I told you, wherever you go, I go. I'm not leaving.*"

"*Margo,*" he nearly shouted.

"*Theo, I love you.*"

There was silence.

"*I love you so much.*"

"This is all very touching." Saskia smirked. "But, my patience is running thin, and I'm getting bored with this."

"Saskia, this is the last thing you do before you die. Is this really what you want your last moments to be?"

"You don't get to choose how you die," she growled. "Alexei and Malachi didn't get to choose how they died."

"Alexei and Malachi? That's your brother and mate?" Theo asked gently.

"Don't say their names. You don't get to say their names."

"Is this what they would want you to do?"

"I think it is." Her eyes with sadness

"I hope you're happy with the way things end then."

She paused at Theo's words and slipped her finger out of the pin. She closed her eyes for two seconds, whispering a soft but notable, "I'll see you soon."

I closed my eyes at the same time and sent Theo one last, "*I love you.*"

He didn't get to answer. I opened my eyes again. I wanted him to be the last thing I saw.

I didn't get to join my parents, though.

Before Saskia's finger could even enter the pin, a heap of blonde hair flashed behind her, lifted something over her head, and brought it down violently on Saskia's arm.

An ax cut through Saskia like a marshmallow, just below her elbow. Her vocal cords must have burst with the scream she let out.

As her severed arm hit the ground, Saskia turned and gripped Albia's throat with her other hand. Her claws elongated as she held onto Albia, cutting through the tendons and veins in her neck.

Albia's eyes widened, sinking forward as Saskia's claws sliced through her windpipe. The ax dropped to the floor loudly. Her claws remained in Albia's neck, her other arm soaking the floor with her thick blood.

I couldn't look away, none of us could.

The bomb laid at Saskia's feet. Theo noticed at the same time as I did and started forward to take it before Saskia's uninjured arm pulled the pin.

Saskia's claws left Albia's neck with a nerving, *squish*. She was going to pass out soon from the blood loss, and she turned to us with a dizzying look.

Theo reached for the bomb seconds before Saskia did.

He looked up at her just as the ax sliced through her neck, from one side to the next. Her head hit the ground first, and then her body tumbled after her.

Pilar shrieked.

I looked up from Saskia's head to Sloane, who held the axe in her hand, heaving to breathe, blood splattered on her shirt and face.

"Mom?" Theo asked, standing up slowly and reaching for the axe. There was a faraway look in her eyes, dazed almost.

"No one messes with my family," she breathed, sliding the ax onto the ground next to Saskia's body.

Reese turned, and Olympia dove into his arms. Gabriel quickly rushed to Pilar, who was shaking.

I didn't notice any of them. All I could see was Theo, covered in Saskia's blood, and looking at me with such relief, I nearly cried. I jumped childishly onto him, wrapping my legs around his waist, and my arms curled around his head. He held me, inhaling my scent, touching me.

"I thought we were going to die. I didn't know if my mother could get here in time," he admitted with his face stuck in my curls. He yanked my head back to look at him. "Margo, don't ever do that to me again. If I tell you to leave, you leave."

"Theo." I grabbed his face in my hands, Saskia's blood transferred onto my fingers. "I will never, ever, leave you." And I kissed him, ignoring to iron taste on his lips.

He set me on my feet gently, and we looked at the two

bodies on the floor.

Sloane knelt down next to Albia and slid her eyelids down over her eyes.

"She's with her mate now," she said depressingly. "I'll tell Emily."

"We'll tell her together," Gabriel told her, resting a hand on his mother's shoulder.

"Where did you get the ax?" Reese asked.

Sloane's lip twitched. "Your father liked to chop his firewood himself. I keep it by my bedside, it makes me feel safer."

"How did you get from the basement to your room?"

"Sons, there are many things you don't know about this house and this pack," she reminded them. "You should go get cleaned off," she told Theo. "We'll get someone to take care of this mess."

Theo pulled me down the hallway to a bathroom. He grabbed a towel and soaked it in water before wiping his face violently. When he rang it out, he turned and wiped the bloodstains from my lips and fingers.

We didn't speak.

There was no reason to.

COLOR THEORY

Theo disappeared three days after Saskia's death.

On the first day, we burned Saskia's body in the front yard. Theo chopped up the wood with his father's ax. Most of the pack came to watch her burn. News traveled fast that someone had tried to kill the Alpha's family and the Enforcer. No one shed any tears, although I felt a strange feeling in my stomach like somehow, I understood what she did.

On the second day, we held a funeral for Albia. Even though she had betrayed us, we respected Emily enough not to tell her what her daughter did before her death. There was no reason to ruin her name now that she was gone.

When I woke up on the third day, Theo was gone from our bed. My heart raced until I found a small note on the night-stand that said, "Needed to take care of some things. Be back soon. T."

I rubbed the sleep out of my eyes and tried to mind-link Theo, but the link was blocked. I started to worry and tried again. I tried all throughout the day, and then I started to get annoyed.

I walked around the house gingerly, looking over my shoulder constantly. Even though Saskia was dead, the feeling of dread didn't leave my body for months to come. I constantly expected her to be waiting in the shadows and around every corner.

I made myself dinner with an extra portion for Theo. I put it in a container in the fridge for him to eat later. The guards outside the house knew nothing of his whereabouts.

When I woke up the following day, Theo hadn't come back. Sloane showed up at our doorstep with a tray of soft cookies, claiming to know nothing about her son's trip. She came in, and we talked for a long time. She loved Pilar and Olympia already, claiming they were exactly what her sons needed.

Eli and Verona were still at the pack's hospital. She hadn't woken up yet, but most of her superficial wounds had healed, and they were just waiting for her to wake up to send her home with her mate.

Sloane stayed until nighttime. She cooked dinner with me, and we put on one of Theo's old movies. Gabriel and Pilar came and drove her home when it got dark; no one wanted her walking home alone.

The third day that Theo was gone was the worst. I stayed in bed for most of the day, rolling in and out of sleep. The door opened at four in the afternoon, and I rushed downstairs.

Eli stood in the foyer with an anxious expression. I flew down the steps and to his side.

"What's wrong? Is Theo okay? Is Verona okay?" I asked.

"You need to get dressed and come with me. Right now." He grabbed my hand and pulled me upstairs.

"Eli, what's going on?" I tried to ask as he threw clothes at me. I put on the simple blue dress he gave me.

He grabbed my hand again and dragged me outside. We stalked through the woods, his hand gripping mine. I stumbled over my feet; even being a werewolf didn't help my coordination. I realized we were heading towards the packhouse as it came into view.

We were almost the back of the house when Sloane came out and grabbed me from Eli's hands.

"Sloane, what is going on?" I asked desperately. She smiled calmly and fixed my hair.

"Come on, dear," she said kindly.

The pack was gathered at the back of the house, many of them standing in the woods behind the clearing due to the size of the pack. Theo stood on the small stage where I had first been introduced to the pack in a tailored black suit.

It would be an understatement to say I was confused as Sloane pushed me up onto the stage.

"Where the hell have you been?" I angrily whispered as I got closer. He just kept smiling at me. When I was close enough, he stepped forward and took my clammy hands in his.

"Margo," he said mischievously. "I'm sorry that I've been gone the last few days, but I had to get a few things in order, and I think what I'm about to say will make up for it."

I waited, leaning back slightly in apprehension. Theo laughed nervously.

"My whole life leading up to the day I met you was black and white. When I was little, there was nothing I wanted more than to meet my mate, and as I got older, my hope started growing smaller every day. The day I met you was one of the greatest days of my entire life. You took my black and white world, and you lit it up like a firework.

"I have enjoyed every moment since that day. Every time you laugh, my world turns bright green. When you smile, it turns yellow. When you cry, it turns blue, and when you kiss me, it turns bright red, kind of like your cheeks right now." His thumb lifted to my cheek and touched the blushing flesh.

"I'm sorry that I've been gone the past few days, especially after everything that has happened. I visited Caddy's pack," he said to my surprise. "I know that he's the closest thing to family that you have and if I'm going to do this, I wanted to do it right. I know this is an old human tradition and it probably hasn't been done in over fifty years. I know that sometimes you want to hit me and pull out my hair because I annoy you so much. I know that every day isn't going to be perfect, but I do know I don't want to spend them with anyone but you.

"So." He let go of my hands and knelt on one knee and pulled out a small black box. The ring that was nestled inside was a thin gold band with one small, diamond-shaped gem on the band. "Margo Celina Anderson, will you do me the greatest honor of my existence and marry me?"

His eyes were nervous. My eyes had filled with tears long before he asked me the question.

I started nodding, then realized that it wasn't romantic and said, "yes," over and over. His smile sent chills down my spine as he got off his knee and slid the ring onto my left hand.

As he kissed me, the pack burst into cheers of happiness. I was sure my entire face was blushing red as we parted.

"Caddy gave me his blessing. He said this was your mother's ring, the pack kept it. It was buried in an old safe, it took us two days to find it."

Warmth spread through me as I touched the small diamond. I had never been happier than that moment.

Sloane walked up on the stage with us, holding a small

screen in her hand. She hugged us tightly and kissed my cheek before she gave Theo the device. He clicked it on and showed me the videos.

"These are from packs across the country. They gathered to celebrate our engagement," Theo said softly, clicking through the different packs. I noticed Caddy's pack, Duncan's, Joella and Felix's, and many others. They were kneeling, the same way they had knelt down before the fight.

I glanced over at our pack, kneeling, arms clasped over their chest, heads down. I didn't know what I had done to deserve the love of so many people.

I turned back to Theo, who had set the screen down. He had knelt at my feet, arm over his chest, head bent for just a moment.

He lifted his head and smiled at me. I could have flown at the moment.

"You are my queen, little one. I will follow you anywhere," he swore.

LILACS

"He's perfect," I said in awe.

Joella smiled and held her newborn son closer to her face. "He is pretty gorgeous, huh?"

"It seems like just yesterday he was just a little bump in your belly," I said wistfully. Only two and a half months later, Rowan came into the world, pink and wrinkled. He had grown into his body more over the past two weeks or so and was curled, sleeping in his mother's arms.

He was covered in a small white onesie with a black long sleeve sweater on top, like a small suit.

"I can't believe you came all the way here, I would have understood, Jo," I told her, playing with Rowan's tiny hand.

"And miss this? No way in hell." She laughed. "Gosh, I've got to stop swearing, or his first word is going to be damn."

"Margo," Verona called sweetly, peeking in the bedroom door. "It's almost time. I have your bouquet."

"Thanks, V," I told her, letting go of Rowan and ushering Joella out of the room.

"You look gorgeous," Verona told me, standing behind me as I stood in front of the tall mirror.

Sloane came over the day before, sent Theo to the pack-house for the night, and turned our bedroom into a dressing room. She set up a vanity, lights, mirrors, and tubes of makeup I didn't know existed.

She primed, plucked, and plumped me into perfection. Olympia sat on the bed, snickering every time I whined. I begged Sloane not to go overboard, which she thankfully adhered to.

My dress was made by one of the women in the pack. It was sleeveless with triangles of fabric covering my breasts; the stomach of the dress was tight, and it flowed out from the waist. It was soft, elegant, simple. It was perfect.

My hair was left down in its usual curly mess with a white flower pinned on the side, showing off Theo's mark on my neck. My heart raced as I looked at myself in the mirror, palms sweating, hands shaking.

"You're going to be okay," Verona fixed the back of my dress, tucking the fabric in snugly. "Everything looks beautiful."

"I know." I smiled. "This is just the last human thing I really have to do."

"This isn't the last thing," she said lightly. "You and Theo are going to have babies, even if they are little werewolf babies. And you're going to be there on their first day of school, and when they have their hearts broken. You're going to grow old together."

I turned and pulled her tightly to me, arms squeezing her small shoulders. She laughed and patted my back, careful not to mess up my hair; Sloane would have her head.

Someone knocked on the door loudly.

"Margo?" Caddy's voice called. Verona opened the door, looked at me once, and then left us alone. "How are you?"

"Honestly?" He nodded and sat on the edge of the bed. "I'm okay. I just wish..."

"You wish your parents were here," he filled in. I nodded, smiling grimly. "I do, too. But they're here, they're watching over you. They never left you, Margo."

I sat next to him, resting my head on his shoulder. He put his hand on my knee, his warmth coating me. A female voice screamed my name from the first floor, and Caddy removed his hand.

"It's like we have somewhere to be or something." He chuckled playfully. I stood up and fixed my dress.

"I guess it's our time to shine, Caddy." I followed him out of the room. He watched me carefully as I descended the stairs in my long dress. Verona, Olympia, and Pilar were waiting at the bottom of the steps, adorning lilac-colored dresses.

Verona handed me a small bouquet of lavender and white hydrangeas. They walked towards the back of the house, right in front of the back doors that were covered in sheer fabric. The girls walked out first. I wasn't able to see anything but white flower petals on the ground.

Tansy pushed her way in front of me, her basket filled with pink flower petals. She took her role extremely seriously and practiced many times before the big day came. She exited with a grand smile, followed by Joella carrying Rowan in her arms. An emerald dress laid beautifully under her fiery hair, and she bounced Rowan happily as she carried the rings for the sleeping baby.

Caddy squeezed my arm. Somehow, my nervousness faded the moment Caddy opened the door. I held onto his arm as he escorted me towards the altar where Theo waited. There was a simple wooden arch in the center, flowers, and vines woven into it.

Along the walkway, there were small bouquets of white flowers and simple wooden chairs. There weren't many people sitting there.

Pilar, Olympia, and Verona stood to one side; Gabriel, Reese, and Eli to the other next to Theo. The rest of the chairs were filled with family and close friends, Emily and her mate, Sloane, the woman who sewed my dress, Cam and Gemma, Bodhi, Beau, and his mate Juniper.

I took everything in within ten seconds, and for the rest of the walk, I looked at Theo. He closed his eyes and opened them again, blinking rapidly. His eyes became glassy, and he ran his hand over his face to shake off the feeling.

I blushed and smiled. He looked so handsome, standing in his black suit with his hair combed back. A small sprig of lavender was pinned to his lapel, the same as his brothers.

We reached the alter faster than I imagined. Caddy let go of my arm, kissed me on the forehead, and took his seat next to Bodhi.

Pilar took my flowers, and I turned to my mate. There was no need for an officiator. It was a simple, short ceremony. We exchanged our vows, handwritten on sheets of paper we wrote one night after a few glasses of wine. We wrote them lying on the bed, constantly trying to peak at the others.

Theo unfolded his from his pocket; there were only a few lines written down.

"Margo. I've never been to a wedding before, and I've never heard vows, but I imagine it's something like a promise. So, I promise you that I will always wake you up gently in the morning. I promise I will never interrupt you when you're reading. I promise I will kiss you every day for the rest of our lives, no matter what gets in the way. Most of all, I promise you that I will be there for you forever. You're never going to get rid of me."

I could barely see with the tears clouding my vision. I giggled stupidly as I wiped the tears away. Pilar handed me a sheet of paper.

"Theo. You are the first person I want to see when I wake up in the morning and the last person I want to see before I go to bed even if you try to keep me awake every night. You're the only person I want to come to when anything happens, good or bad. I promise I will never voluntarily let you win a race or win the discussion on whether films are better than books."

"Films," he murmured childishly. I rolled my eyes and laughed.

"I promise you, you'll never have to go to a business meeting alone, even if I have no idea what's going on. But, more than anything, I promise you that you'll never have to go a day without knowing that I love you."

I folded the paper back up and gave it to Pilar. Joella stood up with Rowan and came forward. She handed Theo my ring and gave me his plain black band.

"Margo, do you take me as your husband?" Theo smiled, holding my left hand in his.

"I do," I said firmly. He let my hand go, and I took his left hand in mine. "Theo, do you take me as your wife?"

"I do."

He grabbed my face in his large, warm hands, and kissed me. We were both smiling, trying to kiss each other, but laughing too much to make it anything more than a small kiss.

He let my face go, and we turned to our friends and family who were cheering, although Sloane was crying loudly.

"After you, Mrs. Weston," Theo whispered in my ear, taking my hand to escort me back down the aisle.

"Thank you, Mr. Weston."

We had a large dinner in the house, talking over each other, passing plates and bowls of food down the tables messily.

When we finished eating, Sloane insisted we have our first dance, as was human tradition. She played some slow, acoustic song, and we swayed softly. I didn't let go of him when I was supposed to. Cam asked Gemma to dance, the same with Caddy and Bodhi, and every other mated couple.

The inside of the house had been redecorated, stripped, and left with only strings of soft lights and flowers around the room.

"I can't wait to take you to bed tonight, wife," Theo whispered roughly in my ear.

"As I recall, you owe me one night of me in complete control," I said playfully, trying to hide my laughter.

"Margo, I'm all yours. Anything of mine is yours; my body, my hands, my heart, it's all yours to do what you please."

"That's a big responsibility," I noted lightly, face still pressed against his chest.

"I trust you," he told me.

"You have my heart, too, Theo," I reminded him.

"Good. It took me long enough to earn it," he teased me. I pinched his arm but kept my head on his chest. "I'll never let you down."

"Your mom would have your head if you did," I said, pulling my head away to glance at Sloane taking pictures of everyone.

"You're going to be a great mom someday," Theo smiled.

"You're going to be the best father ever."

"Whenever you're ready," he said solemnly.

I knew female wolves could only get pregnant if they were in heat, and mine hadn't come yet. It was indefinite how long it would take for my heat to start since I was a turned shifter, but there was plenty of time to worry about that later.

I bit my lip as I looked at him, remembering for the first time in a while just how much taller he was compared to me. He grinned, lips just slightly parting.

"One day," I promised simply. He seemed happy at that and leaned down to kiss me. A bright flash snapped next to us as Sloane captured our sweet moment.

She giggled slyly and disappeared into another room.

"I never thought I would feel this way about someone," I admitted to Theo shyly. "This is so strange to me still. I mean, I'm happy, don't get me wrong, I'm ecstatic. I don't know, it still amazes me sometimes how you make me feel."

"How do I make you feel?" He smiled crookedly, smugly.

"You make me feel like I'm home. Like it doesn't matter where we are or what's happening, but like I'll always be home as long as I'm with you. And-"

He kissed me to stop my anxious rambling. I silently praised him. Then, he pulled away and tucked my hair behind my ear.

"You're my home, too, Margo."

EPILOGUE

"Come on, Margo, push!" Reese screamed in my ear.

I nearly growled at him as another bead of sweat wiggled down my forehead. I grunted, animalistic noises coming from my mouth as I struggled to push.

"You're almost there, Margo," Theo praised, pushing his brother away from me.

Olympia, Pilar, Verona, and Sloane stood somewhere in front of me, cheering me on. I couldn't see them, though. I threw my head back, nearly crying at the pressure.

"Come on, little one, I know you can do this," Theo teased me. "You're tiny, but you're strong."

"Theo, I'm gonna fucking kill you when I'm done," I screeched. He laughed anyway and stayed by my side.

"Think about the result," he urged. I continued to push, my legs nearly seizing up as they spread and contracted.

"You're nearly there," Sloane squealed happily. I nearly

stopped because of how tired I was.

Theo yelled at me as my eyes closed for half a second.

"No, Margo, just a few more pushes."

I gritted my teeth, and with one final heaving push, I was done.

I slumped over onto the ground, panting.

"I told you, you could do it!" Theo picked me up under my arms. I stood on my shaking legs and looked at my accomplishment. I had managed to choose a sizeable boulder, around the size of Reese's.

"I can't believe I just did that." I surprised even myself.

"I knew you could," Theo's head shook with pride. He picked me up, and I attached myself to his chest like a toddler.

"I think I deserve a reward," I giggled in his ear before biting it. A low growl vibrated against my stomach. "Will you take me home, mate?"

"As you wish, my queen," Theo kissed the side of my head. He turned, and we all began walking back to our house.

The peace that surrounded us in that moment wouldn't last forever, we both knew it, but with Theo at my side, I knew we could conquer anything. My rock sat proudly, nestled next to Theo's, right where it belonged. I closed my eyes and leaned into Theo's scent, like sweet, burning wood, and I knew I was home.

Made in the USA
Middletown, DE
22 October 2020